MIRROR, MIRROR

A TWISTED TALE

JEN CALONITA

𝔇𝔦𝔰𝔫𝔢𝔭 PRESS
Los Angeles • New York

Printed in the United States of America
First Hardcover Edition, April 2019
1 3 5 7 9 10 8 6 4 2
FAC-020093-19046
Library of Congress Control Number: 2018953269
ISBN 978-1-368-01383-3

Visit disneybooks.com

THIS LABEL APPLIES TO TEXT STOCK

Mom, thanks for convincing scared six-year-old me to ride Snow White's Scary Adventures at Walt Disney World, even though I was afraid of the Evil Queen. (It paid off!)

—J. C.

Prologue

The castle looked different from the outside.

It was the first thing the princess thought of when she saw it again. It felt like years since she had laid eyes on it, but in reality, it had only been a few weeks. Now, as she stared at the monstrosity looming high on the hilltop, she felt her breath catch in her throat. Those walls were filled with so many ghosts and memories of the life she'd lost.

But they didn't have to be.

If they could do what they'd set out to, they could change all that. The castle and those who sat upon its throne could be a beacon for the kingdom again. But that meant not running away from what the princess knew she'd find inside that castle, even if every inch of her body wanted her to.

"We should hurry," Anne said as she slashed at the brambles to make her own path, which would lead them right to the village outside the castle without being seen. "We haven't much time before the celebration begins."

The princess quickened her pace, following her friend.

She was going home.

It didn't feel like home. It hadn't for a long time, but technically that's what the castle was. Or had been once upon a time.

If she concentrated hard enough, she could picture the castle the way it had been when she was a child. In her mind's eye, the kingdom was beloved and beautiful, with a castle the people took pride in. (After all, they were the ones who had placed every stone to build it.) Overgrown ivy didn't trail across the gray stone walls. Every bush, every tree, every flower was manicured. The aviary was brimming with the songs of birds. Windows gleamed. The lake at the base of the hill glimmered with hope as visitors frequently came from other shores. The gates to the castle were almost always open, and it wasn't uncommon for parties to spring up at a moment's notice.

But now things were different. The windows appeared dark and the curtains were always drawn up tight, giving the castle an abandoned appearance. The waters surrounding the castle looked like glass, for no ship dared cross into their kingdom's borders. The gates, rusted and leaning, were locked. The grounds were, except for a few faithful guards, deserted. Her kingdom's renaissance was long gone.

When King Georg and Queen Katherine had sat upon the throne, they had looked benevolently upon their province. The land's soil had been rich enough for farming, and held a thriving diamond mine beneath the earth. The pair celebrated the province's growth by throwing frequent festivals in the castle's courtyard, where subjects from every walk of life were welcome. When she closed her eyes, she could see herself being swung through the air as a fiddle played and people danced. But the memory quickly vanished, replaced by the sound of Anne splintering more tree branches.

For too long, she had spent her days and nights inside that fortress wishing someone would break her free. She'd lived without love in that castle for so long, with little laughter or company to bolster her spirits. Maybe that was why, despite the castle's splendor, it had always felt tainted and tarnished. The princess had accepted her fate in an effort to make the best of things, but she refused to do so any longer.

It wasn't till she was outside those walls that she'd realized the truth: the only one who could truly break her free was herself. That's why she was back. To claim what was truly hers. Not just the castle, but the province and its throne. Not just for her own happiness, but also for that of her people.

Now was the time to strike. It was why she had traveled so far, risked so much, and found strength within herself that she hadn't known she possessed. Queen Ingrid's popularity had never been strong, but in the last few years, the kingdom had gone from indifference to downright terror. She couldn't allow her people to suffer this way any longer. It was time.

"There!" Anne had slashed through the last of the branches, and sunlight was now shining through the shadows. "We've reached the road. It's just a little bit further down, and then we can slip through the castle gates near the butcher's shop unseen. The queen has demanded everyone be at the celebration, so there should be crowds near the gates today."

She hugged the brown cloak Anne had made her tightly. It was quickly becoming one of her most prized possessions. Not only did it keep her warm, but the jacquard pattern reminded her of a traveling coat her mother used to wear. It felt like her mother was with her somehow, or at the very least, making sure she found the right companions to keep at her side. She was grateful for Anne's friendship and all the subjects she'd met who had helped her. Their kindness wouldn't be forgotten.

She turned to Anne. "Won't that make it harder for us to get through?"

Anne took her hands. "Don't worry, my friend. You will have an easier journey than Prince Henrich and I had this morning. These crowds are the perfect cover for you to slip inside."

"Have you heard from Henri at all?" the princess asked hopefully.

Anne shook her head. "I'm sure he's safe. If he wasn't, we would have heard something." Anne pulled her along. "It's *you* I worry about. Once you cross the gates, everyone will recognize you. We need to get you indoors before you're noticed. We must move quickly and get you to your love. He's waiting for you."

Your love. The words caused a small smile to play on her lips. She and Henri had been through a lot in the last week, and more before that. Her steps quickened.

As Anne predicted, the road to the village was deserted that morning. They didn't pass a single carriage on their hike in. No one was traveling on foot at the moment, either, though she saw plenty of footprints in the dirt. She'd expected the village entrance to be guarded, but there was no one manning the post when she and Anne walked through the open gates. A declaration had been nailed to a wrought iron post. She read it quickly as she passed:

Queen Ingrid demands all loyal village subjects join her for a celebration in the castle courtyard today at noon. In preparation for this momentous occasion, all village establishments will be closed. Those not at the celebration will be noted.

She shuddered. Anne was right about the celebration being mandatory, but it was an odd request. It wasn't that she was surprised by Queen Ingrid's insistence, but there hadn't been anything close to merriment or official festivities in the kingdom for years. The people were so frightened by their queen that they avoided doing anything to make themselves noticeable. Instead, they spent their days with their heads down, living in the shadows. Being drawn out for a rare celebration—if that's what it really was—had to be unnerving. What was the queen playing at?

They were both silent as they made their way onto the dusty village road that led up to the castle. The princess had spent some time in these streets—albeit limited time— but she was still surprised by how quiet things were. The small wood homes with thatched straw roofs that lined the road were closed up tight. The monastery's bell tolled solemnly to mark the time as noon, but there was no one around to hear it. Evidently the people had heeded Queen Ingrid's warning. She sighed heavily and Anne looked at her.

"You don't have to do this alone. You know that, right?" Anne's voice was gentle. "Let me come with you and Prince Henrich and fight!"

"No." She shook her head. "I appreciate all you've done for us, but this part of the journey I must take alone."

Anne stared at her as if she wanted to say more, but they were interrupted by shouting. A man came running toward them, his face filled with terror.

"The queen is a witch!" he shouted. "Steer clear of the town square—run! Hide! Or Queen Ingrid will curse you, too."

The princess was so startled she couldn't comprehend what the man was saying. Anne looked equally frightened. What had the queen done to her people now? She started running toward the town square to see what was going on.

Anne went after her. "Wait! You heard the man. This could be a trap!"

If the queen suspected she was near, so be it. Her gut told her something was seriously wrong. She needed to know what had happened.

As she approached the castle, she could see what looked

like the entire village gathered in front of it. Heads bobbed up and down as villagers gawked at whatever was behind the closed gates. Clearly this was no celebration. She watched villagers anxiously jockey for position, trying to get a better look. Some screamed and cried while others lifted children onto their shoulders to get a better look. Anne and the princess struggled to get a better view.

"Don't look," she heard one mother say to a young boy. "We must go now! Before one of us is next."

"Does anyone know who it is?" asked another.

"Looks like royal blood if you ask me."

The princess pushed her way through the crowd, trying to make her way to the front. Anne clung to her arm, not wanting to lose her.

"Excuse me," she kept saying. "May I please pass?"

But the townsfolk continued to goggle, talking and staring as if they didn't see her.

"It's witchcraft, I tell you!"

"A warning!" said another. "She is not to be crossed!"

"Is he sleeping or is he dead?"

"He hasn't stirred. He must be dead."

He? She pushed harder, going against all the manners she'd been taught so long ago to reach the front of the gate and see what the others were so upset about. As soon as she did, she wished she hadn't.

"No!" she cried, pulling her hand from Anne's and grasping the bars in front of her.

It was Henrich. Her Henri. Lying in what appeared to be a glass coffin on display on a raised platform. His eyes were closed and he was dressed in the finest of garments. His face looked almost peaceful. Clasped in his hands was a single white rose. It was a message for her, that much was clear. Was he dead? She needed to know.

"Wait," Anne said as her friend pushed on the gates, slipping inside so fast the guards couldn't stop her. "Wait!"

But she kept going, the cloak falling from her shoulders as she ran.

"It's the princess!" someone shouted, but she didn't stop. She didn't care who saw her. She rushed up the platform steps and leaned over the coffin, lifting the glass lid. "Henri! Henri!" she cried, but his eyes remained closed. She clasped his hands. They were still warm. She leaned her head on Henri's chest. There was shouting and commotion behind her. Screams and cries rose up from the crowd.

"It's her!"

"She's come back for us!"

"Princess, save us!"

She blocked out their yelling and listened for the most important sound in the world: a heartbeat. But before she had the chance to register one, she was ripped off the platform and spun around. She instantly recognized the large, burly man holding her.

The man smiled, his gold tooth gleaming. "Take the traitor to Queen Ingrid. She's been expecting the princess."

She held her head high as he marched her past Anne and the crowd and whispered in her ear.

"Welcome home, Snow White."

Snow

Ten years earlier

Flakes fell softly, covering the already frozen castle grounds. When she stuck out her tongue, she could feel the flakes land on it. The little droplets of frozen water had the same name she did: Snow.

Was she named for the snow or was the snow named for her? That's what she wondered. She was a princess, so the weather *could* have been named after her.

Then again, snow had been around a lot longer than she had. She was only seven.

"What's that smell?" her mother called out, pulling Snow from her thoughts.

Snow flattened herself to the castle garden's wall so she wouldn't be seen and tried to stay quiet.

"Smells delicious and sweet . . . Could there be a goose in the garden with me?'"

Snow giggled. "Mother, geese don't stay at the castle in the winter! They fly south. Everyone knows that."

"Everyone also knows that if you talk during hide-and-seek, you can be found faster." Her mother rounded a bend and pointed to her. "I've found you!"

Maybe she was biased, but Snow thought her mother was the most wonderful person in the world. Father said she looked just like her, and if that was true, Snow was pleased. Her mother had kind eyes the color of chestnuts and ebony hair, which, today, was pulled back in a loose chignon. She had removed her favorite crown—Mother didn't often wear it during games in the garden, especially in the winter months—but she'd need to place it on her head when they went back inside in a few moments. Her mother had to get ready for the castle's annual masquerade ball. Snow hated that she was too young to attend and had to take her supper in her room with her nursemaid. She so wished she could go to the party. She preferred her mother's company to anyone else's.

"I'm going to get you!" her mother sang, pulling up the fur-trimmed hood on her red velvet cloak. Snow particularly liked the gold buttons on this cloak. She would play with them when she was standing close to her mother during processions through the village streets. It loosened the buttons and drove their tailor mad, but it made Snow feel safe and warm, like her mother did. She rarely ever wanted to leave her side—except during games of hide-and-seek.

"But you haven't caught me yet!" Snow cried, and she took off through the garden's maze of bushes. Her mother started to laugh.

Snow wasn't sure which way to turn. Every path looked the same. The high, neatly trimmed green hedges blocked all but the view of the gray, snowy sky. Most of the flowers had been pruned for the season, leaving much of the normally beautiful grounds bare and Snow's position in the gardens more visible than usual. If Snow kept weaving around the corners, she knew she would reach the center of the maze and her mother's beloved aviary. The two-story wrought iron dome looked like a giant birdcage. It was her mother's pride and joy and the first thing she had commissioned when she became queen. She'd always had a love of birds. Snow's mother kept several species inside the netted walls, and she patiently explained each bird's nature to Snow in detail. The two had spent countless hours watching the aviary, with Snow naming all of the creatures inside it. Her favorite was Snowball, a small white canary.

As Snow rounded the turn and spotted the dome in front of her, Snowball fluttered to a perch and spotted her, tweeting loudly and giving away Snow's position. That was okay. Sometimes Mother catching her was half the fun.

"Here I come!" called Mother.

Snow giggled even harder, her breath leaving smoky rings in the cold air. She could hear her mother's footsteps growing closer, so she rounded the aviary fast to hide on the opposite side. But she wasn't being careful—her mother always told her to be careful—and she felt herself begin to slip on a patch of ice. Soon Snow was falling, sliding out of control into a rosebush.

"Ouch!" she cried as she pulled herself free of the thorny branch that was pricking through her cloak and into her right hand. Snow saw the blood trickle down her pale white palm and began to cry.

"Snow!" her mother said, drawing down close to her. "Are you okay? Where are you hurt?" She leaned in and Snow's vision began to blur, as if the snow was falling harder now. Even through the haze, Snow could still see her mother's dark eyes peering at her intently. "It's all right, Snow. Everything is going to be all right." She took Snow's injured hand, pulled an embroidered handkerchief from her pocket and dabbed it into the snow, and then pressed it against her daughter's wound. It cooled the burn from the cut. She wrapped the handkerchief tightly around Snow's hand. "There. All better. We can clean you up when we get you inside."

Snow pouted. "I hate roses! They hurt!"

Her mother smiled, her image softening along with the sound of her voice. She seemed so far away. "They can, yes, when you get nicked by a thorn." She plucked a single red rose off the bush. It was petrified from the snow and frozen, but still perfectly preserved and almost crimson in color. Snow peered at it closely. "But you shouldn't be afraid to hold on to something beautiful, even if there are thorns in your path. If you want something, sometimes you have to take risks. And when you do"—she handed Snow the rose— "you reap wonderful rewards."

"You shouldn't be here, Your Majesty."

Snow looked up. Her mother's sister and lady-in-waiting, her aunt Ingrid, was staring at them sharply. Almost angrily. Somehow, Snow knew this look well. "You're already late."

Seventeen-year-old Snow awoke with a start, gasping for air as she sat up in bed. "Mother!" she cried out.

But there was no one there to hear her.

There never was. Not anymore.

Instead, Snow was greeted by the sound of silence.

As she wiped the sweat from her brow, she wondered: had this been another dream turned nightmare, or was it a true memory? She had them more frequently now. It had been more than ten years since she'd seen her mother's face; sometimes she wasn't sure.

She hardly ever saw Aunt Ingrid these days. No one in the castle did. Her aunt had become all but a recluse, letting very few into her inner circle. Her niece, whom she was begrudgingly raising, was not one of them.

Aunt Ingrid always looked the same in dreams, maybe because on the rare occasion Snow crossed her aunt's path in the castle, she always had on some slight variation of the same gown. Although they were mostly similar in cut, she wore only the most beautifully tailored dresses, with the finest fabric their kingdom could offer, and only in shades of purple. The castle was indeed drafty, which could have been why Aunt Ingrid was never seen without a dark-hued cape that she coiled around her body like a snake. Snow couldn't recall the last time she'd seen her aunt's hair (she couldn't even remember the color) because Ingrid always covered her head with a tight-fitting headdress accentuated by her crown.

Snow, on the other hand, couldn't remember the last time she'd been given something new to wear. Not that she minded that much—who even saw her?—but it would have been nice to have a gown that didn't tug at her arms or end at her calves. She had two dresses she rotated, and both were covered in patches. She'd mended her burgundy skirt, which she had made from old curtains, more times than she could remember. She didn't even have any fabric left over to patch it anymore, so her skirt had become a rainbow of colors with beige and white patches covering the holes where the dress had torn on the stone steps or a rosebush.

Roses. What was the bit about the roses in her dream?

She couldn't remember. The dream was already beginning to fade. All she could picture was her mother's serene face. Maybe it was best to leave the memory alone. She had a lot to do today.

Snow pulled herself out of bed and went to the large window in her room, drawing open the heavy curtains. She'd resisted using the drapes to make a warm cape for herself so far, but if the next winter was as bad as the last one, she might have to resort to it. She let the bright light of day in and looked out at the grounds below.

Summer was in full bloom, giving the aging castle a glow it needed badly. While there was no denying that the castle's exterior had deteriorated in the last ten years, she felt a sense of pride as she looked out at the garden and her mother's beloved aviary. She had pruned the bushes, giving them a neat shape, as well as overturned and weeded the flower beds. Fresh blooms hung from silver canisters on the brick walls, making the garden come alive. It didn't hurt that she'd been slowly cutting back the ivy that threatened to take over the entire castle. She could only reach so high, but at ground level the stone was clearly visible again, even if it did need a good scrubbing. (She'd add that to her list.) She could only imagine how the facade looked outside the castle gates. Her aunt forbade Snow from leaving the castle's grounds. She said it was for Snow's safety, but it made her feel like a prisoner. At least she could still come and go in the gardens as she pleased.

Being in the open air rather than cooped up in this castle was her own personal form of heaven. She wasn't supposed to speak to the few guards her aunt still kept in employment, but at least when she passed another human being on her walk through the castle to the garden each day she didn't feel quite so alone. Her aunt hadn't let her make a public appearance in years (though there rarely *were* appearances these days, even for Queen Ingrid), and the castle seldom saw visitors. She sometimes wondered if the kingdom even knew there *was* a princess anymore. But there was no one to ask.

Snow tried to stay busy keeping up the castle. When she had too much time on her hands, she began to think a lot about all she'd lost over the last ten years. Her beloved mother, Queen Katherine, had fallen ill so quickly Snow never had the chance to go to her bedside to say goodbye. Her father had been too distraught to comfort her, instead turning to Aunt Ingrid, whom he soon married. Snow could still hear the whispers about the union, which seemed more like it was done out of necessity than love. She assumed her father had wanted her to have a mother, and Ingrid had appeared to be the next best thing. But she wasn't. Snow noticed her father never again smiled the way he had when her mother was alive.

Perhaps that was the true reason her father had run off only a few months later: he'd had a broken heart. At least, that's what she told herself. It was too hard to believe what Aunt Ingrid told everyone—that her father had lost his mind. Aunt Ingrid said that without Katherine around to help him govern the kingdom, King Georg had become overcome with grief. Snow once heard her aunt tell the court that Georg spoke to Katherine as if she were still alive, frightening guards, servants, and even his own daughter. But Snow didn't remember him doing that.

Her last memory of her father was in the aviary. She had snuck out there to take care of her mother's birds. Sensing someone's presence, she'd turned around to find the king watching her with tears in his eyes.

"You remind me so much of your mother," he'd said hoarsely. He reached out and gently stroked her hair. "I'm so sorry she isn't here to see you grow up."

"It's not your fault, Papa," Snow had said, and this only made him cry harder. He knelt down, grasping her shoulders and looking her in the eye.

"Don't make the same mistakes I did, Snow," he said. "Don't be fooled by love. It only comes once. Trust your instincts. Trust your people. Trust what you've learned from your mother, most of all. Let her spirit guide you when you rule." He cupped her face in his hands. "You will make a remarkable queen someday. Don't let anyone make you lose your way."

"I won't, Papa," she remembered saying, but his words had frightened her. They felt like goodbye.

The next morning, he was gone.

She hadn't realized it at first. It wasn't until she got dressed and headed to her father's chambers to have breakfast with him as they always did that she heard people talking about the king's sudden disappearance. Queen Ingrid—recently coronated—had been pulled into "urgent business" and hadn't found Snow to tell her herself. Instead, Snow had heard the news from two gossiping guards.

"Queen says he's a madman. That we're better off without him. Hasn't been the same since Queen Katherine died," one said. "What king runs off and abandons his daughter?"

"What king abandons his own people?" the other replied.

Snow didn't know the answer to that. All she knew was that she'd never felt more alone. After Father had gone, Aunt Ingrid seemed to disappear, too. The new queen didn't have time to have breakfast with Snow, let alone study birds in the aviary. She was too busy meeting with her newly appointed court, a group of people Snow had never seen before. Everyone her father had worked with had been dismissed, and the smaller staff of advisors had been handpicked by Ingrid. Even so, Snow heard the whispers about her aunt's new nickname: the "Evil Queen," they called her, when she wasn't within earshot. Other than meeting with them, the queen rarely took appointments or met with visiting royals. After a couple of years, her aunt stopped letting anyone new into the castle. The rumor was that she was fearful of traitors, which seemed to prove true when most of the staff were dismissed except for a select few.

A vain woman, Queen Ingrid couldn't do without her personal tailor, Margaret; the ever-present guards; or a small group of cooks; but she certainly didn't hire anyone to care for Snow. Instead, Snow had raised herself, growing up mostly alone in her big, empty room that reminded her of a tomb. Being alone with her thoughts could have driven her mad. But she kept her mind busy by making mental lists of things to do to get her through each day.

Today was no exception. Turning away from the window, Snow removed her dressing gown, then washed up at her water basin, which she had filled at the wishing well the day before. She put on her gown with the patched-up tan skirt and smoothed out the creases on her white-and-brown blouse that almost matched. She slipped into her clogs, which she had recently cleaned. Looking in her freshly shined mirror—she'd tidied up her room yesterday, as she did every week—she put on the blue headband she'd made from scraps her aunt's tailor had left for garbage. Satisfied, Snow went to her wardrobe.

It was almost bare. The few dresses hanging on the rack she had outgrown years before, but she kept them both for sentimental reasons and in case she ever needed to use the fabric for patches or material. She hated the thought of cutting up her history—there was her seventh birthday dress, and the gown she'd worn to a meeting with her father and the visiting king of Prunham—though sometimes it was necessary. For now, the dresses served as reminders of a different life, as well as a wonderful hiding spot. Snow pulled back her birthday dress and glanced at the portrait hidden behind it.

Her mother's and father's faces stared back at her. So did a younger version of her own. The portrait had been commissioned right before her mother had taken ill. It had been the family's first time sitting for an official painting since Snow was a baby. It had hung in the castle barely more than a few weeks before the king had ordered it taken down. Her aunt claimed he'd done so because it was too painful for him to see the former queen's face every day, but Snow felt differently. Any chance she had to see her parents she took.

Morning, Mother. Morning, Father.

Snow had her mother's face, but her father's eyes, while bluish gray, were the same shape as her own. They looked kind, which was how she tried to be, even when it was difficult. She lightly touched one finger against the coarse painting. *Father, why did you leave me?* she wondered, trying not to let bitter feelings well up inside her. Knowing she wouldn't get an answer, she tucked the portrait away again.

Snow went to her room's double doors and opened them quietly. As there was every morning, a tray of breads and fruit awaited her. Snow suspected this was the work of the remaining servants, and she appreciated the gesture more than she could say. Breakfast was always left in front of her room, but dinner was more unpredictable, everyone busy with the queen's most lavish meal. Snow didn't mind going down to the kitchen to get something for herself. Tucked back in the kitchen, away from prying eyes, the main cook, Mrs. Kindred, didn't ignore Snow the way others in the castle did. For just a few moments a day, it meant she had someone to converse with.

"Please, sir, I haven't eaten in two days."

Snow was picking up the tray when she heard the plea.

Startled, she ducked into the shadows of her doorway to eavesdrop.

"If they didn't leave you food, then you get no food."

She knew that voice. It was Brutus, one of her aunt's faithful guards. Snow didn't recognize the other voice.

"But they promised with this post I would be fed two meals a day. It's not for me, sir. I bring most of it home to my wife and child. We can't go a third day without food."

"Your job is to guard these halls, not grumble about grub."

"But—" the guard started to say just as Brutus interrupted him.

"Are you questioning the queen's judgment? You know what happened to the boy in your position before you, do you not?" Snow peered through the shadows as Brutus got in the young man's face. "He was never seen again. Some say he was turned into one of the snakes slithering through the grass on the grounds. I wonder what would become of your family if you weren't here."

"No!" The man's voice was urgent. "Don't bother the queen. I'll wait for food to be delivered . . . whenever that might be."

Snow audibly inhaled. She'd heard the chef and other servants talk about how her aunt practiced witchcraft. "It's how she stays looking so young," some said. "It's why no one questions her decisions—they're afraid she'll turn them into a toad or an insect or worse," said others. They talked about a chamber where the queen spent most of her time talking to someone—even though no one else was ever seen coming or going from the room. Snow wasn't sure what to think, but she knew people who crossed the queen disappeared. And she knew the queen's very presence struck fear through everyone in the castle. Brutus's role as her henchman could be equally frightful.

"Smart boy," Brutus said, and headed down the hallway toward Snow, a playful grin on his lips.

Snow pressed herself against the cool wall to make sure he didn't see her. When he was out of sight, she peeked again to look at the guard. He was young and very thin. Not much older than she. And he had a family he was feeding on meals that weren't arriving. She looked down at the warm bread and the fruit on her breakfast tray.

Her belly was still full from the night before. She could make it until dinner without anything more. Looking both ways to make sure the hall was clear before stepping out of the shadows, Snow walked swiftly toward the guard, her eyes cast downward. The guard looked surprised when she placed her tray at his feet.

"Your Highness," he said, struggling for words. "But that's *your* meal."

Snow was too shy to speak. Instead, she waved the food away and pushed the tray closer to his boots. With a small nod and smile, she hurried back to the safety of her chambers before anyone could see them conversing and tell the queen, but not before she heard him speak softly.

"Thank you, kind princess. Thank you."

She didn't feel much like a princess these days, but she was proud to help anyone when she could. Back in her chambers, Snow prepared to go about her day. Since the court wasn't meeting with her aunt, she knew it was safe to mop the castle foyer. It had been looking a little muddy when she'd walked through yesterday. There were also several stained glass windows on the second floor that she hadn't had a chance to clean recently. And there was a rug she wanted to scrub near the throne room. She hated getting too close to her aunt's quarters, but that rug was the first thing visitors saw when they came to meet with her, however rare that might be. What people thought of the castle was one of the few things about the kingdom Snow could control, and she took pride in the work . . . even on days when her back began to ache from scrubbing tiles or her hands grew callused from all the pruning she did in the garden. She tried to break up her day between indoor and outdoor activities when the weather allowed it. Today was a fine day, so she hoped to get out to the garden as soon as possible. She wanted to gather flowers to make bouquets for the castle vases. There wouldn't be many who had the opportunity to see the flowers, but at least the servants' day would be brightened.

She gathered her cleaning supplies and was heading down the hall when she heard footsteps. Once more, she instinctively moved into the shadows to stay unseen. It was the queen's seamstress, Margaret, as well as Margaret's apprentice: a daughter about the same age as Snow. Snow had overheard them talking on their many trips to the castle and knew the daughter's name was Anne, but the two had never spoken.

"I told you: I don't know why we were summoned," Snow heard Margaret say as she wheeled a cart with spools of fabric and sewing materials down the hall. With every turn, the cart made a clicking sound that echoed through the corridor. "I'm sure it's nothing to worry about."

"What if she changed her mind again?" Anne prodded, her brown eyes holding a world of worry. She pushed a stray strand of hair off her tan face. "We can't afford to throw out any more fabric, Mother. The queen won't let us sell the discarded gowns to anyone and she won't let us keep them. One day she wants all purple, the next black, and the following blue. The Evil Queen can't decide!"

"Don't you dare call her that! Hold your tongue!" Margaret looked around worriedly and Snow pushed herself farther into the shadows. "Do you know how fortunate we are to have this position? She is the queen, and as you well know, she can do whatever she pleases—including doing away with us."

Anne hung her head, staring down at the basketful of spools in her arms. "I'm sorry, Mother. It just feels so wasteful! Her tariffs and rules mean so many go hungry. If we could give the unwanted clothes to those in need . . ."

It pained Snow to hear the subjects talk like this. She was forbidden to spend time outside the castle, so she didn't know for sure, but she sensed that most of the people were struggling. She hated feeling like her life was frozen in time. She'd have given anything to help the people, but she knew her aunt would never entertain her concerns.

Margaret stopped the cart. "Enough now! I mean it!" Anne grew quiet. "I am grooming you to take over this position when I am too old to thread a needle. Do you want the job to go to someone else?"

"Honestly?" Anne started to say, and Snow couldn't help laughing.

Anne seemed like a funny girl, one Snow wished she could spend time with. But that was out of the question.

"What was that sound?" Anne said in alarm, and Snow grew quiet. Anne was looking in her direction.

"See what I mean?" Margaret hissed. "She is always watching, girl. Always! Enough griping. Whatever the queen doesn't want today, you put with the rest of the waste we leave behind."

Anne sighed. "Yes, Mother."

More rags! Snow thought. She wondered what the queen would think if she knew her unwanted clothes were being torn up and used for cleaning. (The staff joked that the castle had the finest cleaning rags in the land.)

Snow watched them both continue down the hall and waited till they turned into the queen's corridor before she stepped into the light again. Then she heard movement and froze, turning around slowly. Anne had come back around the corner and was looking right at her. The two stared at one another for a moment. Snow wasn't sure what to do, so she stood there, still as a statue. Then Anne smiled and did something surprising—she curtsied in Snow's direction.

"Have a good day, Princess," she said. And then she was gone.

Snow grabbed her cleaning supplies and disappeared before Anne could return again. As lovely as it was to be acknowledged, she knew she couldn't respond. Not there, out in the open. Not without the queen hearing about it and punishing Snow—or worse, Anne, for "endangering the princess" with her company. She walked down the hall in the other direction, taking the stairs down two levels, past the banquet hall, the dining area, and the empty living quarters, and heading straight to the doors that led out to her mother's garden.

Blue. It always amazed her how blue the sky was on a cloudless day. Was it always this color, or was it just more stunning because it had been so long since she'd seen it? It had rained the last three days, forcing her to stay indoors, which was painful. The sun made her more grateful today. Her mother was very much on her mind after last night's dream, and being in the gardens near the aviary always made her feel closer to her.

She looked down at the stone steps beneath her feet. Moss had started to creep up the walkway and was turning the white stone green. She would start there. With a sigh, she dropped to her knees, wet her sponge, and began to scrub, humming a tune to herself as she worked. A few moments later, a group of white birds landed on the steps to watch her. "Hello there!" she said and removed some birdseed from her pocket, laying it on the steps for them to eat. When they were finished, they stayed to watch her work. She didn't mind. It helped to have company, even if they couldn't talk. She found herself talking to *them* sometimes. True, some might call her mad for conversing with animals, but who was paying attention?

The moss began to vanish under her scrubbing, and the steps looked almost new again. Pleased, she went to the well to get a fresh bucket of water. Perhaps if she finished with this in a timely manner, she could visit the aviary. The birds followed, watching as she hoisted water from the well, and she couldn't help smiling.

"Do you want to hear a secret?" she asked the birds. "This is a magic wishing well. Let's make a wish."

Her mother had been the one to tell her the well had the power to grant wishes. "What do you wish for?" her mother would ask, and Snow could recall closing her eyes and thinking really hard. "I wish," she'd say . . . and then she'd ask for the thing she wanted most in the world at that moment. One time it was a pony. Other times a doll or a tiara that looked like her mother's crown. All her wishes were granted within days of asking for them at the well. She was old enough now to know her father and mother had made her wishes come true, but still, she loved the idea of the well being magical. She hadn't made a wish since she was a child, but the movement felt so natural she couldn't resist doing it again now. Snow closed her eyes. "I wish . . ."

What did she wish for?

She no longer needed a pony or a doll. What she needed was her parents' love, but no well could turn back time and change her fate. She had accepted her mundane, solitary life and made the best of it . . . but she couldn't help wishing there was someone to share her days with.

"I wish for love," Snow announced, the statement simple and profound at the same time.

She opened her eyes and looked into the cavernous well.

No love—true or otherwise—was waiting at the bottom.

One could always dream. And she was still outside, enjoying the beautiful day. It made her want to sing. She thought of her mother and hummed one of her favorite tunes—one she'd said she sang to Snow's father when they were courting. The birds stayed near to listen to Snow's melodic voice.

She was so caught up in the music that she didn't notice the boy till he was in front of her, seeming to appear from thin air.

Snow

Stranger!

Snow was so surprised to see a young man walking toward her that she knocked over her bucket and ran for the safety of the castle. Her heart was pounding as she rushed inside. Had this intruder come for her, as Aunt Ingrid had always warned? *There is a mark on a princess's head. Mark my word!* she'd say whenever young Snow asked why she couldn't leave the castle grounds in the early days, back when Queen Ingrid had been around more. And now a man had appeared. What should she do? Alert the guards? She could hear yelling—was he calling to her? What if someone heard him? She ran up the steps to the first landing, went to the nearest balcony, and cautiously looked out.

The stranger was looking right at her.

Snow did as she always did: she retreated into the shadows again.

"Wait!" she heard him call. "Please wait. I am so happy I found you."

Found you? she thought. Why was he looking for her?

She knew Aunt Ingrid said strangers couldn't be trusted, but he appeared to be the same age as her, if not slightly older, and looked like he had a kind face. His voice wasn't menacing, so maybe he meant her no harm. But why was he looking for her? She risked another peek from the balcony to get a better look. She inhaled sharply.

His eyes were as blue as the blue jay that sat on her windowsill most mornings, and his hair, while a bit messy, was a lovely shade of brown. She liked how one curl fell over one of his eyes, and he had such a luminous smile that she couldn't help blushing. His clothes were fine, indicating that he held a high station somewhere; he had on a dark red traveling cloak over a clean white dress shirt, blue pants, and a royal blue and gold vest. His brown suede boots were muddy, as if they'd been well-used, but still seemed high quality.

It had been so long since she'd concentrated on someone else's face. Reluctantly, she avoided eye contact. Her aunt didn't want her to appear friendly. *It opens you up to trouble!* she'd say whenever she called upon Snow in the early years to scold her for eating with the cooks or bringing flowers to a servant. Maybe he wasn't there to hurt her, but nothing would save him from Aunt Ingrid when she learned he'd climbed over the castle wall.

"You should leave," Snow said, forcing herself to look away from him.

"Wait!" he called after her. "Did I frighten you?"

Yes. Snow didn't answer him. Instead, she hid herself behind the curtains.

"I didn't mean to," he said. "Your voice is so lovely. When I heard it, I had to see who was making such beautiful music."

She smiled to herself. He thought her singing was beautiful?

"Would you please come out?"

Snow looked down at her tattered dress and hesitated. That's when she heard her mother's voice in her head again, another memory from long ago. They'd encountered some beggars in the village and she recalled asking her mother why they dressed so differently. *You must look past appearances, Snow,* she remembered her mother telling her. *A person's true worth is always found within.*

Snow did what she could with what she had, and she should be proud of that. She touched her hair to make sure it was in place and stepped out onto the balcony.

The young man smiled, removing his feathered cap. "There you are. Are you going to come down?"

She hesitated. "I really must go," she said. "I have much to do."

"Please stay, if only for a moment," he begged.

Her cheeks felt warm again. No one had ever spoken to her this way before. "For a moment," she agreed, stepping closer to the railing.

He looked at her curiously. "You look far too young to be a queen."

"Oh, I'm not the queen," she said, her fingers gripping the stone rail tightly. For some reason, he made her feel almost dizzy. "I'm just the princess."

"Just?" He cocked his head to one side.

A small brown bird with a blue head landed on her shoulder, and she handed it a seed from her pocket.

"That's a bearded reedling," the young man said in surprise. "You rarely see those anywhere but in the woods. It must really like you to stay here."

"Yes," said Snow, surprised at his knowledge. She hadn't met anyone other than her mother who shared her love of birds. "This one frequents here a lot, but isn't a permanent resident." She motioned to the gardens, where her mother's beautiful aviary reached high into the sky. "My mother commissioned this aviary, and when I was a child she taught me all there was to know about the species that live in our kingdom. We have many sparrows and even a few middle spotted woodpeckers," she said, noting the small black-and-red birds on the ground.

He turned around to look at the domed structure. "It's beautiful. The birds must love having such a lovely cage to reside in."

Cage. She had never called it that before, but it's what it was, wasn't it? A prison. A beautiful prison, but a prison nonetheless. A lot like the one she grew up in. The thought suddenly saddened her. "Yes," she said. "I hope they are happy here."

He studied her face. "I'm sure they are. You give them all they need—food, shelter, water. What's not to love?" She didn't reply. "It's the perfect setting. All these winterberry bushes you have—they attract a lot of birds." He began to look around, his boots scuffing the pebbles on the ground. Then he glanced up at her again, his eyes bright. "You know, if you wanted to see more cardinals, you could ask the palace to plant grapevines. They love sitting on those in my kingdom."

"I will try that," she said pleasantly. There was something about him that reminded Snow of her mother. "Where are you from?"

He bent down and let a bearded reedling climb onto his

arm. "My kingdom borders yours in the north. I'm Henrich, by the way, but my friends call me Henri."

Did that mean she was a friend? She couldn't help smiling. "I'm Snow White."

"Snow White," he repeated, staring at her intently. "I hope our paths cross again. I'm here to see the queen, although I don't have an appointment."

"Oh." Snow's face fell. "She doesn't like being called on unannounced."

"Perhaps you could tell her I'm here, then?" he asked. She opened her mouth to protest. "It's important I talk to her. My father, the king, asked me to, and I don't want to let him down." His face fell slightly.

"May I be so bold as to ask what for?" Snow couldn't believe the words coming out of her mouth, but she didn't want him to leave yet. Having an actual conversation with another person was so much nicer than she remembered. She'd had no idea how much she craved such contact.

"Your kingdom is known for its diamonds and good farming, and ours is known for raising sheep. We've always had a robust trade between the two kingdoms that we both benefited from," Henri explained. "But the past few years the queen has taxed us heavily when we want to buy crops, and keeps cutting our profits on wool. Recently, she stopped taking orders. We've heard she's started looking elsewhere to trade. I wanted to appeal to her to keep the original agreement we had with King Georg."

Snow felt a pang hearing her father's name. "I'm not sure she's going to honor that agreement, especially if you bring up the former king," Snow said thoughtfully. "But perhaps you could offer her something more in return. Something that lets her know that trading with your kingdom is something she couldn't possibly refuse. Is there another export you have that would be worthy to her?"

Henri paused for a moment. "We have a lot of cattle. We'd certainly be willing to trade some of our stock." He looked at her. "You're very wise, Snow White."

She looked down at her clogs. "I like figuring out things and keeping my mind busy." She glanced up at him again. "I'm not sure I have much pull with Queen Ingrid, but at least now you know what you can offer her."

Henrich's grin lit up like a thousand fireflies. "I'm indebted to you, Princess." She suddenly noticed he looked very tired. She wondered how long he had been traveling. In the distance, she heard the village clock chime. How long had they been talking? She needed to leave before the queen learned what she was doing. "I should go, and you should, too, I'm afraid."

"Yes," Henri agreed, placing his cap back on his head and bowing to her. "Perhaps I will try to make an appointment. Thank you again for your help." He looked back at the wishing well where he had first seen her. "May I take a drink before I go?"

"Of course," she said, and she watched as he walked to the well and filled a canteen from his pocket. With a final nod, he headed back to the wall. He grabbed on to some hanging vines and gave them a tug to see if they would hold. Slowly, he began to climb. When he reached the top, he looked back at her.

"Thank you, Snow," Henri said. "Till we meet again?"

"Till we meet again," she repeated. *I hope it's soon,* she thought, despite herself. *I hope it is very soon.*

Snow was so busy watching Henri that she didn't notice she was also being watched. High above, the Evil Queen looked down unhappily from her window.

Ingrid

The queen watched the scene in the garden with disgust.

How many times had she told that girl not to converse with anyone, especially strangers?

And yet, there she was in that ragged dress of hers, talking to a young man. Just the sight of them together, smiling and laughing like old acquaintances, had caused the queen to dig her fingernails into the stone railing so hard she left a mark. Who was that boy and what was he doing on the castle grounds without her knowledge? It wasn't just his intrusion that angered her. It was something else she couldn't put her finger on yet. But she would.

Whirling away from the window, the queen moved toward her wardrobe door. She pressed a lever on the wall, which allowed her to open a secret doorway that led to another room. She quickly closed it behind her. Once in the darkened chamber, she stepped up onto the platform at its center. Then she threw open the blue curtains that hid her most prized possession. Her private quarters were off-limits, but one could never be too careful. Yes, she had protection charms in place—ancient symbols that she had painted on the white stone walls around the artifact to keep it from being removed—but she was suspicious by nature and didn't like to take chances. The mirror was worth protecting.

Even though they had spent practically a lifetime together, she still marveled at the object's beauty. With an oval silhouette, the mirror took up almost an entire wall. Its frame—made of ebony and intricately gilded—was magnificent enough, but it was the snakelike gold rope wrapped *around* the frame that had first drawn her eye when she'd found the mirror hidden in her master's shop. The rope lay smooth on the lower half of the mirror, but became more erratic and vine-like near the mirror's top, where it seemed to breathe out of two serpents' mouths like tongues. The jewels that adorned the mirror, too, were worth more than any of the diamonds in the kingdom's mines. If she didn't keep the mirror hidden, some fool would stumble upon the thing and plunder the jewels for their worth, never realizing the object's *true* gift. The mirror had never told her how it had come into being, but she knew every part of it was vital and irreplaceable. How much of her day did she spend in this tower room staring at those rubies that peered at her like two snake eyes? How often did she turn to the mask in the glass over all others?

She closed her eyes, raised her arms, and heard the thunder and wind that were summoned with greater ease with each passing year. Lightning illuminated the room as she began to speak.

"Voice in the magic mirror, come from the farthest space," the queen began. "Through wind and darkness I summon thee. Speak! Let me see thy face."

The mirror began to smoke and an image began to take shape. Sometimes it came through rather smoky, or so fuzzy she felt like she was looking at it through a distorted piece of glass. But this time, the jester-like beige mask appeared clearly—its eyes missing from its sockets, its eyebrows arched almost permanently in a curious expression, a mouth nothing more than a thin pink line. The first time she had seen the bodiless man in the mirror, she had thought him loathsome. Now his was the face she craved to see more than any other. She knew the features on the mask as well as she knew the lines on her own face . . . lines that disappeared over time, thanks to the mirror's magic. She looked as young and vibrant as Snow on most days, and she dressed infinitely better. Her purple gown with its sewn-in cape was made of the finest silk and fit her like a well-made glove.

"What wouldst thou know, my queen?" asked the mirror, sounding steady and strong. The mirror's voice always had a profound effect on her, perhaps because she knew it was always right.

There was also a smug satisfaction that came from knowing the mirror still bowed to her every whim. Despite the ritualistic exchange they had each day, it never questioned her need to hear her heart's desire. Ever since she was a young girl, she had craved a type of beauty and wealth she had not been born into, and she never tired of hearing that she had finally achieved it. She said the familiar words: "Magic Mirror on the wall, who is the fairest one of all?"

She waited for the familiar answer. And yet . . .

"Famed is thy beauty, Majesty. But, hold, a lovely maid I see," the mirror replied. "Rags cannot hide her gentle grace. Alas, she is more fair than thee."

Ingrid's blood ran cold. She tried to remain calm, but the answer had rattled her. Somewhere in the recesses of her mind, the presence of a boy—much like the boy who had once captivated her sister's heart—always made her worry. She had done everything she could to prevent this day from coming, but somehow she had always known it would. "Reveal her name," she demanded, understanding this was only delaying the inevitable.

"Lips red as the rose, hair black as ebony, skin white as snow . . ."

She didn't wait for the mirror to finish. "Snow White," she gasped. Despite having known this might be the case, it felt like all the air was being sucked out of her lungs. She tried to steady herself, exhaling slowly. She ran a pale, slender hand over her head, which was covered with a tight black headscarf. Her hair had always been unusually thin, unlike her sister's or Snow's. She hated how wiry it was and how it wouldn't curl like theirs. Now she kept it locked up tight.

"The future holds more than one outcome. If your will is to pass, you alone know what must be done," the mirror told her.

She understood where the mirror was going with this. They'd had this discussion before. It was one the mirror kept circling back to, just as it had all those years ago.

Ingrid turned away to compose herself. She looked around the almost bare room. To her knowledge, no one knew this room existed. Hidden behind her bedroom closet, she'd had the room built when she had moved into Georg's tower after her sister's death. Georg was too consumed with grief to even wonder what she was having built into her wardrobe. Katherine, on the other hand, had found out about the mirror and its power. She had not trusted it. And she had paid for those fears dearly.

Katherine. Ingrid glanced at a sudden movement in the shadows, her pulse quickening. But there was no one there. She breathed a sigh of relief and turned back to the mirror, trying to focus on the things she could control in this moment. "Tell me about the boy."

"You have long known this day would pass," the mirror replied. "To succeed, you must keep him from the lass."

"Tell me again," she said impatiently. She knew the mirror hated that tone, so she reconsidered her attitude. "I don't recall this conversation. Where did the young man come from?"

"From a kingdom in the northern land," said the mirror, "hails Henrich—a prince, brave and true. He shall not leave till he asks for her hand."

"She just met the boy," Ingrid said dismissively. "They won't cross paths again." *I could also see to it that he doesn't cross paths with* anyone *again,* she thought. If that was what she had to do, she would.

"My queen, take heed, and do not laugh," the mirror said. "If you do not act, he shall again cross her path."

Ingrid felt the anger bubble up inside her at the mirror's words. She curled her hands into tight fists. Just an hour ago, she'd been down in the dungeon, working on a potion, before sensing the mirror had a message for her. Now she had a problem that needed to be dealt with. Immediately.

The queen wasn't sure how she always knew the mirror was calling, but the more she gave in to its powers, the more in tune with it she became. And she knew that everything it was saying now was true. No matter how hard she had tried to keep the girl hidden away and keep her from the finer things a princess should be afforded, the girl's beauty and nature shone through. No rags, no dirt could hide Snow's luminescence. That child was a perfect rose. Now that she was of age, there was no hiding that.

"The maiden may be under lock and key, but beloved by the people she will be," the mirror continued. "You, my queen, they are less pleased to see."

It was as if the mirror suddenly delighted in telling her what she didn't want to hear. "I know that! Don't you think I know?" She lunged at the mirror as if about to strike it, but stopped herself. She wouldn't dare. "That child diminishes my authority over the people. Even hidden away in her ivory tower, they seem to know she's there. I'm sure they wish she'd do something to rid them of their 'evil queen,' but she doesn't have my strength, my power."

"Power does she lack," the mirror agreed, "yet strength is another matter. If given a chance, she will take the throne back."

The mirror let the words linger in the damp, still air. The room smelled so musty that she sometimes felt ill. But it wasn't as though she could ask anyone to clean it. She walked to one of the lanterns and lit it to give the room a warm greenish glow. Her eyes instinctively went to the corner of the chamber again, but still, no one was there. Maybe today she would get some peace from *that* at least.

"Till Snow White's heart beats no more, the people will look to her. And an end to your peace will be in store," the mirror said, reading her thoughts.

She hated when it did that, though she sighed with silent agreement. For too long she had allowed that child to exist, afraid to do anything that might disturb her newfound power. But ignoring Snow would not make her go away. It was time to take action, to do what no one else would, as per usual. "I will take care of this," she proclaimed quietly.

"My queen, you are wise. The late hour has yet to strike. Do not let her be your demise."

She would have it done today. She had delayed the inevitable for far too long. There would be no more indecisiveness. The threat was now too great. Rushing to the secret entrance, she pressed the lever that would let her back into her wardrobe. Then she emerged out of the closet and into her main chambers. She went straight to her door and opened it. He was waiting, as she knew he would be.

"Brutus," she told the burly guard standing by. "Find me the huntsman. Bring him to my throne immediately."

It always pleased her when people moved quickly.

By the time Ingrid got to her throne room, Brutus told her the huntsman had arrived. Whether the huntsman had to come from a great distance or not, she did not care. All she cared about was that she wasn't kept waiting. Making other people wait was another story.

She had learned over the years that time might not have been her friend when it came to aging (at least not before she had come across the mirror), but in terms of making visitors uncomfortable and anxious, time was a blessing, indeed. Which was why she took her time getting settled on her throne that day. She loved sitting in that chair.

Georg, the fool that he was, had kept the same old, unassuming design as his father had before him. And Katherine, never caring much for décor, hadn't made a peep about changing that fact. Ingrid, on the other hand, couldn't wait to make alterations to the receiving room. As soon as she married Georg, she had workers build a platform for the thrones. As king and queen, should they not sit higher than those coming to ask favor of them? Armor was hung from the walls, giving anyone who entered a clear picture that this kingdom was not to be challenged. She added red velvet curtains and had her throne covered in blue velvet. But her favorite part of the opulent chair was the peacock feathers that fanned out behind her head, wreathing her in a sea of greens and black.

Poised upon it now, she gave the guard permission to let the huntsman in.

He walked in, gaze downcast, his brown hair falling in front of his eyes. As soon as he got close enough, he knelt before her.

"Rise, huntsman, as I have a task for you," she said. It occurred to her at that moment she didn't even know the man's name. He'd carried out many tasks for her over the last few years. Unspeakable tasks that he would take to the grave, and yet she still greeted him as if he were almost a stranger. It was for the best.

The huntsman removed his cap and looked at her, waiting for more direction. He had learned the hard way that she didn't take kindly to interruptions.

"I would like you to take Snow White into the forest where she can pick wildflowers." A devilish smile played on her lips. "And there, my faithful huntsman, you will kill her."

He looked taken aback. "But Your Majesty! She's the princess!"

"Silence!" she commanded, her eyes flashing like fire. "You dare question your queen?"

"No, Your Majesty," he said softly, hanging his head again.

She drummed her fingers on the throne. It thrilled her to know he had no choice but to follow her command. If he didn't, he and his family would suffer the consequences. "You know the penalty if you fail."

He did not look up. "Yes, Your Majesty."

His word you cannot trust! she heard a voice in her head say. She knew it wasn't her own. The mirror knew everything. *Ask for proof, you must.*

Proof.

Yes.

Her eyes landed on the red box she kept on her throne. She used it to collect taxes from the foolish men her guards brought to her when they failed to make their payments. The box was empty at the moment. She'd cleared it out only yesterday. Lifting it, she examined its design more closely than she had in quite a while. It featured a heart with an arrow sticking through it. How poetic.

Queen Ingrid held the ornate box out to him. The huntsman looked at her worriedly, which was thrilling. She could not believe how long it had taken her to do this. Oh, how she would enjoy it. "But to make doubly sure you do not fail," she said, the words sounding deliciously slippery on her lips, "bring me back her heart in this."

Ingrid

Thirty years earlier

They sat on the floor, facing one another, knees touching in front of the warm fire. She spread the wooden figures out in front of them on the small linen towel.

Her younger sister, Katherine, clapped excitedly when she saw them. "Oh, Ingrid, you made more!"

Katherine picked up the small wooden knobs upon which Ingrid had painted faces, and looked at them lovingly. They were wearing scraps of cloth Ingrid had found in Mother's old sewing basket. Father thought he had thrown all of her things out when she died, but Ingrid had shrewdly hidden the basket under her bed. She knew they'd need it for mending and sewing new clothes. The dresses they had weren't going to last forever.

Her father had no head for girls. He left them to fend for themselves most days while he worked in the village at the blacksmith's. It was a long time for the two of them to be alone—before the sun rose and after it set—but that suited Ingrid just fine. She didn't much like having him around.

"Yes," Ingrid told her, holding up a small king with a paper crown on his head. "Here is King Jasper and Queen Ingrid and Katherine, the good fairy."

Katherine laughed. "You're the queen! That's okay. I quite like being a kind fairy." She touched the small paper wings Ingrid had glued to the back of the wooden dowel. "Do I have magic powers?"

"Of course you do," Ingrid told her. "So does the queen, of course. Everyone should know magic."

Katherine's sweet face clouded over, the flames making shadows dance on her button nose. "Good magic, right?"

"Of course," Ingrid said. They'd heard Father talk about ridiculous rumors of witches who dabbled in the dark arts, but he swore it was all rubbish. And on this fact, Ingrid tended to agree with him. Magic didn't exist. She was sure of it. If it did, she would have found a way to save Mother from her illness.

But Katherine was only ten. She *should* believe. At thirteen, Ingrid was older and wiser, or so she told herself, and in Mother's absence, she tried to teach her sister all that their mother would have if she were still alive. That meant she tried to teach Katherine how to write and read, among other things. Father had stopped their schooling when Mother died.

"Your place is to keep house," he told Ingrid. "Cook, clean, look pretty, keep your mouth shut, and be ready to serve me when I get home."

Like he was a king. He wasn't, that was for sure. Ingrid couldn't stand the sight of him when he came home some nights—later than he'd say he'd be, smelling like the devil. Some evenings he wouldn't even eat what she'd cooked. He'd just stumble into his bed and stay there till they woke him in the morning. Ingrid liked those evenings best. She and Katherine could eat without saving him the biggest portion, and they didn't have to hear his belligerent mouth. He was so angry all the time, as if he hated them for living when Mother had died.

So, if Ingrid had to tell Katherine some white lies to keep her from hating their life the way Ingrid did, she would.

"Katherine is a good fairy, and good fairies and sprites have the best kind of magic," Ingrid said, taking her sister's wooden dowel and flying it above their heads like a bird.

They played for what felt like forever, and Ingrid finally allowed her shoulders to relax. Dinner was cooking in the fire—a stew that would feed them for days—and with any luck, Father wouldn't be back till the sky was black as night.

So when they heard the door thunder open while the sun was still high, both girls jumped. Father had come home early.

Ingrid hated that she looked like the man. She wasn't balding, of course, but she had his wiry brown hair, whereas Katherine's was black like Mother's had been. Ingrid had his eyes, too—black as coal—while Katherine had Mother's brown ones. It seemed unfair that her sister should get to look like the parent they both loved fiercely, while she had to be reminded of the man they loathed.

"Why are you both sitting on the floor like dogs?" he bellowed, one hand gripping the doorframe.

"Sorry, Papa!" Katherine jumped up and one of the dowels began to roll away from her, coming to a stop at their father's feet.

He bent down and peered at the dowel. It was Fairy Katherine. "Toys? You two were playing with toys?" He moved toward them quickly. Ingrid instinctively put her hand in front of Katherine to keep her out of Father's way. "You are supposed to be doing chores! Cooking! Women don't sit on the floor, Ingrid. You are too old to behave like this."

"Supper is already on, Father," Ingrid said calmly as he stomped around the room. "We weren't expecting you for a few hours."

"Got dismissed," he muttered. "Docked a day's wages for showing up with half a mind."

He was unsteady on his feet. Why had he come home? Now they'd be stuck with him in as foul a temper as ever. Ingrid felt the walls closing in.

"Why don't you go to sleep?" Ingrid suggested.

His eyes narrowed. "I don't need sleep! I need pay, stupid girl!" He raised his hand to strike and she moved out of his reach. He stumbled toward them again. "You two should be out there working instead of me. Earning your keep. Stop playing with toys!" He took the dowel and tossed it into the fire.

"No!" Katherine cried. She started to weep as Fairy Katherine crackled and vanished in front of her eyes.

"Stop crying! You hear me? Stop your crying this instant!" Father shouted.

Ingrid watched his hand wind up like it needed to connect with something. Ingrid always took the blow for Katherine. She couldn't stand to see her younger sister hurting. But seeing Father's expression, and hearing about the job, she knew today he wouldn't settle for just whipping Ingrid. He'd come after them both. He grabbed a strand of Katherine's hair and tugged. Katherine cried harder.

"Is that all you're good for, girl? To make me angry?" he shouted again.

"Let her go!" Ingrid said, pushing his broad chest. It didn't faze her father. Instead, it made him laugh. Ingrid felt her insides harden. Her anger was going to consume her.

"Ugly, stupid girl," he said to Ingrid. "You're even more worthless than she is."

He pulled his hand back again.

The anger bubbled up inside her like a cauldron ready to overflow. Ingrid was tired of being called worthless and ugly. How could she be pretty when she lived in this hovel, wearing these rags? She would not let him hurt her again, and she wouldn't let him dare go after her little sister. Pushing Katherine out of the way, Ingrid grabbed the fire poker from the hearth and struck him with it, hitting him in the head. He fell to the floor with a loud thump.

"Ingrid!" Katherine screamed.

But Ingrid didn't blink. The look of shock that registered on his face after she hit him made her feel good. *How do you like it?* she thought.

She stared at her father as he lay on the ground, blinking rapidly as if he were in shock. She didn't wait for him to get up. Instead, she grabbed Katherine's hand and ran from their cottage. She rushed them down the path and didn't stop till they were deep into the trees in the thick of the forest. Katherine cried most of the way.

"Where are we going? What are you doing?" Katherine kept asking as they ran.

But Ingrid didn't have answers. All she knew was she had to get them as far away from that home as she could. She didn't really think Father would come after them. Why would he? He didn't love them. But she also knew she didn't want him to find them, either. And so they kept moving.

"Are we going home?" Katherine asked after a while.

They'd been walking for what felt like hours now, and the sky was beginning to darken. Ingrid looked around for a way out of the forest. Finally, she saw a clearing.

Ingrid looked at Katherine's tearstained face. "You want to go home to that man?" she asked. "You want to be treated like dogs? Mother wouldn't want it! I don't want it! And you shouldn't, either."

Katherine's little lip started to quiver. "But where will we go?"

Ingrid had heard those words before. She remembered saying them to Mother at her bedside when she was near the end of her life. Her mother had told her to be good to her sister and to raise her well. Ingrid had promised, but she, too, had wondered where they should go. She knew Father wouldn't be there for them. Not in the way Mother had. And Mother, somehow, understood. "*Where* doesn't matter," Ingrid remembered her saying, her breath staggered. Ingrid had wiped the sweat from her mother's brow. "All that matters is that the two of you stay together."

She wouldn't break that promise to her mother. Ingrid pulled Katherine into her arms as her sister cried. "Wherever we go, it will be better than that place. The most important thing is that we stay together," she said, echoing her mother's words. She took Katherine's hand again and led the way down the path.

When the two of them finally stepped out of the woods, they were no longer near their village. Nothing looked familiar. They'd traveled farther than she'd ever been before. She glanced around the planting fields in front of them and stared off at the mountain in the distance. A castle's turrets peeked out from behind some trees. She wasn't sure where they were, but this was as good a place as any to start their new lives.

When the farmer and his horse came out of nowhere, she didn't even startle. Instead, holding Katherine's small hand, she flagged the man down. His face was weatherbeaten and his clothes ragged, but he looked kind.

"Please, sir," Ingrid said, using her sweetest, most endearing voice, the one she usually only used for Katherine. "Would you have any need for my sister and I to do work on your farm? We'll work hard, sir. We are orphans," she lied quickly, before he had a moment to hesitate. "All we ask for is a place to sleep and some food to eat. In return, we will be loyal apprentices."

The man looked from Katherine to Ingrid and back to Katherine again. Then he motioned to the back of his cart. "Come along. We'll see what we can do."

Ingrid helped Katherine up into the hay and climbed in after her. She didn't realize how tired her legs were till they were sinking deep into the dried wheat. Katherine put her head on Ingrid's shoulder as the man pulled them through the field. Ingrid put her arm around her sister, but she kept her eyes on that castle on the hilltop. She'd never seen such a beautiful structure before. Foolish though it was, she allowed herself to imagine what life might be like there—a place with abundant food and clothing and no mean fathers. And perhaps some magic, after all.

Whoever lived there had power, and power was something she'd learned that she needed in this world. It was something she wanted with every fiber of her being. Once she had it, no one would ever be able to push her down again.

Snow

"Your Highness?" Snow felt someone shaking her awake. "It's time to get up now."

Was someone in her room? She opened her eyes and was surprised to find a servant standing over her bed. What was she doing here? No one ever visited her room. She blinked and looked around. Her room was still dark and her curtains drawn. Was it still the middle of the night? Was the castle under attack? Snow had heard the servants talking on more than one occasion. With Aunt Ingrid not being very beloved, a coup was never out of the question.

Snow recognized this servant—a woman who managed the washing of her aunt's fine clothes. "Mila, what are you doing here?" Snow asked, sitting up. "Is something the matter?"

The older woman jumped back as if burned. "You know my name?"

"Yes." Snow suddenly felt shy again. "I have heard other servants address you, and . . ." She thought for a moment. "You sing beautifully."

Mila touched her chest. "Thank you. I . . ." Her voice petered out. "I'm sorry we've never spoken before, Your Highness. The queen . . . she doesn't like us to . . ."

Snow knew what she was trying to say. Her aunt felt the servants' job was to serve *her*, not her niece. "It's quite all right," Snow assured her.

Mila smiled. "But today is different. Queen Ingrid asked that I come help you get ready for a journey!"

"A journey?" Snow had to still be dreaming. Her aunt didn't allow her to go anywhere outside the castle.

"Yes!" Mila pulled back the heavy tapestry bedding and helped Snow out of her bed. "Your aunt thought you might like going into the woods to pick wildflowers today."

"She did?" Snow still wasn't sure she believed it. "Are you sure?"

Mila put her hands on her hips and laughed. "Yes, Your Highness! She gave me the instructions herself last night and told me to help you get ready. She's sent a gown for you to wear and everything. She wanted you to leave early, before the weather got too warm."

Snow watched in wonder as Mila performed the chores Snow had done for herself for years. The servant poured water into the basin and helped her wash up. She made Snow's bed and tidied her things. She combed Snow's hair for her and helped her finish it off with a red piece of fabric tied in a bow. Snow couldn't help feeling weepy. No one had helped her do any of those things since her mother died. Aunt Ingrid had convinced her father she was old enough to fend for herself, but she missed this personal contact. She missed the company of her mother. Looking in the mirror as Mila tied her bow, Snow couldn't help thinking of her mother doing the same thing. To Snow, one day blurred into the next. But today . . . today would be different! Her aunt had somehow heard her heart's desire to leave the castle and see another part of the kingdom . . . if only for a few hours.

She was surprised at the gesture, especially after what had happened the day before. Aunt Ingrid had summoned her to the throne room that afternoon and questioned her about Henrich, after spotting him talking to Snow in the gardens. She hadn't seen her aunt in ages (could it have been a year?), but she looked exactly the same. It was as if she never aged.

"You allowed a stranger to walk our grounds and did not alert the guards! You disobeyed me," the queen scolded as a few of the guards stood watch. "How many times must I tell you not to talk to strangers?"

Snow looked at her clogs. "I'm sorry, Aunt Ingrid, but Henri seemed so kind. He wouldn't have hurt me."

"Henri?" Aunt Ingrid repeated, raising one perfectly arched eyebrow. "So you spoke to the intruder long enough to learn his name?"

Snow's cheeks flushed. Her aunt was not pleased, but maybe she could appeal to her senses. "He'd come to discuss a trade agreement with you. I told him you'd be upset he came uninvited and suggested he try to make an appointment. I told him to leave."

Aunt Ingrid sat forward on her throne, both of her milky white hands gripping the seat's armrests. "And?"

"And?" Snow was confused. She liked to tread lightly when in her aunt's presence. It happened so rarely; she didn't want to do anything to upset their relationship further. She still had a hard time understanding what she could have done to cause her aunt to pull away in the first place. When her father had disappeared, she'd assumed her aunt would try to draw her closer. Instead, the queen had closed the gates—both literally and figuratively. In addition to getting rid of much of the palace staff, she'd discontinued all the balls from years past, limited visitors, and stopped socializing with anyone—including Snow. It made her wonder if it was her doing. But nothing was ever said about it. Did her aunt even notice how much she did around the castle to keep it from falling into despair?

Aunt Ingrid sighed deeply. "What else did he say? What did he really want?"

"He didn't mean any harm," Snow said. "He was hoping to meet with you, but I told him visitors were rarely granted an audience with the queen."

Her aunt still didn't look pleased. "Well, he won't be getting that meeting now. And you will not disobey my orders again. Understood?"

"Yes, Aunt Ingrid." She supposed her aunt had a right to be angry. Snow had gone against her wishes. But if only Aunt Ingrid would agree to meet Henri, she'd see he was harmless.

And yet, just a day later, her aunt had decided to give her a bit of freedom. Maybe their relationship was finally changing.

Mila held out a dress so lovely that Snow gasped. She lovingly touched the blue bodice with the cap sleeves that had red accents woven throughout and the shining yellow satin. She hadn't had anything new to wear in a very long time. She almost hesitated to put the dress on—what if she ruined it in the woods? But when else would she have a chance to wear such a fine gown? She slipped into it with glee.

Next the maid offered Snow a biscuit and some tea from a tray that was already inside her room. Pleased, Snow stared out the window. The sky was still a bluish pink and the sun had not yet risen.

Mila coughed. "I'm afraid you'll need to finish your breakfast quickly, Your Highness," she said regretfully. "The queen's escort is already waiting for you."

Snow stopped mid-sip of tea. "Already? But it's not even light yet."

"Exactly," Mila said with a nod. "Your aunt worries for your safety outside the castle walls. Since she isn't able to travel with you, she feels it's best that you travel under the cover of darkness so that no one knows you're leaving."

"Oh." Snow hadn't thought about that. She spent her everyday life unnoticed.

"Besides, it's a long journey. I took the liberty of packing you a lunch. Off you go now!"

She was leaving the castle! For that, of course she'd do whatever the queen wanted. Snow was so elated she didn't even remember to glance at her parents' portrait before she was whisked out the door to meet her escort.

Snow recognized the man as soon as she saw him. He was tall and muscular, with dark brown hair worn in a small ponytail, and he had on clothes meant for traveling. She always liked the chance to look someone in the eyes, but this man's were cast downward. She wanted to ask his name, but he didn't seem overly social. All she knew was that he had long worked for her aunt, leading hunts to acquire meat for the castle. He was known simply as "the huntsman." She couldn't believe her aunt was giving up his services for the day to accompany her.

He bowed. "Good morning, Princess. We should begin our journey before it gets too light."

"Of course," she said, anticipation drumming inside her. She looked back at Mila and smiled shyly. "Thank you for your help today." Mila blushed. "Please tell my aunt I'll bring her back a magnificent bouquet of flowers."

Mila curtsied. "Of course, Your Highness."

The journey wasn't as long as Mila had made it out to be, but Snow still enjoyed the ride in the carriage. She had it all to herself since the huntsman was also her driver. She breathed in the fresh air as the horse and carriage bumped along through the quiet streets of the village, where people were just beginning to rise. Soon they were down the mountain and into meadows so lush with greenery that Snow couldn't believe they were real. The sun was starting to rise in the sky on a cloudless morning, and to Snow, the kingdom had never looked more beautiful.

Were the fields always this bright and filled with flowers? Was their farmland always this vibrant? Did the apple orchard always have this many trees? She knew her mother had cultivated one herself when she'd lived with a farming family as a girl. They had taken her and Aunt Ingrid in, and her mother had worked tirelessly to return the favor, helping their orchard grow and bloom. She would have loved to stop and look at those trees and picture her mother picking the finest fruit from the branches, but she didn't want to be so bold as to ask the huntsman to do that. She was truly grateful to be outside the castle at all. It had been too long since she'd been allowed to see the countryside full of small cottages with people taking care of crops or horses and cows. She wanted to soak in every image and never forget a moment of it. Who knew when she would be able to take another journey?

After the carriage came to a halt, the huntsman came around to her door and unhooked the latch. He still didn't make eye contact with her. "We are here, Your Highness," he said stiffly.

"Thank you!" she said, hurrying to get out and be free. A northern lapwing—one of her mother's favorite birds—flew past her, chirping excitedly, as if it, too, knew how momentous it was to see Snow in this very spot. She gathered her things and looked around the meadow. They were in a hilly grove, with tall grass and flowers growing freely in patches. There were so many varieties and colors;

she couldn't wait to start designing the perfect bouquet. She started gathering blooms right away, humming to herself as she walked. In the distance she could see a forest that light didn't seem to touch. The trees that rose from it were mostly dead. Perhaps a fire had destroyed this land once before. It struck Snow as strange that two contrasting worlds could be so close to one another.

"We'll head that way," the huntsman said, pointing to the dark woods. He flung a sack over his back. It seemed rather heavy.

Snow didn't want to doubt her escort, but it seemed an odd choice. Then again, perhaps he knew something about the terrain she did not. He surely had more experience in these parts than she did. They ambled toward the dead trees, Snow stopping every few steps to observe their beautiful surroundings more closely.

Spotting a daisy in her path, Snow knelt down to pick it up. She held it close. "Are you hungry?" she asked the huntsman shyly. "I'm sure Mila packed enough for the two of us."

He looked at her for a moment before replying, "No, Your Highness." He put out his hand to allow her to go first. "After you."

"Sir?" Snow moved ahead, picking a few wild roses that grew like vines along the grass. "I don't even know what to call you. What is your name?"

"You may call me the huntsman. That is what my queen calls me."

Maybe it was the newfound freedom—it was making her bolder than she'd ever been. "I'm sure you have a name," she prodded. "It would be a much more enjoyable outing if I could call you by it."

"There is no need," he said, wiping his brow as he looked around.

Oh, well, Snow thought, giving up the effort. She supposed he did have a job to do, after all. Maybe he couldn't protect her and be social at the same time. Either way, she wouldn't let the huntsman's mood dampen her spirits. Snow pulled the beautiful new cloak she'd been given around her shoulders. The air was still a bit cool this early in the day, but it felt good on her skin. Perhaps she could gather enough blooms to make several arrangements for the castle. And once they had wilted, she could collect those that had seeds and try to replant them by the aviary.

The thought of the aviary and the gardens reminded her of Henri. They hadn't spoken long, but she could tell he had an easy charm about him. If only he could convince Aunt Ingrid to meet with him, she'd surely see he was an honorable man. Though, in truth, he was probably already on the way back to his kingdom. The thought saddened her. Why hadn't she been bold enough to suggest they meet again?

Then she laughed. She'd never thought such things before! It had to be the mountain air giving her such wild ideas.

A sudden sound made Snow stop in her tracks. Something was floundering in the grass up ahead. Rushing over, she spotted a baby bird. It must have fallen from its nest or flown into a tree. It kept hopping around, attempting to fly and then fluttering down to the ground again. She scooped it up in her hands.

"Are you all right?" she asked the bird, as if it could answer. She stroked its feathers and felt it shaking beneath her touch. "Poor thing. I think he must have fallen," she said, trying to engage the huntsman in conversation again.

If he was still behind her, he didn't say anything. Snow decided to keep talking.

"I can't tell if he's hurt or just stunned. Don't worry, little friend. I've got you." She had a sudden flashback of her mother doing the same thing while she stood watch. She smiled at the thought, then turned her attention back to the bird. "Do you want to try to fly again?" she asked it, happy to have someone else to talk to for a moment. She placed it back on the ground. "Go ahead. Give it a try." As if following her instructions, the bird hopped twice, then flew off.

Pleased, she watched the bird take flight. She was ready to tell the huntsman about her mother's love of birds when a shadow fell over her. She looked up in surprise to see the huntsman's grave face.

It was mere seconds before her surprise turned to gut-wrenching fear. The huntsman held a knife high above her head.

Sweat pooled on her skin, and her limbs began to shake. Even with her animal instincts taking over, it took her a moment to register what she was seeing. The huntsman had a knife. Her blood ran cold as she realized she was backed up against a large boulder, with nowhere to run. She knew what was about to happen. Snow felt herself falter, tripping backward as her hands came up to protect her face. It was silly, really. There was no stopping the knife, and yet she screamed, the sound of her voice echoing through the meadow. She heard some birds take off from a nearby tree at the sound, but there was no one else to hear her. *So this is how I die,* she thought, holding her breath and waiting for him to strike.

Instead, she heard the knife clang to the ground.

Snow moved her hands from her face and saw the huntsman bend down in front of her. He looked up. It was the first time she had seen his eyes. They were green.

"I can't do it!" he wept, his face crinkling with despair. "Forgive me. I beg you, Your Highness. Forgive me. She's mad, jealous of you. She'll stop at nothing."

His words didn't make sense. Someone was jealous of her? Why? But there was no time for questions. The huntsman could pick his knife back up at any second. This was what her aunt had always warned her about; being princess made her a target. This was why she had kept Snow so secluded. It turned out her aunt had been right.

Shocked, she started to run, her heart still pounding like a drum. She'd taken only a few steps when she fell forward. She threw her hands out in front of her and braced for the fall, landing hard in a patch of flowers. Her finger tore on a thorn from a rosebush.

Mother, help me, she thought as she stared at the blood trickling down her finger. She heard her mother's voice clear as day, just as she had the other night in her dreams. *If you want something, sometimes you have to take risks,* she had said. What would her mother do right now?

The answer was clear. Her mother had never been one to balk at a challenge. In everything she did, she was bold and unabashed, no matter what tradition or precedent dictated: from her ruling to her aviary to her role as a mother, she had set out to find solutions and to help. Yes, it was clear to Snow that her mother would want *answers.* She'd want to know who wanted to kill her, and to make sure that person could not harm her or anyone else.

Still shaking uncontrollably, Snow picked herself up

and slowly turned back to the huntsman. Her steps were sluggish but steady as she reached the man, still kneeling on the ground. Every fiber in her being told her to run again, and yet she held her ground. "Who? Who wants to kill me, huntsman?"

He looked up, seeming surprised she even had to ask. "Why, the queen!"

Ingrid

Twenty-four years earlier

Katherine dropped the basket on the table with a thud. "That's the last bushel for the week. Ten in all! If that won't bring in a fair sum at the market, I don't know what will."

Ingrid stared at the basket overflowing with perfect red apples. The apples were so ripe they practically oozed at the touch. Not a single one was bruised; none had the faintest indent or even a rotten mark. Katherine never would have allowed it. She fawned over the apple trees in the orchard as if they were her children, making sure they were watered and pruned daily. The farmer and his wife adored Ingrid's sister and were pleased with the work she did around the farm. When Katherine took an interest in the apple trees the farmer had failed to nourish, the very next year they'd produced a good apple harvest. And now, just a few years later, Katherine's apples were said to be the best in the kingdom. She'd come up with her own hybrid, which she named Red Fire. They had a hint of tartness like a green apple would, but ample sweetness to balance the flavor. There was even a rumor that the king himself ordered Katherine's apples by the bushel to have them juiced for his morning breakfast. At least that's what Ingrid had heard at the market. It wasn't like anyone from the castle ever came down to this simple corner of the kingdom to grace them with their presence.

Since the farmer had taken them in at Ingrid's behest several years back, she and Katherine had worked hard to earn their keep. Katherine instantly took to farm life, but it wasn't long before Ingrid found it dull. While her sister called farming "being one with the earth" and loved the challenge of getting a reluctant plant to bloom, Ingrid grew tired of always having grime beneath her nails and soiled skirts. She didn't want to spend her life turning soil and harvesting corn, spending her days roasting in the sun.

She tried to talk to Katherine about moving on from the farm, but her sister wouldn't hear of it. "They've been so good to us, Ingrid," Katherine would say in that pragmatic way of hers—as if that meant they owed their very last breath to a couple who treated them like hired help.

Six days a week, they rose before the sun to pick ripe fruits and vegetables and toiled in the fields till the sun began to set. On the seventh day, they should have been resting, but instead, they were forced to head up to the village to sell their bounty.

Truthfully, Ingrid didn't mind the seventh day, because it was her one chance to escape the farm. The farmer trusted them to venture into the village on their own to sell Katherine's precious apples and the other produce, even allowing them to take the wagon. If only she could've taken the wagon and never returned to the horrid place. . . . But she couldn't leave Katherine.

"There are twice as many bushels this week as there were last," Katherine said before they set out for market day. She had arranged the apples in the basket as carefully as she would cradle a fresh batch of eggs. "Uncle Herbert couldn't believe how many we sold last week."

"He's not your uncle," Ingrid snapped, and Katherine stopped fussing over the fruit to look at her. "Sorry. It's just—he's not. He has no dowry for you. He will not find you a hand in marriage. He owes us nothing, Katherine, and one day he will take the life we've become accustomed to and pull it out from under us just like Father did. If you'd realize that, you'd want to leave as badly as I do."

Katherine sighed. "Oh, Ingrid."

They'd had this argument before.

Sun slipped through the cracks in the barn and shone on Ingrid's younger sister. Though the hours in the sun had tanned her complexion (as she always refused to share Ingrid's large, worn straw hat) and hard work had callused her hands, Katherine sported these features with pride. Her dark hair was always tied simply and practically off her face, no matter how many times Ingrid had told her to wear it in the latest fashion like she tried to do. Despite this, Katherine endeared herself to all she met—from the farmer to the people at the market, unsure whether they wanted to spend the money for a premium apple. (The farmer insisted Katherine charge double the amount for hers.) Perhaps it was the sweetness that radiated from behind her amber eyes. But those eyes no longer worked on Ingrid.

"I'll be nineteen at the end of the next month," Ingrid said as she helped Katherine lift the baskets into the back of the wagon. "It's time I make a life for myself. If you want this one, you can have it. I want more."

Katherine frowned. It was not something she did often. "Where will you go? What will you do for food and clothing? Maybe if you ask Uncle—*Herbert*—for help finding work in the village, you could continue to live here and still have more freedom."

Ingrid tilted her head. She hadn't considered that

option, but it could be the best one . . . for now. "Maybe." She dropped the tarp over the back of the wagon, and the two began the long ride into the village, arriving just before the morning rush.

The marketplace was set up in the shadow of the church-yard. Some vendors sold out of the backs of their wagons; others walked around with baskets. Katherine preferred to set up a table and let people touch and smell the food they were buying. "It gives them a choice," she always said. Ingrid had initially thought she was foolish. Who wanted to buy corn that someone had already half husked? Once again, she was proven wrong, because Katherine's method always produced a line. Today, the villagers were waiting before they even arrived to set up their table.

"Hello, Katherine!" the owner of the butcher shop called as the girls began to unpack their wares.

Everyone knew Katherine. It was Ingrid's name they had trouble remembering. She understood neither of them were the fairest in the land, but Ingrid pinched her cheeks in an effort to give them the right shade of pink and kept her clothes clean. She studied books and could hold a conversation, unlike so many of these peasants. Was it really so hard for them to remember her name, too?

"Hello, Sir Adam!" Katherine said, because she, of course, remembered everyone's names as well.

"Your apples look even more beautiful this week than last. Anything new on the market?"

Ingrid hated ridiculous questions. "The crop is the crop," she said plainly. "We don't magically grow beanstalks overnight."

Adam looked at her strangely, and she knew she had gone too far. Katherine touched her shoulder.

"Why don't you let me sell this morning while you look around?" Katherine said lightly. "I'm okay here by myself."

The move would help Katherine as much as it did Ingrid—Katherine always sold better when she was solo. She had that kind, patient persona that the villagers lapped up like a street dog with a bowl of water.

Ingrid glared at Adam. "Fine." She grabbed a handful of apples and stowed them in a small sack. Sometimes she could sell them to the other stalls. "I'll be back soon. Don't give away the produce."

That was another problem. Katherine was a sucker for a poor soul. If someone drooled over her apples but couldn't afford to buy one, Katherine sometimes took pity and gave it to them for free. It drove Ingrid mad. They'd never been given handouts. Why should others get them?

Aimlessly wandering the stalls of the market, Ingrid turned up her nose at the fish on ice at one stall and someone selling soaps at another. It was the same offerings week in and week out. Even the freedom of the market was beginning to lose its appeal. She stopped momentarily at a jewelry stand to admire a strand of black pearls on display. She'd never seen ebony-colored pearls before. They certainly weren't from around here. She touched one of the pearls with the tip of her finger.

"See anything you like, pretty lady?" the shopkeeper asked.

"Yes, these are—"

"He was speaking to me," a woman next to her said.

Ingrid looked up. The woman was clearly a noble. Her violet dress was made of fine silk, and she wore a gorgeous sheer ivory scarf wrapped around her head. Several white pearl bracelets adorned her matching ivory gloves, her face was beautifully made up, and she smelled like roses—obviously wearing perfume. Ingrid's mouth opened slightly. This was the type of woman who garnered attention and respect. This was the type of woman she wanted to be.

"What would you like today, madam?" the shopkeeper asked the noblewoman as they both ignored Ingrid.

"These." The woman held up the black pearls. She hadn't even tried them on.

Ingrid walked away, feeling dismayed.

Life was not fair. She could be that type of woman—commanding, beautiful, controlled—if given the resources. Resources she clearly would never have living in a musty farmhouse. She wished she could become someone else entirely.

"Wish, my lady?"

Ingrid kept walking. Whoever it was clearly wasn't talking to her. That much she'd learned.

"I said, would you like me to grant your wish, my lady?"

Ingrid turned around.

The man was old, his face weathered and his grayish-white beard far too long. His gray eyes held hers with interest. She shifted her gaze to his small, cluttered stall filled with trinkets of every shape and size. He also had mirrors, vases, trunks, and small bottles of what appeared to be spices. She looked back and saw that he continued to stare at her.

"Are you talking to me?" Ingrid asked.

He didn't answer the question. "You look like someone who wants her wishes granted." He motioned to her sack. "I'll grant one if I can have an apple."

She was no fool. "You expect me to believe you'll grant my wish in exchange for a piece of fruit?"

He smiled thinly. He was missing several teeth. "Yes. I could even offer you something better than a wish, if you'd prefer. I could offer an apprenticeship with me."

Ingrid couldn't help laughing. "And why would I want that?"

"To get away from the farm, of course, and to chart a

new path," he said, and she stopped laughing. "That is what you want, isn't it?" He stepped out of the stall and moved toward her. "I can teach you how to grant your own wishes. I can give you power."

She felt her body shiver. It was as though he knew her intimate thoughts. How was that possible? She looked closer at the wares in his booth. She spotted the black feathers, the cauldron, the potion bottles with the poison symbols. She suddenly noticed how nervous the villagers were as they passed the stall. This man was feared, and for that, she was in awe.

Could it be? The rumors of the black arts her father had spoken of long ago . . . had they been true?

"What do you want in return?" she asked, attempting to sound more confident than she felt.

"As I said, I need an apprentice," he told her. "My eyes are not as good as my head anymore. I need someone to help me prepare . . . *things* . . . and in exchange I will share all I have learned in this life." He took her hand in his. His nails were dark and dirty. She had to tell herself not to pull away. "Do we have a deal, young Ingrid?"

She didn't ask how he knew her name. Her heart pounded. "Yes."

"Ingrid!" Katherine's voice rang out in the aisle. She rushed to her sister, and Ingrid dropped the man's hand. Katherine's face was flushed with excitement. Her smile faded as she looked from Ingrid to the man and back, but it brightened again in an instant. "I've been looking for you! You will never believe what just happened. The king has personally requested my apples be served at his next dinner! He loves the Red Fire." She laughed gaily and grabbed her sister's hands. "Isn't today magical?"

"Yes," Ingrid agreed, looking at her new teacher instead of her sister. "Magical, indeed."

Snow

The queen wanted her dead?

It was inconceivable. It couldn't be possible! She must have heard the huntsman wrong. But he'd had a knife pointed at her and now he was kneeling on the ground, weeping.

Could it be true?

Her heart was beating so fast she feared it would burst out of her chest. The wind seemed to pick up and roar in her ears. Every nerve in her body told her to leave him, but she felt rooted to the spot. This did not make sense. *Aunt Ingrid wants him to kill me?*

Curiosity got the best of her. "Why?" she whispered, her voice shaky.

The huntsman didn't look up. He had slipped back into his habit of avoiding eye contact. "She's jealous of you, much like she was jealous of your mother, the old queen," he said. He paused, seeming to struggle to find the words. His long sigh turned into a sob. "She suffered the same fate the queen wanted for you, I'm afraid."

Her mother? Snow felt her knees buckle. "No! That's impossible!"

"It's the truth," the huntsman swore, and he bowed his head again. "You're not the first the queen has tried to strike down." He looked around. "Your mother's death came at the hands of my family, I'm afraid to say."

Snow was too stunned to speak. This man was clearly out of his mind. Her mother hadn't been killed. She'd fallen ill . . . hadn't she?

She remembered her father's voice breaking as he gave her the news. Snow had already been in bed, waiting for her mother to come say good night, when her father had come in with tears streaming down his cheeks. She immediately knew something was wrong, but she never would have imagined something had happened to her strong, radiant mother, a woman who had always seemed so full of life. She'd seen her mother that morning before she'd headed out for the day on official business—what type of business, Snow did not know. But that was not unusual. The queen was always off meeting with folks in the kingdom and outside of it, listening to concerns, mediating differences, attempting to solve the latest problems that had arisen . . . including a terrible plague that had sprung up. She had kissed Snow's cheek and gone on her way, saying she'd be home before dark. By evening, she was dead. But the plague had been rampant at that time, killing so many others in the surrounding kingdoms, and it was said to be fast-acting. Snow had been shocked, but she'd never questioned the cause of her mother's sudden death. . . .

She looked at the huntsman again. Could he be telling her the truth? Had her mother been killed by her own sister instead of a disease?

Suddenly, she felt a pressing need to hear what he had to say about her mother. If Queen Katherine had been betrayed by Ingrid, who had then taken her crown, Snow needed to hear it. She felt a surge of adrenaline mixed with sudden anger course through her veins. She wasn't leaving this place till she knew exactly what had happened all those years ago.

"Huntsman, tell me what you know," she said, her voice stronger than she'd ever heard it. She knew the situation was delicate. The knife still lay on the ground where it had fallen, mere feet from the two of them. "Please, sir. You owe me that much." She could feel her hands shaking again. She tried to keep them steady.

The huntsman stared at the ground. "Your mother

died at my own father's hands, I'm afraid. He was the castle huntsman before I, but his work for the queen went deeper than hunting and foraging for food. I am told she tasked him with killing the queen so she could marry your father."

"No," Snow said, her voice breaking. It felt like the world was spinning. *"No!"* she said more forcefully, willing the words to not be true.

"Yes, Your Highness," the huntsman said, his voice cracking. "My father confessed this to me on his deathbed." His face crumbled. "It seems my father was her personal slave, much as I've become. Your aunt told him that if he aligned himself with her, he'd have great power when she sat upon the throne. And he believed her. He died this past winter, but he didn't want to take this evildoing to his grave. This deed had tortured him for years." His eyes were wild. "Once I knew, who could I tell such a thing? Would anyone believe me? The king had long since disappeared. The stories of the other things done to her own people are foreboding. I have a family. I couldn't . . . she's too powerful." He wiped his brow. "But I won't repeat my father's mistakes. I will hide my family away before I return to accept my fate. I won't put your heart in a box and hand it to her like a prized pig on a platter."

Snow closed her eyes tight, the idea almost too much to bear. Her mind was whirling. How could this be possible? It was sickening. Her mother had trusted her own flesh and blood. She'd made Aunt Ingrid her lady-in-waiting. She was Snow's godmother. She had been given a home in the castle. Her job had been to help protect her sister, but instead, her aunt had ordered the unthinkable. She'd stolen her mother's crown. Her husband. Her daughter.

Why?

Because she's the Evil Queen, a small voice in her head said. There was a reason Snow heard people whisper the nickname. Her aunt showed no mercy. Snow knew this. It's why a small part of her had feared being in the queen's presence these past years. For so long, she had lived in her aunt's shadow, frightened the woman would one day tire of her completely and throw her out into the streets. Funny, though—she never would have dreamed Queen Ingrid would have her killed.

"I'm so sorry, Princess," the huntsman cried. His green eyes no longer appeared strong and stoic. They looked sad and fearful. "I know the consequences I will face if she finds out I didn't do her bidding, but I can't kill you. I will not continue to destroy our family name at her behest."

Benevolent Queen Katherine, her beloved mother, was gone because of her aunt's jealousy and rage. How could Snow have been so blind? She froze. What about her father? Had he really run off, or had her aunt done away with him, too? Who else had died because she had been busy keeping her head down?

"Please, Your Highness," he said, startling her once more. "You are our kingdom's only hope. You're the only one who can stop the Evil Queen!"

They both heard the branch snap at the same time and startled. Snow looked around. No one was there. Not in the meadow, not in the neighboring grove. But there were the beginnings of a fog seeping out of the woods, like a snake weaving its way through the grass. They both saw it.

"You must go quickly!" the huntsman shouted, his voice stronger. "The queen . . . she has eyes everywhere. She could be watching. She might already know the truth. Run, child! Run away! Hide! In the woods! Go!"

A new feeling washed over Snow. One she wasn't familiar with—it was the will to conquer. First her aunt had taken her mother, then her father; now she wanted Snow and her home. The Evil Queen wanted to take everything from her.

Snow stepped up to the huntsman and looked him squarely in the eye. "I won't let her do this."

Then, into the tree line and fog she darted, hiding from view.

Every ghastly tree looked the same: decrepit, stripped of bark and black as a raven's feathers, not a single leaf left on its branches. The trees in this forest were indeed all dead. Their trunks were thick and knotted. Their branches scrolled and twisted over and under one another, up and down the tree trunks, littering the path with vines that one could easily trip over, or get caught in. Snow blinked hard, trying to walk steadily over them, fearing she'd fall and never be able to get up again. No one would come looking for her. If they did, it would only be to finish the huntsman's job. She kept walking, feeling the air grow colder and the fog thicken like pea soup, till soon she could barely see in front of her hand. A crow cried. Or maybe it was a raven, there to watch her die. How foolish she had been, humming and singing and thinking of Henri and the flowers she would bring back to the castle, never realizing this rare outing was really an excuse to lead her to her death. Where *was* she going, anyway? Every turn she took looked the same. Was she traveling in circles?

She stopped when she heard a sound. It wasn't a bird. The wind seemed to have disappeared now that she was so deep in the forest, but there was a distinct howling sound. She looked up into the fog and could barely see through the tightly wound dead branches to view the sky. She listened harder and wondered, worriedly, if she was hearing spirits. Ghosts of the lost souls like her who were doomed to wander this forest forever.

Get ahold of yourself, Snow. There are no spirits.
The only thing haunting you is your own past.

The path was dark and growing darker the deeper she went into the woods, and she didn't like the look of some of the trees. Some were rotted out, with hollowed-out holes in their stumps that looked like eyes. She had the unnerving feeling they were staring at her, which was silly, really, but she was already worked up. When she stumbled by a tree with large holes that looked like piercing eyes and a mouth that appeared to be screaming, she stepped back to get away. But the ground behind her was unsteady, and she felt herself begin to fall into a cavernous hole. Crying out, Snow descended into the darkness, splashing down into a murky pond. Quickly, she picked herself up and tried to tread out. That's when she saw two things in the water slithering toward her. Were they logs? Or were they crocodiles? She tried to move faster to get away, but her skirt was now heavy with water and holding her back. When she finally reached the edge and pulled herself out, she still felt trapped. Where was she? A cave?

Snow pushed her wet hair out of her eyes and looked around, her vision soon adjusting to the low light. Was that an opening up ahead? She could see a parting of trees in the distance. Maybe it was a way out! She rushed into the clearing, feeling like she could breathe again as the world opened up once more around her. As she ran, her shoe caught on something and she tumbled forward, landing hard on her knees, her hands sinking into the dirt. She looked back and saw the long tree root her foot was caught on. She tried to yank it free and heard a tear. Her skirt was caught on a branch thickly wound along the ground. It was as if the tree wanted to hold her prisoner in this forest forever.

Maybe she should just let it.

The anger she had felt only hours ago at her aunt, the huntsman, and her father and mother for not seeing the Evil Queen for who she really was had given way to self-pity. It was obvious that she was completely alone in this world. And that she had been naive enough to trust the most terrible of foes. All there was left to do was cry.

Snow lifted her head. There was that whispering sound again. It sounded like the rustling of leaves—if there *had* been any leaves on the trees or dried up on the ground. But the branches and dirt were bare. It felt like the wind was following her. Could her mind be playing tricks on her? She closed her eyes for a moment and listened.

I will catch you! she heard her mother shout. She could almost see her younger self running past her mother in the gardens by the aviary. *I've got you! I'll always catch you!* her mother would say.

If the queen catches you in here again, Princess, she'll sentence you to do the dishes right alongside me! she heard another voice ring out.

No one was there, but Snow knew the voice. It was Mrs. Kindred, the cook who had survived her aunt's dismissals over the years. When Snow's mother was alive, she'd encouraged her daughter to be friendly with those who helped them in the castle, and Mrs. Kindred had always been Snow's favorite person to chat with. She could see herself sitting on a chair, no more than six or seven, watching Mrs. Kindred chop onions, carrots, and leeks and throw them all into a giant pot of broth. She and Mrs. Kindred only stole a few moments together most days now—she suspected her aunt must have forbidden the cook from talking to her, what with how Mrs. Kindred always quickly sent Snow on her way—but back then she had always peppered the cook with questions. ("How do you cut the carrots so small? Why do leeks have sand in them? What spices are you going to add? How do you know how much to put in?") On one such occasion, she'd been such a distraction that Mrs. Kindred had finally picked her up, holding her high on her broad chest, and let her stir the pot herself. Eventually, she taught her how to dice and chop, too, since Snow wouldn't stop talking. By suppertime, young Snow had convinced herself she'd made the whole meal. She had been so proud, too, carrying the dishes out to the dining table that night. She walked so slow that she hadn't paid attention to the fact that everyone at the table was arguing till later. It had been her parents and her aunt, actually. She'd thought they'd be so happy—all of her memories with them tended to be good ones, but this time she saw the memory differently.

No one had noticed her at first. Her parents were sitting next to each other and Aunt Ingrid was across from them. Normally they would been fawning over the soup, but this time they were too angry to see she had entered the room. She'd never heard Aunt Ingrid raise her voice to her father before, but they were definitely not seeing eye to eye about something. As her mother's lady-in-waiting, Ingrid always walked a few steps behind the king and queen, waited for directions, and only spoke when spoken to whenever they were in public. Sure, Snow had seen them be more informal when they were in private quarters, but there was always some sort of impenetrable wall between her father and aunt. Why would her mother have asked Aunt Ingrid to be her lady-in-waiting if they had disliked one another, though? She had never understood how her father had fallen in love with a woman like Aunt Ingrid. The memory of that night just reinforced her feeling that something had not been right between them. Aunt Ingrid and her father had definitely been angry with one another. She just wished she knew why.

Images of her mother with her aunt flashed by. Her mother getting dressed in a navy blue gown with crystal stitching before some celebration. Her aunt combing her mother's hair for what felt like hours as they talked about the queen's appointments and duties. Was it all a ruse on her aunt's part? Had she secretly been plotting Queen Katherine's death from the moment she set foot in the castle? Or was it before that? But they were *sisters*! Snow did not have a sibling, but she could not imagine ever harboring such hatred for one.

Snow heard more whispering. Was it spirits or her imagination? She struggled to sit up, but both her skirt and foot were still caught in the thorny branches.

You think you're so clever, don't you?

It was her father's voice now playing tricks on her. She could picture him sitting in the throne room, awaiting visitors, and she could remember laughing with her mother. They were constantly playing little tricks on him. Snow remembered calling him the wrong name on purpose. She would call him Fritz, and he called her Ediline—her mother was Frieda. Then they'd all pretend to be mad at one another for using the wrong names. Once Snow had even convinced two visiting dignitaries to call her father Fritz over and over. Then she and her mother had jumped out from the shadows to let him in on the joke.

"Only you, young Ediline, could make me laugh like this," he'd tell her. "You are the light of my life."

"Of both of our lives," Mother had said.

Aunt Ingrid had taken away all of that.

Snow lifted her hands to her face and wept again. For her parents, for herself, and for the life together Aunt Ingrid had stolen from them. Instead of challenging her aunt about her father's whereabouts or the closing of the castle gates, she'd looked away. She'd allowed her aunt to dismiss most of the staff and had never questioned why her aunt would disappear into her own private chambers for days. Why had she allowed her aunt to stop trading with other kingdoms? To make such hard demands on their people and tax them so heavily? Why had she let them all live in fear? Unlike her parents, she had just let the kingdom die on the vine, much like these haunted woods.

As far as princesses went, she was a pretty pitiful one.

Tears fell down her cheeks, running off her chin and settling on her hands, which still covered her face.

Are you going to give up?

Snow wiped her tears and sat up. "Mother?"

It was her mother's voice, clear as day, but she wasn't really there. It was just another memory. Another moment meant to tear her heart in two.

Are you going to give up? Mother had said. But when? And to whom?

She lay there and tried hard to recall where these words came from. Finally, she remembered. She'd been sitting in the royal carriage. She remembered the feel of her mother's hand tightly wrapped around her own small one. The carriage had given a sudden lurch and then stopped. There had been shouting, guards jumping off the carriage and people running. Her mother had sat up and looked out the window.

"No!" she had shouted. "Unhand her!" She looked back at her daughter. "Stay here, Snow."

Snow was too curious. She had climbed out of the carriage and hurried behind her mother. The guards were standing over an old woman, shouting. Her mother quickly stopped them and knelt down by the woman. She didn't appear injured, but she looked sad. Her clothes were equally so—haggard and patched up, much like Snow's own were these days. Lying beside her was an empty basket. A rotten apple lay in the mud beside it.

"I will have the guards escort you home. Where do you live?" her mother asked.

"I have no home, my queen," the woman said. "The earth is my dwelling, and all I need comes from it."

"Your Majesty, we must be on our way," a guard interrupted.

Her mother hadn't moved. "Not until I am done speaking with this woman," she commanded in a strong voice. She turned back to the beggar. "The world is a beautiful home, but I would feel better if we gave you some warm clothes to wear and perhaps something to eat." Her mother hurried back to the carriage and grabbed the picnic basket that always accompanied them on small trips. Snow knew it was full of food, and they rarely ate all of it. "Take this." She untied the cloak around her neck. "And this, too. It will keep you warm on your journey." Snow had watched in wonder as her mother reached out and embraced the woman. "I wish you well, my dear."

"God bless you, my queen," the beggar had said, and then Snow and her mother returned to the carriage. They both waved as they drove by the woman.

"Small acts of kindness are so important," she remembered her mother telling her as they had pulled away. "I once stood in the same spot she is now. I came from nothing."

"I don't know what I'd do if I had nothing," Snow recalled saying.

Her mother had lifted Snow's chin and looked her straight in the eye. "If that day ever comes, are you going to give up? No. You will carry on just as I did. I didn't give up, and someone took a chance on me." She straightened and leveled her gaze on young Snow. "Always remember your past, Snow, and let it help you make decisions on how to rule your future. But never, ever give up."

The memory startled her. She knew her mother had always been generous and kind, but she had long forgotten this memory. And it had been so important.

Suddenly, the air felt cold and she heard another voice.

Your tears won't change your fate!

It was Aunt Ingrid. She had said those words to Snow the day after her father had left—been banished, killed, who knew?—when Snow had refused to come out of her room to have supper with her. Her aunt had sent for her twice, and Snow still wouldn't come. She was too distraught. Instead of taking pity on the child, Aunt Ingrid had been outraged. She had flown into Snow's room and unleashed her full wrath.

How different her aunt was from her mother. And that's when it dawned on her: *This* was who ruled their kingdom? A woman whose cruel words and actions spread like venom? Wasn't Snow the rightful leader in her father's absence? She was of age. Her father's rule had begun when he was only sixteen, a year younger than she was now. Her mother never forgot where she came from. Was Snow going to? Would she just lie there in the grass and give up on herself? On her kingdom?

Or would she take the knowledge her parents had given her and change her future?

Are you going to give up? No. You will carry on just as I did.

Snow set her jaw, and this time she used all her strength to pull her foot loose from those vines. She twisted, she pulled, and finally she broke free from its grasp. Then she stood up, letting the new dress she had marveled at only that morning tear at one of the seams. It was just a dress. She'd get another. With a deep breath, she began walking again.

However long it took, she would wander through this darkness till it led to the light.

Ingrid

Twenty-three years earlier

"Concentrate," her master commanded.

Ingrid did as she was told and closed her eyes, blocking out the sounds of the world. She could feel her breath rise and fall in her chest. She waited till she could feel the tips of her fingers and even the weight of her toes before she imagined what she wanted to happen.

Light, light! she said in her mind, and when she opened her eyes there was, indeed, a flame atop the wick of the candle where moments before there had been none.

"Good!" her master appraised. They were standing in the middle of his shop, working before the doors opened for the day. Before the shop opened, after it closed, and on Sundays when everyone was home, he taught her all he knew about magic and spell work. She drank it in like a delicious elixir. Never had she been given the freedom to learn like this before. Her father had just wanted her to keep house and stay out of his way. All the farmer cared about was his crops. But her master was there to feed her soul.

Katherine had been devastated when Ingrid announced at dinner that she would be leaving the farmstead to work in the village. She didn't say where and the farmer had not asked. She told them that it was a good opportunity for her, one that would lead to her eventually leaving home completely. This seemed to please the farmer, who had never warmed to her the way he had Katherine.

In exchange for allowing her to keep boarding with Katherine, she told the farmer she'd give him half her wages. She hated parting with the money she earned, but her new master had no place for her to stay, and she was not about to sleep on the shop floor. It was torturous leaving the life and energy of the village every night and heading back to that sad little farm, but there was one bright spot: her sister was there. And so, she continued making the journey back and forth every day, dreaming of the moment when she could open her own shop and have the power to leave the farmer completely. She'd take Katherine with her, of course. She could never leave her sister.

"Concentrate on the flame," her master instructed. "See if you can burn it brighter. Bigger!"

Ingrid concentrated, focusing on the flame, envisioning

her goal. The flame began to swirl like a cyclone and spiral up till it almost reached the rafters. Ingrid and her master watched in awe, Ingrid wondering if the flame would burn the building down, but then her master commanded the flame to extinguish and they were left in almost total darkness again.

"I think that's enough for today," her master said, sounding a bit shaky.

"But we've just started!" Ingrid protested.

"And you always want to rush things!" he snapped, hurrying to put away all the books Ingrid had opened. They were filled with spells she wanted to try—love potions, creams to turn one's skin milky white, even spells that could make a person beautiful. She craved those sorts of things more and more lately. Her face had become windburned from all the travel, and her hands were splintered and nicked from all her work in the shop—just like her sister's callused hands, though without the apple stains. And yet, more and more men began to notice Katherine, while Ingrid began to feel more and more like an old hag. The farmer never received suitors that had come calling on *her*. They only came for Katherine.

Well, she didn't need the farmer's help. She didn't need anyone's. She just needed a good spell.

"There will be more time to work after the chores are done and the customers leave," her master said, thrusting a crate of small vials at her to clean and fill with elixirs. "Don't be impatient." He hobbled to the front of the shop and unlocked the door.

That was his constant critique of her: she had no patience. And it was true.

She wanted to know everything she could about magic, everything *he* knew, and she wanted to know now.

The bell at the front of the shop rang and a woman with wiry graying hair walked into the shop. Their first customer of the day. Ingrid sighed and started to clean the vials. Once the customers came, looking for beet juice and ragweed, she would have little time to do anything but assist them and keep the place presentable. She quickly put on a brew that was meant to rejuvenate the spirit. The last time she had made it, the entire batch had sold out within the day.

For a shop shrouded in mystery, they had a lot of patrons. Some traveled from very far, and some met with her master in private, not trusting his apprentice to give them what they needed. She hated customers like that. And she hated the busywork that was required of an apprentice— the cleaning, the mending of items that had been handled improperly, the sweeping of the shop. She was not a servant, no matter how she had spent her days before working there. She wanted to be her master's equal, but that sort of trust took time.

There was that impatience again, creeping up on her.

"Ingrid?" her master called. "Ms. Yvonne and I will be going on an errand together to get some herbs."

"I will get my cape and join you," she said. There were several herbs she needed for a face cream she wanted to try, which was supposed to give the skin a shimmer.

"No," her master said flatly, before lifting a cloak over his head to hide his face. She sighed as Ms. Yvonne did the same. "Watch the shop. We will be back soon."

They weren't. As the sun rose high in the sky, and no customers came, Ingrid became more and more aggravated she hadn't been allowed to accompany them. Why was her master trying to hold her back rather than teach her all his ways as he'd promised? Wasn't she the rightful heir to his shop? Shouldn't she know all there was to know about magic, to benefit them both? Why wouldn't he let her skills strengthen the way she knew they could?

Because he fears the power you wield, your master halts your progress. He puts up a shield.

Ingrid spun around. "Who said that?"

Look closely within these walls; great power you will find. Along with the knowledge to leave this place behind.

Great power? Where? The shop was not that big. Her eyes ran over the shelves stocked with books, potion bottles, urns, vials, and a few live rats and birds that were occasionally used for spells. None of the creatures could speak, of course.

"Reveal yourself!" she commanded, her voice so thunderous that the candle her master had put out reignited.

It is clear thou art exacting and strong. Lightning in the eye of the storm. The wait to become thy own master shall not be long.

Ingrid continued to search for the voice. When nothing jumped out at her in the shop, she entered the back room. The items in storage were mostly broken or no longer of value. Her master didn't even bother telling her what many of the items were. He kept saying he needed to dispose of these things, but there was a system to doing so. Items with dark properties could not just be thrown out like rubbish. "Broken magic is the most dangerous type of magic there is," he had once told her.

There seemed to be no one back there, either, and yet her instincts told her the phantom voice was close by. She immediately moved to the bookshelf in the back of the room, wiping off the dust and reaching her hand behind it, where there should have been a wall. Instead, she felt an indention that revealed a hidden nook. Carefully pulling the bookcase away, she spotted some shoddy rags. She pulled them off and found . . . a mirror?

Its glass was so dirty it was almost black, but it did not appear to be broken. Its gilded frame, with serpents twisting around it, was nicked and the paint was peeling, but she could tell it had once been impressive. Ingrid couldn't understand why her master would have let an item like this fall into disrepair.

Do not fear magic you do not understand. Give yourself over to me, and become the fairest in the land.

Ingrid stumbled back as smoke seeped from the glass. The voice was coming *from the mirror.* And, what's more, it seemed to be reading her thoughts. How?

"Thy fate is not sealed," said the mirror in a deep baritone voice. "Touch the glass. All shall be revealed."

Ingrid placed her palm on the cold mirror and felt a surprising flush of pain shoot through her arm. But she didn't let go. With her hand on the glass, she could see the journey of the mirror: it had been welded out of molten lava, cloaked figures reciting incantations around it as the glass was formed and cooled. She watched as a large tree in what was known in these parts as the Haunted Woods was chopped down, and an intricate frame with snakes and symbols was carved from its wood. The cloaked figures were careful with it. They hid it away in a cave in the darkest recesses of the forest, visiting from time to time to care for the mirror and commune with it. Their cloaked appearance made it hard for Ingrid to make out faces, but there were a lot of them, always standing around the mirror, chanting. On the ground, paths of fire spread from their feet to the wall on which the mirror hung.

Somehow, she could tell the mirror was pleased with their devotion, but it desired more—a task. One of the cloaked figures seemed to understand that, and this figure, too, wanted something more. Beauty. The Fountain of Youth. Immortality. The mirror offered the figure these things for a price. In time, the figure was revealed to be a woman who seemed to age backward. She grew more beautiful with every visit and appeared happy. But soon the woman's beauty led her to argue with the others. Someone called the mirror evil. They threatened to destroy it. A fight broke out among them. The next image she saw was of death, the woman who had loved the mirror lying on the ground. One of the cloaked figures took the mirror from the forest and brought it to this very shop, to plead with her master. "It's dangerous and needs to be disposed of," he said, speaking clearly.

"I will see to it that it is not trusted again," Ingrid's master replied. Ingrid let go in surprise and the images swirled and faded away.

"There is much more to see . . ." the mirror started. It was only then that she realized the glass, while foggy, emanated purple and black shapes, which seemed to swirl like fire. Was there a face staring back at her? Was it her own distorted image or someone else's entirely? A mask of some sort? It was hard to tell. It appeared only in shadow. She was mesmerized by it.

"What more is there? Show me," she hissed.

"When my lifeblood is renewed, I shall help thee."

Lifeblood? Somehow she could sense the mirror's magic was dying. She couldn't allow that to happen. "What do I do?" she asked, afraid she wouldn't be able to get it done in time. This mirror was the most unique and powerful thing she had ever seen. She couldn't let it disappear.

"Mandrake and nightshade you must find. Do it quick. Concoct a brew for the magic to bind."

The mirror's voice was fading already. She rushed into the front room again and found some supplies, including the tonic she had been brewing to rejuvenate the spirit. Hopefully it was already strong enough. Mixing it all together, she ran back into the room and looked around for something with which to apply it to the mirror. Already, the glass had darkened. She grabbed a rag from a pile of clean laundry she had yet to fold and quickly began applying the varnish to the mirror's glass, extending even to its frame.

The mirror remained dark and quiet. For a moment, she worried she was too late. But as she sat back on her heels and waited, the mirror slowly began to glow, like an ember growing to a full flame. Heat filled the room and Ingrid wondered for the second time that day whether the shop was about to burn down. But the light faded again and the mirror's glass began to swirl with black and purple shades once more. The once tarnished frame began to shine and soon the glass was as clear as crystal. The masklike face slowly swam into view.

"Ingrid," the mirror said, sounding strong again, "my master you will now be. I owe my life to you, and you, in turn, belong with me."

Master? What had she done when she'd touched that mirror? "But *my* master has you in this room for a reason. I'm not sure I can set you free," she said, hating that she suddenly sounded fearful. She was talking to a mirror. This was absurd.

"Do I appear broken? Does a river run after the rains return? Because of you I have awoken." The voice was stronger still. "Put your hand on the glass. Your fate hangs in the balance. Let me show you the future, not the past."

Once more, she touched the glass and the visions came to her, but this time she was *in* them. She saw herself in a lavish room, the likes of which she had never seen before. She sat in a chair high above all others, wearing a beautiful gown and jewels much finer than those the nobles who frequented the village wore. The images kept changing—her standing in front of a roomful of people, her commanding a group of guards, her speaking from an opulent balcony, but she was always there, and each time she appeared, she looked younger and more beautiful than she ever had in real life. The last image was the most powerful of all. Suddenly, a crown was being placed upon her head. She looked young, vibrant, and powerful. Ingrid let go of the mirror, gasping in surprise. "I could be queen?"

"This fact does not wane," the mirror said. "You are meant to be queen, and long will you reign."

It's what she'd always wanted—power, attention, respect—and who had more of those attributes than a queen? King Georg was a young man, of courting age. He was not yet engaged to be married. Perhaps *he* was her future. Perhaps this was what the mirror was telling her . . . *If* it was accurate.

"Place your faith in me," the mirror said. "Grant me your trust. This will be the path that is meant to be."

Ingrid hesitated for a moment, then touched the mirror again. This time she felt a surge of pain, then numbness, but saw no vision. Something was wrong. She let go and looked down at the palm of her hand. A burn mark appeared on her weathered palm. Before she could even consider it, it began to fade away, taking the roughness and dirt she could never seem to be rid of completely with it. The wrinkles and weather-beaten skin smoothed away, replaced with a flaw-less complexion. The unsightly vein that usually throbbed in her hand disappeared. She cried out in surprise and relief. Her hand was beautiful. She looked at the mirror. She wanted her other hand to match.

"You need only ask," the mirror said, reading her thoughts. "Working together, your dreams shall be an easy task."

Queen. She could see it. *Feel* it. Just then, she heard the shop door open.

"I will get you out of here," she promised. "I will come back for you later. I won't let him destroy you."

The mirror became quiet once more. To be sure it was truly safe, she moved it to a new location, hiding it behind a large painting against a different wall in the back room. When the master left for the evening, she would say she had tidying up to do and come back for it. She'd figure out where to keep it permanently later. The bell on the desk chimed, which meant whoever had arrived was a customer. Her master wouldn't ring for her—he would yell. The bell chimed again. This was a customer, and an annoying customer at that.

Ingrid wiped her hands—one dirty with varnish, but the other glowing with the beauty that befitted a future queen—and walked out of the back room. "Can I help you—?" she started, before seeing who it was.

"Sister!" Katherine ran to her and hugged her fiercely. "You'll never believe what happened!" She waved a cream-colored paper in front of Ingrid. "I received an invitation to the palace's masquerade ball!"

"You?" Ingrid sputtered, grabbing the piece of parchment

and reading it hungrily. "'King Georg cordially invites you . . .'" she read. *The king* was inviting her plain sister? Her stomach dropped, along with her hope. The mirror had said *she* would be queen. Not Katherine. "How did you get this?" Her beautiful hand was shaking.

Katherine didn't seem to notice. Her eyes were crystal clear and her cheeks were flushed. "It's my apples!" she said, her voice bursting with pride. "The king has been asking for batches weekly now, and this week I was asked to deliver them myself! He's such a lovely man, Ingrid. You would love him. And now he's asked me to the ball! Can you believe it?"

"No, I cannot," Ingrid said flatly.

Katherine hugged her sister tightly again, which was for the best; there was no hiding the look of jealousy on Ingrid's face.

Snow

She was free.

After what felt like an eternity of being trapped in the woods, the trees had parted and she'd come upon a clearing. Snow inhaled sharply, feeling as if she had held her breath, along with her fears, for too long. The whispering that had plagued her as she wandered vanished, replaced with the welcome sound of chirping birds. As her eyes readjusted to the light of the midafternoon sun, she took in her surroundings. The ground was green, and the earth alive with flowers and trees, but she was definitely not in the meadow where she had begun this journey. In fact, she couldn't recall the last time she'd seen a rocky terrain such as this. The boulders rose out of the ground like mountains.

She noticed a cave opening among the rocks and a small wooden sign in front of it, which meant civilization couldn't be far from here. That was a good omen, because she had no plan to explore that cave. A cavern meant more darkness, and she had finally found the light.

Snow walked past the cave opening and kept going, hoping she'd find a path or a road that might lead her . . . where? That was the problem. She couldn't go back to the castle, not when the queen wanted her dead. She sighed, trying to clear her mind and will her aching feet to keep moving. She needed to find somewhere to rest, gather her thoughts, and decide what she was going to do next.

A northern lapwing flew past her, tweeting excitedly as though singing a song. Mesmerized, Snow followed it. It seemed funny that it was the second time that day she had seen her mother's favorite—once in the meadow with the huntsman and now again. It was as if her mother were somehow with her, pushing her to go on. She watched the bird bob and weave over the meadow before landing on . . . a house? It was a cottage with a thatched roof and it sat in the middle of a grassy knoll like a mirage. The bird tweeted again, as if beckoning her to come see it for herself. Then it took off.

After hours of nothing, she had suddenly stumbled upon this small home in the woods. It had to be a mirage.

But as she walked closer, her legs growing more and more tired, the home blessedly did not disappear. The closer she got, the more detail she noticed. The cottage had a hand-carved door with a small bird etched on the front. That same bird was carved into tiny shutters that dotted each window. Snow felt her heart leap; that seemed to be a good omen. Maybe that lapwing had been good luck.

Out front, she noticed a firepit with burned embers that still glowed. That meant the cottage wasn't deserted! Maybe there were people there who might give her a quick respite. She hastened her pace to the front door and knocked softly. She could only imagine what they'd think of her appearance. Her dress was torn and soiled, and her hair had a few leaves tangled in it. But even if she looked like she normally did, in all likelihood, they wouldn't recognize her. Those outside the palace walls hadn't seen the princess in years.

No one answered the door, so Snow leaned her ear against it and listened. Inside, it seemed all was quiet. She knocked one more time to be sure, but no one came. She sighed, feeling the rush of adrenaline and hope drain out of her.

She couldn't keep wandering. She would just have to wait for the owner of the cottage to return. She looked through the dirty window next to the front door. She could see a comfy armchair inside. Oh, how she longed to sink into that chair, if even for a little while. With a boldness she hadn't known she possessed, her hand went to the doorknob. Turning it, she heard a small click. The unlocked door opened slightly. Snow looked around. There was no sign of anyone approaching. Would it be so terrible of her to wait inside?

"Hello?" Snow called. There was no answer.

If she'd had any doubts that someone currently lived in the cottage, they dissipated the minute she stepped over the threshold. There were bowls of porridge sitting all over the room on small tables, as well as on the chair upon which she had hoped to rest. Clothes and small single socks littered the floor and tables, along with open books and . . . was that a hatchet? *Who* lived here? Curious, she began to look around.

One thing was for sure: the cottage could really use a good tidying. The large room, which appeared to be for cooking and resting, was musty and warm, as if windows had never been opened to let in fresh air. The dining table was covered with dirty dishes. When was the last time these dishes had seen the sink?

That chair looked divine, but she knew what would happen once she sank into it (after removing the bowl of porridge, of course). Her thoughts would return to the darkness. Her mother had been murdered—by her own sister. Had her father known what really happened to her mother? Was that why he'd always seemed so sad? Had Aunt Ingrid done away with him, too? The thoughts could easily paralyze her, and she needed to be sharp. She needed a plan. For now, it was easier to do something useful with her hands. Cleaning had kept her busy all those lonely years in the castle. It could keep her busy again for another few hours.

She picked up the dirty dishes and carried them to the sink to wash them for her hosts. That's when she noticed the seven small dining chairs.

Did a group of children live here? Taking a closer look, Snow noticed the socks on the floor were tiny, as was the shirt hanging on a hook by the door. She didn't see any larger clothes or chairs. . . . Did the children live on their own without parents or caregivers? Her heart gave a sudden lurch. If that were true, they were orphans, just like her. Poor darlings. She wondered where they were now.

Well, at least they will come back to a clean home. Finding energy she was surprised she had left, Snow began gathering the dirty clothing and placing it in a basket to be washed. She cleaned all the dishes and swept the floor. She washed the dirty windows with a rag she found. Then she ventured into the small garden out front. She was delighted to find some ripe and delicious-looking vegetables. Her stomach rumbled at the sight of them and she realized she hadn't eaten since her breakfast at the castle, which now felt like days ago.

Gathering the vegetables, she headed back to the kitchen and started on a soup she had learned to make from Mrs. Kindred as a girl. As it began to boil, an appealing herby aroma filled the room. She left it to simmer, then set the table. When she had finished, she still wasn't satisfied, so she headed back outside—a bouquet of fresh golden-rod flowers would brighten up the place. (What a strange completion to the task she had started what seemed like a lifetime ago!) When she returned with the flowers in tow, she couldn't find a vase, so she placed them in a pitcher, which she then set in the center of the dining room table. *Now* the table looked presentable.

Next she turned to the staircase against the back wall. If the downstairs were this messy, she could only imagine what she might find in the loft. Part of her actually hoped it would need as much care and attention; she could use more tasks to distract herself.

Heading upstairs, Snow found seven small beds lined up in the small space. None of the beds were made, so she tidied them, too, fluffing pillows and placing the small slippers she found in every corner at the foot of each bed. The frames appeared to be hand-carved, and they had odd names etched into the headboards. But they couldn't be their actual names. . . . *Dopey? Grumpy? Sneezy? Bashful, Happy, Doc, and Sleepy?* Whoever these children were, they clearly had a sense of humor. And very comfy-looking beds. Just looking at them, Snow felt herself begin to yawn. There was a small window against the far wall, and the light was dimmer up there. She peered out to see the sun was already starting to set. Could it be evening already? This had been the longest day of her life, and the first time she'd ever been away from the castle come nightfall.

The castle. Mother. Father. Aunt Ingrid's dark deeds. Now that all her busywork was done, she felt the thoughts come rushing back to her like a waterfall. Thankfully, the urge to sleep was coming on just as fast. She felt her limbs grow heavy as she sank down onto the nearest tiny bed and lay across them. The beds felt soft and safe. Maybe she could lie down for just a little while and rest her head. She'd surely hear the door and be downstairs in time to greet her hosts. . . .

It was only a matter of seconds before Snow fell fast asleep.

Snow awakened with a start. Seven figures were leaning over her, watching her sleep. She quickly sat up and blinked at the people surrounding her, feeling disoriented. It took her a minute to remember where she was and why she was there. Oh, yes, the childr—actually, they weren't children at all. They were grown men. They were quite small in stature, but there was no mistaking the mature look to their faces— not to mention the facial hair. One even had a white beard. Their clothes were quite dirty and ash smudged their foreheads and cheeks. Now she felt foolish. How could she have thought a group of children lived on their own? She was the only child she could think of who'd been left to raise herself.

One of the men glared at her angrily. "Who are you, and what are you doing in our house?"

She gaped, trying to remember why she had thought it was a good idea to venture inside the cottage instead of waiting outside, but her head still felt so heavy.

"Now, is that any way for us to talk to our guest?" said one man with a round belly and long eyelashes. He smiled at her. "We're sorry, miss. It's just us out here and, as you can see, we're not used to having visitors."

"Especially not visitors who . . . *achoo!* . . . clean the house," said one with a bright red nose.

Sneezy, it would seem.

"Are you all right, miss?" asked one with tiny spectacles. Another man peeked out from behind his shoulder. He seemed quite shy. Perhaps that one had the nickname Bashful. "Have you fallen ill?" the spectacled man continued. "I can fix you a tonic to help you feel better." She shook her head. He lowered his glasses and looked at her clearly. Maybe he was the one called Doc. "Are you sure? Not many make their way to the edge of the kingdom near the mines by foot."

So she was near the mines. She'd heard Father talk about the diamonds being some of the kingdom's most valuable riches. At least they had been, once. It was said the mines were all dried up now, which cost many villagers their jobs and the kingdom valuable assets—very likely part of the reason the kingdom had become so poor.

"I apologize for the intrusion," Snow said, feeling more embarrassed about her foolishness by the moment.

"Why, that's all right!" one said, sounding jolly. She assumed this one must be Happy. "We never get visitors, which is a shame. It's nice to have company. Right, men?" No one replied.

"I lost my way in the woods and stumbled upon your cottage," Snow explained. "I tried knocking, but no one was home and the door wasn't locked, so . . . I was so tired I let myself in." She looked down at her torn dress, feeling her cheeks flame. "It was quite rude of me."

"So she *does* speak," said the angry one, who Snow deduced must be the one called Grumpy. He looked her up and down. "But you still haven't told us who you are. A spy?"

"You're so distrustful," said another man, who yawned

before looking her over mildly. "The girl obviously just needed a rest. She's not here to steal our gems."

"Don't tell her we have gems!" Grumpy barked, and they all started arguing.

"I'm not here for your gems," Snow promised. "Precious jewels should be kept safe when the kingdom has so few left."

Grumpy raised his right eyebrow and grunted. "So few left? Hogwash! The queen closed the mines so she could keep all the diamonds for herself!"

"No, the mines were closed years ago because they were all dried up," Snow said, confused.

Grumpy grunted again and looked at the others. "That's what people were made to think, but why do you think we're covered in soot? Because we like spending our days in caves?"

"Because we don't wash much?" Sneezy suggested. Grumpy nudged him.

"Because she's got her best miners secretly still doing her dirty work!" Grumpy declared. "The diamonds are still plentiful! But now we mine the caves, and she keeps the riches. The Evil Queen is poison, I say! Poison!" The other men shushed him.

The Evil Queen. So the nickname extended beyond the palace walls. How many others had her aunt's cruelty and greediness affected? She needed more information. "My apologies. I fear I've turned a blind eye to much of what's gone on in the kingdom."

Grumpy grumbled. "Like most, I'd say. But who are you? You still haven't said."

The men looked at her curiously, and she hesitated. Did people still know her name? When she'd been small, her parents had taken her everywhere and endeared her to their people. But, of course, since Aunt Ingrid had become her caretaker, she'd spent her days locked in a less than ivory tower. Did their people think she'd abandoned them the way her father had? That was what Aunt Ingrid always claimed, saying there was a high price on her head. But now she wondered. Maybe they knew she was as much a prisoner as they were. "My name is Snow White."

"Snow White!" the men repeated in unison, and there were a few audible gasps.

"You're the princess!" said Doc, removing his cap. "It's an honor, Your High—"

"Get out!" Grumpy commanded at the same time, and Snow winced.

"That's no way to talk to the princess," Happy argued. They all started to quarrel in disagreement.

Grumpy jumped up. "She's the princess, you fools! Do you know what that means? If the Evil Queen finds out she's here, and that we told her the truth about the mines, we're done for!"

"She thinks I'm dead," Snow said flatly. "She tried to have me killed this morning." Some of the men removed their caps. The room was silent.

"Your Highness, no." Doc sounded breathless. "We're thankful you're all right. We truly hoped someday you would escape. We've always thought you were our kingdom's last hope."

That's what the huntsman had said, too. Why had she never seen it that way before? She had failed her mother. Failed her father. Failed their kingdom. Well, not anymore.

"I'd like to be, but . . ." Snow paused. "I escaped death for the time being, but this has still been the longest day of my life, which is strange because I've had quite a few long days." She couldn't help thinking back to the day her mother died and the night her father disappeared. "When I found your cottage, I was completely spent and unsure I could even go on. Your home seemed so welcoming that I couldn't resist." She looked at their forlorn faces. "To repay you for your kindness, I tidied up and made supper. But I can leave before you eat."

Grumpy seemed to like this idea, but Snow could tell the others disagreed.

"Stay for dinner, Your Highness," Happy said. "We'd like to know more about your journey."

"Thank you all," she said, feeling grateful to stay with them for even just a little while longer. Feeling overcome, she reached out and squeezed the hand of the man closest to her. "Thank you so much."

He backed away nervously, but didn't speak. He smiled at her from the safety of the other side of the room. Had she overstepped?

"Dopey isn't much for talking," Happy explained. "But he's a good man to have on your side. Come, Princess." He motioned toward downstairs. "Let's continue our talk at the table. We haven't had a nice home-cooked meal in years!"

"Hey, are you calling my goulash rubbish?" Grumpy asked.

"It's edible . . . sometimes," Sneezy replied.

"Why don't you all wash up and I'll put the food out?" Snow asked. Her aunt would be horrified at the thought of a princess serving people, but it felt good to be so useful for a change and to be in others' company. Still, the men looked at her strangely.

"Yes, wash up," said Bashful. He nudged the others. "Come on, men."

There was some grumbling, but they all went to the sink while she ladled soup into bowls on the table. Dopey lit a fire, which made the room toasty. Then they all sat and ate. The men slurped loudly, but there wasn't much talking. Grumpy kept watching her, but every time she made eye contact, he looked away. Between the fire and the lanterns glowing in various corners of the room, Snow suddenly realized that she felt quite safe and warm, a sharp contrast to how she had felt only a few hours before. Maybe that's what continued to make her feel so bold.

"That was delicious, Princess," said Happy, patting his round stomach.

"I'm so glad you liked it," she said. "While we all digest, I was hoping you could tell me more about the diamond mining and how the queen has altered your original arrangement."

Grumpy dropped his spoon onto the table with a thud. "See? Told you she had a motive."

"If I'm going to stop my aunt's reign, I think it's important I know what she's done to those in the kingdom. Don't you?" Snow asked, looking at Grumpy, then at Doc. "As you said, I may be our kingdom's only hope." She hoped she hadn't gone too far, but now that she'd gotten kernels of information about the happenings in the kingdom, she craved more.

Grumpy leaned back in his chair, tipping it so far she was sure he'd fall. He looked her square in the eye. "All right. We'll talk. But we have some questions, too."

"We do?" Bashful spoke up. Grumpy gave him a look.

"Fair enough," Snow agreed. "If you would be so kind, could you tell me the true condition of the mines?"

The men looked at one another. "For years, the queen has ruined our commerce," Grumpy complained.

"King Georg always had us meet a quota, but as payment for a job well done we could keep a percentage of our findings," Doc added.

"But this queen wants it all! She is so selfish she has led the kingdom to believe the mines are dried up, when they are not," Grumpy spat.

"We've heard stories up and down the land of the jewels she's claimed as her own," said Happy.

"The rugs and the gold that are meant for trade wind up in the castle, locked in her quarters, while in the streets, people are starving!" Sneezy added.

"And still she sends her henchmen to check our mines to make sure she gets it all," Bashful told her.

Snow clenched her fists. "I had no idea this was happening. How has she gotten away with this?"

"Her guards keep her well protected and her court is afraid of her wrath," said Sleepy. "No one will question her decisions."

"We are honorable men," Happy added. "We may not be family in the traditional sense, but we have stuck together for years, and we are barely scraping by."

"Look around you, Princess," Doc piped up. "Do we look like we are living beyond our means? No. We can't afford her taxes."

"We don't touch the diamonds we've hidden away," Sleepy added. "They're only for a rainy day."

"I won't say anything," Snow vowed. "It sounds like you are actually owed money by the kingdom. I won't take away what's rightfully yours. You can trust me."

"Trust. Humph! You're related to her!" Grumpy pointed out.

"But we are not family," Snow said. "She certainly has never treated me as such. Even after my mother died and my father left, she left me to fend for myself." She spotted a carving of a bird etched into the men's fireplace. It made her think of her mother. She'd have loved this humble abode and the people who lived in it. She'd have wanted to hear their worries and their triumphs. She would've tried to help. If the former queen couldn't be there to do it, it was up to Snow to. "The kingdom is falling apart, and as you said, people need help." She thought of her mother and how she had tried to help everyone she met. She thought of her father opening the gates so their people could feel like family. Her aunt did none of that. "She isn't running the kingdom like a queen should."

"And you think you can defeat her?" Grumpy looked skeptical. "Why, before today, it sounds like you didn't even know what was going on in your own kingdom! And she wants you dead! You don't have a chance on your own."

That could be true, Snow realized with a sinking heart. What good was an army of one? The queen had magic. What did Snow have? Maybe she was a fool for thinking she could do more. But still, knowing what she did now, how could she not try?

"But she might with our help," Happy suggested, and Snow looked at him hopefully.

Friends. Allies. That could make a difference. "I would welcome any help you could offer," Snow said.

"She can't stay here," Grumpy said. "We have enough troubles."

"Every month, the queen sends her men to check on us," Sneezy explained. "They just came this week, so no one will be around again for a while. You are safe here for now, but we don't have much to offer. We barely have enough to survive the month."

"Safe? She's not staying!" Grumpy insisted again. "The queen probably already knows you're here, or she's having you followed." He looked out the window again. "They say she's good at dark magic! She can see all!" A few of the men looked alarmed.

"But she thinks I'm dead," Snow reminded them. She rose to her full height. "The queen wanted the heir to the throne disposed of so she could keep it for herself. From what you say, she's clearly not taking care of our people."

She cleared her throat, voicing her anger at the injustices she'd learned about. "Her reign cannot be allowed to continue. I will fight her to my last breath." As she said the words, she knew them to be true.

"What if she tries to destroy us for taking you in?" Bashful asked. In the distance, they heard a wolf howl, and he shuddered. "We've managed to avoid her notice for so long."

"Avoid her? She takes all we have," Doc reminded him. "Soon there will be nothing left and she'll be done with us, too. I say we help the princess." He smiled at her.

Dopey walked over and stood by Snow's seat.

"I do, too," said Happy, as did Sneezy and Sleepy. Bashful agreed, too. Everyone looked at Grumpy, the one holdout. He sat with his arms folded across his chest, staring at the fire instead of her.

"I won't let her continue to harm my people," Snow declared again, her voice commanding. "If you help me, I will work hard to bring peace and prosperity back to this kingdom, as it had once before." She looked at Grumpy. "I know I've let you down, but I won't anymore. You don't know what I've been through. All because I've been afraid." She straightened her shoulders and looked at them with steely determination. "I'm not anymore."

Grumpy studied her for a moment. Finally, he spoke. "Fine. We'll offer our assistance." The other men smiled.

"Thank you," Snow said, feeling relief seep through her. For the first time in a long while, she was no longer alone. Somehow, she had found these small men, and now they were her allies. It felt like fate.

Mother, Father, I won't disappoint you again, she thought.

Snow sat back down. "First, we need a plan."

Dopey ran and found a scroll and some quills. She took a quill gratefully as the other men resumed their places at the table.

She looked at the others. "Now. Let's see how we're going to take back our kingdom."

Ingrid

Nineteen years earlier

They couldn't have been happier.

Ingrid had thought the attraction would fade eventually. The farmer and his wife barely looked at each other. Her own father and mother, in what limited memories she had of them together, certainly hadn't shown affection toward one another in front of their daughters. But King Georg and Katherine were different. Their love only seemed to grow.

The farmer had no qualms about giving Katherine's hand away, but he didn't want to be burdened with Ingrid. Katherine offered her a room in the castle, but Ingrid didn't need her sister's pity. She had taken up residence on her master's floor almost immediately. It wasn't ideal, but at least she was free.

She grinned painfully through the royal wedding, with all its pomp and circumstance. Everyone was thrilled by the idea that a commoner could marry royalty, that Katherine had impressed the king with her innovation and her goodness. The fanfare caused the kingdom to grind to a complete halt. Not a single subject worked that day; no fields were sown nor quarries mined. They were all invited to the celebration. Ingrid thought the move was foolish. The kingdom could have been pillaged as the people danced, but Katherine was sure it would not be. And Georg, of course, listened.

That's all the man ever did—listen to Katherine's suggestions.

It was sickening.

It was Katherine who suggested they open the palace gates to visitors every few weeks for a garden party, where the king could meet his subjects. It was she who suggested they expand the kingdom's agricultural efforts so that the farmer and his wife could head up a marketplace in the village square where all subjects could afford fresh fruits and vegetables. She put time and resources into sprucing up the castle so that it could be revered by all and commissioning a ridiculous aviary in the garden where she could invite people to view the various birds that populated the kingdom.

There was no more price gouging—no charging people

more for the loveliest apples in the orchard. Again, Ingrid thought the choice foolish. How would the kingdom make money if they didn't take opportunities like that? She wouldn't have allowed the kingdom to become so lax with its merchants or agreed to bartering and swapping goods with other kingdoms instead of keeping all the wealth here, where it belonged. She wouldn't have allowed her betrothed to appear soft to his enemies. But Katherine wouldn't be swayed. And Georg loved Katherine, not Ingrid, so he only listened to her. Katherine convinced Georg that being kind to his people was more important than being feared. Ingrid was certain the day would come when they would both rue that ideology, but it hadn't come yet. The kingdom was thriving . . . as was their love.

"Just as the sky is blue and the grass is green, the king is set in his ways. He will only ever listen to his queen," the mirror said when Ingrid lamented about the state of the kingdom.

A few months after the wedding, Katherine arrived at the shop with an entourage of guards around her.

Ingrid's master fled his own shop when he saw the guards, but Ingrid stood her ground, staring at her sister. Katherine was wearing the finest silk the kingdom could find, a gown hand-made just for her. Her hair was now pulled back off her face in a pile of curls placed atop her head, where the tiara still looked too big, as though she were playing dress up.

"What do you want?" Ingrid said, liking how uncomfortable her sister was in her surroundings. Taking in the potions and the herbs and the spell books she didn't understand, Katherine had the low ground. Ingrid couldn't help preferring it that way. She didn't care who Katherine thought she was now that she had a title. She was, and would always be, Ingrid's younger sister.

Somehow, Katherine sensed that. She rushed forward and the guards followed closely behind. "I hate that I don't see you every day anymore."

"*You* left me," Ingrid said flatly. "I never would have left you behind."

"I got married," Katherine said, the hurt registering on her face. "I didn't leave you."

"You did," Ingrid said, looking away, her eyes drawn to the shop's back room, where the mirror was waiting. Always waiting. "Did you think I'd survive staying at the farmer's without you? I lasted a day before I remembered how I wasn't wanted. And now I sleep here, on my master's cold shop floor." Ingrid whirled around. Her eyes blazed as she stormed toward her sister. "Does that make you happy?"

She had taken one too many steps. The guards moved forward, shoving the edges of their swords in Ingrid's face.

"You will not threaten the queen," one guard barked, his voice gravelly.

Katherine put her hand up. "It's all right. Please stand down." The guards stepped back again.

It was comical, almost. Her sister had such power and she had no clue how to truly use it.

"I have offered you haven in the castle repeatedly since my wedding day, and yet you never accept it," Katherine tried again.

"Because I don't want your pity," Ingrid said.

"It's not pity!" Katherine insisted. "I don't like the idea of you here alone, learning witchcraft all day and night."

"It's not witchcraft," Ingrid said. They'd had this conversation too many times before.

"Well, whatever it is," Katherine said, her tone starting to cool. She wrapped her cape more tightly around herself, as if to keep the chill from entering her bones. "I don't like thinking of you here at night, all alone, when your master leaves. So if you won't accept my invitation of a room, maybe you will accept a position on the king's staff."

"What?" Ingrid said in surprise.

Katherine smiled shyly now. "I already spoke to Georg. He said yes, of course. You're my sister. My only family, really, and I want you close by. I want to take care of you the way you took care of me."

Ingrid's face soured. "I don't need caring for."

"I know that," Katherine said quickly. "But I still do. There's so much I have to learn and do, and I can't do it without you. You know that. Please say yes."

Say yes. She heard the voice in her head clearly. *Go and ask for the rest. You know which title will be best.*

Which title. *Yes* . . . "Okay," Ingrid said. "I'll come." Katherine began to clap her hands excitedly. "But I want to be your lady-in-waiting."

"Oh." Katherine paused. "I was already assigned one of those."

"Then give that person another position," Ingrid insisted. If she was Katherine's lady-in-waiting, she could be the voice of reason in her sister's head. And if she was the voice of reason in Katherine's head, she'd be the one in Georg's, too.

You alone can infiltrate the head and the heart. Together, our wisdom you shall impart.

Katherine smiled. "Okay, I will. You're my new lady-in-waiting. Come right now and leave all this behind." She looked around the small shop in dismay.

"I need to gather my things," Ingrid told her. "I'll come tomorrow." She had to find a way to get the mirror out of the shop without her master seeing. It wasn't like he ever went looking for it or even remembered it. The old man was so senile he probably didn't even realize it was there.

"Okay," Katherine said again. She held out her hand. "Tomorrow, Sister, you'll be mine again."

Ingrid gave Katherine's hand a squeeze. "Yes," she said, even though both she and the mirror were thinking exactly the opposite.

Katherine did listen—on some things. But not the things that mattered. Ingrid would have her ear until she was interrupted for something inane like another garden party with the silly subjects. Moreover, Katherine wanted Ingrid to smile more at the servants in the castle. She expected Ingrid to be friendly and kind. Katherine still insisted pricing be fair for crops. She wouldn't allow Georg to go to war with other kingdoms, as much as Ingrid wanted her to. Ingrid had hoped Georg would get himself killed so Katherine would become the sole ruler.

But it was moving the mirror into the castle that had come at the highest price by far. It had taken her weeks to find a way to smuggle it into the castle without Katherine knowing of its existence, but she eventually devised a plan: under cover of darkness, with the aid of two palace guards whom she would pay off (and threaten with their lives if they ever spoke of the outing), she would have the mirror moved to her chambers, putting it in a large dressing closet off her own room. She would keep it locked at all times and refuse to allow any servant in her room, even to dust. "I'm fine taking care of my own affairs," she'd say. Who cared about cobwebs anyway? She had more important matters on her mind.

But when the night arrived and she led the guards to her master's shop, she didn't expect him to be waiting there for her.

"Master." Ingrid had bowed in his presence, something she still did out of habit as much as she loathed it.

"I know why you are here," he said, "and you cannot have what is not yours."

"Master?" she said, her heart quickening. He couldn't mean the mirror. She had been so careful with it, hiding it painstakingly whenever he wasn't around. There was no way he could know she was communing with it. He probably didn't even know he still possessed such an object. After all, when she'd first found it, it was among the broken relics he was preparing to dispose of.

"I am no fool, Ingrid." Her master's voice vibrated with anger. "You think I don't know what you've been up to under my roof? Do you think my eyes have failed me?"

"I am not sure what you mean," she tried again. What if he thought she was coming to steal from him? But she wasn't stealing. The mirror was *hers*. She had cared for it.

She had fixed it. She had given herself over to it. It was part of her now. She wasn't leaving without it. She stepped forward to enter the shop. Her master blocked her path.

Enough was enough. "Let me through, old man. I have things to collect." Ingrid pushed past him.

Her master followed. So did the guards. "That mirror is not yours! It belongs to this shop, which makes it mine." He stepped in front of her. "Who gave you permission to fix it? Did you not think there was a reason it was dying? Did you not wonder why I wouldn't think of something to bring it back to life on my own? A mirror with power like that was meant to die. It is too dangerous for this world."

"Maybe it was too dangerous for you, but it is not for me!" Ingrid thundered. "The mirror saw my potential and it called to me, therefore it is mine, and I am taking it *now*."

She pushed him aside and went straight to the back room, where the mirror was waiting behind the curtain. Even without her presence, it had come alive, smoking and fogging up the room. A swift wind picked up even though they were indoors, and in the distance, she heard thunder. She picked up the mirror and prepared to carry it out to the carriage, where it would be well hidden. But her master blocked her path again. This time he held a potion in his hands.

"I'm warning you, Ingrid," he said. "Put that mirror down or it will be the last thing you touch in this world."

"You would really harm your own apprentice over a mirror?" she asked.

"I would to keep you from letting its darkness bury itself into your soul." He prepared to drop the vial. She didn't want to think of what poison it might possess.

"My lady?" one of the guards questioned.

"Stop him!" Ingrid commanded.

It all happened so quickly there was no time to stop it. Her words, which had seemed so simple, meant something more to the guards. What she'd thought was merely an instruction to restrain her master, the guards interpreted as an order to end his life. Moments later, the old man lay on the floor of his shop, blood pooling around the knife wound in his chest. He had died instantly. The potion bottle was still in his hand. The bile rose in her throat. Her master was dead because of her.

"We must go!" one of the guards said. "Quickly!" He reached for the mirror. Ingrid hesitated a second and then allowed him to take it. "Let's go!"

She looked down at her master once more and stepped over his body. Then she stooped to grab the potion from his still-warm hand. After all, it would be a pity to waste it.

Ingrid walked out of the shop for the last time with her head up, knowing the mirror was truly hers at last.

She had given up a lot for that mirror. The memory of what had happened would haunt her all her days. And even now that she lived in the castle, her master buried and his disappearance barely noticed, it still bothered her that the mirror's original vision for her future had been wrong. Hadn't it shown *her* being crowned queen? Wasn't she the one who was meant to reign?

"She has worn out her use; but if the queen is to live," the mirror told her, "your future I cannot give."

She came *this close* to throwing something at the mirror when it said that, but she didn't dare. The small voice inside her that grew ever louder by the day told her doing something like that would be the death of her. She wasn't sure if the voice meant figuratively or truly, but she wouldn't chance it. She kept quiet, praying the outcome would change, until the day the mirror started to get more persistent.

Stop wasting time with chores! Fulfill your destiny. Take the crown if you want it to be yours.

Ingrid tried to ignore the mirror. This was her sister, and she drew the line at destroying the only person she'd ever truly loved. True, Katherine now loved someone else far more than she loved Ingrid, but Georg was just a nuisance. Someone she'd eventually be able to get rid of.

She never imagined she'd have to compete with yet another for Katherine's attention . . . someone who wouldn't be so easily done away with.

Seventeen years earlier

"Does she ever stop crying?" Ingrid asked, bouncing the baby on her hip as a team of women helped Katherine dress for the day.

Katherine laughed. "Yes! Coddle her, Ingrid. Babies need to be coddled and told all will be right with the world."

Coddled? This baby was selfish.

Two years had passed since she had moved into the castle, and instead of Georg and Katherine's love dimming, it only burned brighter with the addition of their firstborn child. The girl had gotten the very best qualities of both her parents, thank heavens. (Katherine might have found Georg handsome, but he reminded Ingrid of a toad.) They named her Snow White. With porcelain cheeks, the roundest eyes with gorgeous lashes, and thick black curls, the kingdom's new princess was adored by all . . . except one.

When little Snow White stared into Ingrid's eyes, she could swear the child knew the darkness of her soul. Every time she held her—which was plenty, seeing as how she was lady-in-waiting and the princess's aunt—the child screamed.

Fat tears rolled down Snow's cheeks as Ingrid tried to bounce her up and down and shush her. But no matter what she tried, the child could not be soothed in her arms.

"Here, let me show you," Katherine said, scooping

Snow up and holding the six-month-old in her arms. The swishing movement, combined with Katherine's dynamic smile, soothed the child instantly. Within minutes, the baby was actually cooing. The rest of the room gathered round to watch.

"She's a natural mother, our queen," said a handmaiden Ingrid couldn't stand.

Ingrid pushed the woman aside. "Katherine? Are you almost done here? We're supposed to discuss adding more workers to the mines. Truthfully, I think we could just make those down there spend more hours working." One of the handmaidens gave Ingrid a look of disdain. Ingrid didn't care. "If they did that, we could double our diamond harvesting and our profit would be plentiful."

Katherine ignored her for a moment, continuing to coo at Snow White, who lapped up the attention that should have been for Ingrid.

"Katherine?" Ingrid's voice was sharper. "Our appointment time together is only for a half hour. You have a busy day ahead and we haven't much time to discuss things."

"Oh, Ingrid," Katherine said, her eyes still on Snow. "The mines can wait for another day. Right now, come enjoy your niece with me."

"But . . ." This was infuriating! The kingdom needed someone to take a firm hand and shake it alive. They could be drowning in riches and wealth if pathetic Georg would put his foot down! Spending longer hours in the mines, however unstable the miners claimed those conditions to be, would garner them riches like they'd never seen!

Now is the hour. Take thy dream. Seize the ultimate power.

"You keep saying that, but it isn't possible," Ingrid spat, and everyone looked at her. Had she just said that out loud?

Give yourself to me. Put thy hand on the glass. I'll show what you fail to see.

So the mirror wanted more lifeblood. If she was honest, she hated touching the mirror. Every time she made direct contact with it, it seemed to glow brighter, while she felt tired and weak. The feeling had to be in her head. After all, it was just a mirror . . . a mirror that spoke to her soul. She'd done it several times already, and the bond between her and the magic had strengthened. She now knew spells she'd never heard of and had brilliant thoughts about fixing the kingdom. But she hated feeling so drained.

"Did you say something, Ingrid?" Katherine asked. She couldn't even look up to ask the question. It was outrageous! That ridiculous baby took up all of Katherine's time and attention. And royal duties took up the rest.

"No," Ingrid muttered, even though she wanted to scream.

You know what must be done. A life for a crown . . . if you want this battle to be won, the mirror told Ingrid yet again.

But she still wasn't ready to listen.

Snow

"I learned something today that could be of use," Happy declared as the final dish was dried and put back in the cupboard.

The men and Snow looked up from their various positions around the cottage. Happy and Doc were on dish-drying duty, while Dopey and Bashful were sweeping the floor. Grumpy was starting the fire, and Snow, Sneezy, and Sleepy were cleaning up the kitchen.

For the last week, she had lived with the men, or the dwarfs, as she knew they referred to themselves, and she had quickly fallen into a new routine. The men wouldn't hear of her cooking or cleaning for them ("You're the princess!" they protested) so it was agreed they would share the housekeeping duties, with Snow prepping meals while they were at the mines. She didn't leave the cottage during the day—Grumpy had made her promise. ("The queen has eyes everywhere! Don't open the door for strangers!") Instead, she tried to think of ways to thwart her aunt, of unexplored paths she could examine. But though she understood the reasoning behind it, she hated being cooped up all day. It reminded her of life spent trapped in the castle.

Dinner was a family affair. And oh, how she enjoyed it! Who knew there was so much to talk about each day? She loved when the men shared stories about their work in the mines, while she often regaled them with stories about life in the castle when she was a small child or about the types of birds she spotted from the window. And then there were the questions. She found she had many! After staying silent for so long, there was much she longed to know, and she was always interested in learning more about the men and their lives. She wanted to know who had carved the beautiful wooden doorways and furniture around the cottage, and why the deer and the birds seemed to linger at the kitchen window while she prepped meals.

"They must adore you, as we do," gushed Bashful.

"And I you!" Snow would say. She found she could talk to them till the candle burned out each night.

It felt like she was finally waking up and finding her voice after years of silent darkness. And while she promised the men she would not do more than her share of the housework, she couldn't help trying to find small ways to repay them for their kindness when she wasn't busy strategizing. Despite their protests, she prepared a lunch basket for them to take to work each day. She mended tiny socks. And secretly, she was using yarn and needles she had found to knit them blankets for their beds. It might have been summer, but she couldn't help noticing they had few blankets for the winter months.

Knitting helped her pass the time while they were gone, but it also made her think. And thinking about her mother without knowing how to avenge her was making Snow grow anxious. While her aunt continued to dictate orders from the castle, Snow was sitting in a lovely cottage doing nothing. But as Grumpy continually reminded her: "Without a real plan, you are as good as dead. And you dead is good for no one."

And so she waited, and tried to come up with the answers. How could she end the Evil Queen's reign and take back the kingdom? She was only one girl.

One voice can be very powerful when it is heard above the rest.

Those were her mother's words. When subjects had grievances, they would sometimes hesitate, fearing that their voices would fall on deaf ears. Then Queen Katherine would speak up from her throne, as Snow sat nearby and watched, and say exactly that. And most times, the subjects weren't afraid to tell their stories anymore. But how would Snow tell the people she was there for them if no one could even know she was alive?

Sleepy yawned next to her, bringing her back to the present. His eyes already looked heavy from the day. The men worked long hours.

"I overheard Fredrick from Knox Hills say many in his hamlet are thinking of abandoning the kingdom," Happy told them.

"Abandoning the kingdom?" Snow repeated. "Why is that? No work?"

"No," Happy said. "Too much! And too many tariffs. They can't afford to stay."

Snow put down her rag in dismay. "I must talk to this Fredrick. *And* his hamlet. They should not feel forced from their homes because of their ruler."

"You're as mad as a hornet!" Grumpy waved the fireplace poker around. "You have no power to change their fate."

Snow's eyes widened as a thought suddenly dawned on her. "Unless I gather men like Fredrick together and give them something to fight for!" She looked at the others. "If I speak with my people in person, tell them that I am alive and well and ready to take back my kingdom for them, maybe they will help me fight the Evil Queen."

"But if someone goes back to the queen and tells her what you are up to . . ." Bashful looked worried.

Their eyes all went to the kitchen window. A raven had appeared on more than one occasion this past week, and the men had begun to wonder if the queen was watching them. But if she knew where Snow was, Happy argued, wouldn't she have come for her by now?

"Guards don't linger in the hamlets around here," Doc reminded him. "They only come when there are taxes to be paid. As long as we avoid the guards, Snow can talk freely without harm."

"But if the queen learns what she's doing . . ." Sneezy wiped his red nose. His allergies had been particularly rough the last few days.

Snow inhaled deeply. "At some point she will learn I am alive. So I need to move quickly and talk to as many sympathizers as I can. If they will fight with me, then maybe we can stage a coup and overthrow her."

Grumpy stroked his long white beard. "It's risky, but it could work. There must be plenty of sympathizers like ourselves. We could try to organize them, and have them ready to storm the castle on a specific date."

"Two weeks from today," Snow announced decisively, and they looked at her.

"That's not much time!" Sleepy said.

"It's all we have," Snow said. "The queen will learn I'm alive soon and then our time will be short. We must be ready. In two weeks," she said again, trying to sound more confident than she felt. "That gives us enough time to talk to several hamlets and band together."

"Where do we find more who might be willing to help?" Doc asked.

Happy pounded the table excitedly. "I've heard plenty of the men in the mine talking! Their hamlets aren't far from here."

Grumpy ran to a chest in the living room. Unlocking it, he lifted out a rolled parchment and brought it to the table. The others gathered round to watch as he laid the parchment flat, smoothing its creases. It was a hand-painted circular map of the kingdom. The castle was in the center and the kingdom divided into four corners, including the farmland where her mother had spent her youth, the mining area they were now in, a section covered in mostly forest, and one surrounded by lakes. Little homes and names of hamlets dotted the four corners like prizes waiting to be collected. The parchment was yellowed and delicate, but the intricate map of the kingdom was Snow's greatest tool at the moment. If she wanted to end her aunt's reign, she would need more than just the seven men in front of her to help her do it. She would convince people, one by one if she had to, to stand up and fight alongside her. *One voice can be very powerful when it is heard above the rest.*

Snow touched the edges of the map gently. It dawned on her that the lovely places represented on this piece of paper—places she had never seen—made up her kingdom. It was beautiful, and slightly overwhelming. "Where do we start?"

"Here." Happy pointed to a small array of cottages not far from the waterfall. "This is Fredrick's hamlet. The weather in those parts has been stormy of late. We've had so much rain, he's missed some work in the mines because of it."

The men had left for work later than usual the day before for that very reason.

"Much of the kingdom has been covered with rain, from what I hear," Doc added.

"The weather matches the people's mood," Grumpy said.

"If we wait till nightfall," Happy said, "we can avoid you being seen."

"We're going to need some weapons," Grumpy told them. "We can't subdue the guards with our bare hands."

"We have our pickaxes!" Doc reminded him, and the others nodded.

"Not enough!" Grumpy pounded the table. "Have you

not heard what the queen is capable of? She has an army at her disposal—an army that listens to her, not you," he said, looking at Snow. "You're not just facing an evil queen, you're facing a witch of the dark arts."

"Grumpy's right," Happy said, looking anything but. "We're going to need some potions of our own, men, if we're going to fight her."

"I know there used to be a dark magic shop in the marketplace. Perhaps it's still there," Sneezy suggested. "Some say the queen used to work there as a girl."

Grumpy hit him with his own cap. "You fool! Then we can't go there! Whoever runs it is in cahoots with her, you see?" He looked at the others. "Where else can we get some magic?"

They all looked at the map as if it had the answers. But from what Snow could see, there was no little hut or skull that was labeled "witchcraft."

Bashful looked nervous. "In the mines, people talk about what they'd do if they were trapped. How they'd get out. I've heard men talk of an elixir found in the sap of a tree in the Haunted Woods that can change a person's shape. Make you small or big. A bird or an ox. Whatever you need to be to get out of that hole."

"A *tree*?" Grumpy repeated wryly. "The woods have lots of trees!"

Bashful leaned back. "This one is said to have a face, and it looks like it's howling."

Snow shut her eyes tight as a not-so-different memory sprang up. "I've seen a tree like that." She opened her eyes and her heartbeat steadied at the sight of the men. "I wandered through those Haunted Woods. After I ran from the huntsman, that's where I wound up. It was dreadful." She shuddered. "I felt like I'd never see the sun again."

Just the idea of going back in there made her blood run cold. The thoughts that had run through her head, the images she had seen in her mind, the feeling of utter loneliness that had almost consumed her—it was all too much. She wondered if that was part of the tree's power.

"You were alone," Grumpy said, his voice softer. "This time you won't be."

"Spirits can't get you when you have company," Happy said knowingly. The others nodded.

She didn't know if that was true, but the words gave her comfort. She exhaled deeply. Grumpy might be right in that they needed some sort of magic. She wouldn't want the subjects she met with to be led into battle without protection. They were fighting for themselves, but they were also fighting for her. "All right. I'll go back to the Haunted Woods. And we will find that tree."

———

The dwarfs had the next day off from the mines, and they wasted no time setting out for the woods. They walked most of the way in silence—something Snow knew all too well, but on this particular morning she didn't much feel like talking anyway. She was too nervous. Where would her mind lead her when she was back in that awful place? *Hush now!* she told her restless thoughts, steadying her heart and her hands. This time, she wouldn't let it consume her. *I will be brave.*

She knew they had reached the edge of the Haunted Woods when she saw the fog seeping out of the forest. Up ahead, the foliage had turned from green to black and the grass near the edges of the woods was devoid of color. A bird made a lonely cry, seemingly begging them to avoid the darkness. Instead, they walked forward together.

"Don't trust most things. Just the thoughts inside your own head," Grumpy said, sensing her anxiousness.

A raven flew overhead and the men stopped. The same bird had been at their window earlier. This had to be a bad omen. Snow felt like an hourglass was marking her time before the Evil Queen found them—and she could sense the sand was dwindling.

Grumpy looked up at the bird. "And even then, maybe don't trust the creatures in there, either."

"Okay," Snow said, stepping into the tree line.

The sunlight and warmth on her face vanished almost immediately.

Inside, where shadows reigned, the air was colder, and a breeze prickled the back of her neck. As she let her eyes adjust to the light, she heard the familiar whispers from her last visit. She refused to allow herself to decipher what they were saying. Instead, she concentrated on her steps. Ahead of her, she saw the clearing she had run through on her way out of the forest. Beyond it, she knew, were the bleak lake, the trees that had seemingly pulled at her cloak and her dress, and the deep darkness. That's where the tree had been. She was sure of it. "It's that way," she said, trying to keep her voice steady.

"It's dark in there," Bashful whispered.

"So?" Sneezy asked. "You work in a mine. You should be used to the dark."

"But the spirits," Sleepy said, looking more somber than usual.

"Spirits?" Doc said. "That's probably just a rumor the queen made up to keep people away from the howling tree. A tree that powerful needs protection; what better place than a supposedly haunted wood?"

Doc made a good point. Even still . . . Snow held out her hand. "It is quite dark," she said. "Stay close to avoid being separated."

"We will form a chain," Grumpy said, ready as ever to take charge. "Come on, men!"

"Follow me," Snow said firmly as she led them into the blackness ahead. The air was still. The quiet made every sound seem magnified, every crunch of dead leaves beneath their feet echoing in the darkness. Snow concentrated hard to make out the shadows in front of her. It was hard as the fog thickened. Every dead tree looked the same—mangled and gnarled, like its limbs were trying to grab them. She reminded herself it was only her imagination playing tricks on her.

"Anything?" Grumpy pressed.

"Not yet," Snow admitted. There *had* been a tree that looked like it was screaming at her, had there not? She was sure she had seen it. But could that have been in her head like so much else that had happened in these parts? Had she led them into this awful place for nothing?

Snap! Everyone turned sharply at the crackling sound. Snow listened closely; she could swear she heard a familiar birdcall.

"What was that?" Doc shouted.

"It's a ghost!" Sleepy cried.

Snow felt Doc's hand slip from her grasp in his panic. There was shouting, and she heard a few cries. Snow tried to talk over them.

"It's an owl!" she tried to assure the men, surprised she was remaining so calm. But she recognized that call. She and her mother had studied nocturnal birds as well. "There's nothing to be afraid of! It's just an—"

"*No!*" she heard Happy cry, and she whirled around. "No! Retreat! Retreat!"

She heard screaming and the rushing of sudden footsteps. The men's voices sounded far away. What was happening?

"We're not alone!" Grumpy shouted. "Run, Snow! Run!"

Snow froze. She had heard those words before—from the huntsman. Had he come back to finish her off? Was he going to hurt her new friends?

"Turn back, Snow! Run and don't stop!" Doc yelled.

No. She wouldn't run away. Not anymore. "No!" Snow cried. "I won't let him hurt you!" She ran toward the commotion, deeper into the fog and the blackness, and seconds later, she crashed into someone larger than she. She fell to her knees on impact and quickly struggled to get back up. Feeling the dirt beneath her fingernails, she searched for anything she could use to defend herself and the others. Her hand closed around a large stick and she jumped up and swung the stick in the air. She heard it connect with a body.

"Oof!"

It was a male voice. It had to be the huntsman coming for her. She didn't want to hurt him—he had spared her life once—but she would have to scare him off if she couldn't reason with him.

"Leave now and you will be spared, huntsman!" she announced, but even as she said it, she knew the words sounded silly.

"Huntsman?" Grumpy repeated, from somewhere in the darkness. "Men, it's the man who tried to kill the princess! Get him!"

Snow swung the stick wildly and hit her attacker again. She heard him start to cough and the sound of the leaves as he fell to the ground. "Go now and you will not be harmed!" she said again, stepping forward. But her foot slid on wet leaves and she felt herself begin to slip again. She hit the ground hard this time and started to roll, smashing right into him. Her hand was still firmly gripping the branch. She picked it up, fully prepared to use it again, when a sliver of light fell through the trees into the darkness.

"Stop! Please!" she heard him say as he breathed heavily. "I am no huntsman!"

"Snow!" Happy reached down and pulled her up. "Are you all right?"

"Tie up the huntsman," Grumpy demanded. "We will leave him here for the woods to do away with."

"Wait!" Snow said, but the dwarfs held her back.

"Wait!" echoed the man, but his voice sounded different now that the threat was over. "Please! I know not who you speak of." He coughed hard. "I mean no harm. I got lost in the woods. This place is odd. I'm not myself, but time was of the essence . . ." he mumbled. "I'm looking for someone. Please help me."

That voice. It sounded familiar. It was warm. Where had she heard it before? Curious, Snow leaned down to get a closer look before the men could stop her. She removed the attacker's cap and dropped it in surprise. "Henri?"

He tried to sit up fast, but fell back. He ran a hand through his brown hair and blinked twice at her in surprise. "Snow White?"

"You know him?" Grumpy kept a long stick trained on him.

"Yes!" Snow said happily. She couldn't believe she was seeing the prince again, and here, of all places. "What are you doing here?"

He was unsteady on his feet, so she held on to his arm even though it felt strange to hold a man's arm like this. "I've been looking for you, Snow!"

"Me? Whatever for?" Snow asked, her heart beating a bit quicker.

"I was on an urgent mission to get back to your castle to find you and took a shortcut, but my horse was scared off by the darkness," Henri explained. "I got turned around and couldn't find my way out."

"Humph. Some plan," Grumpy mumbled.

"Urgent?" Snow repeated. "Is this about the queen? Has she told the kingdom I'm dead?"

"*You* dead?" Henri's blue eyes held a world of surprise. "You mean *him*? We didn't think she believed he was a threat, but he could be . . ."

He wasn't making sense. Snow reached out and touched Henri's head, then pulled her hand back again just as quickly. Everyone was looking at her. Her cheeks felt flushed. "How hard did you fall, Henri?" she said, trying to keep her voice light. "What are you talking about?"

Henri grabbed her hand. "Snow, I found your father."

Ingrid

Ten years earlier

The second her fingertips touched the glass, she could feel the energy draining from her body. Her fingers felt warm, then warmer, and eventually the sensation moved up her arm, past her shoulders, and spread throughout her body.

She didn't look at the mirror while this change was occurring. For some reason, she always kept her eyes shut and distracted herself with the faint humming sound the mirror emitted. It reminded her of lightning crackling over the hills beyond the castle walls.

Giving more of her lifeblood, as the mirror called it, was a desperate move. After the last time, she'd sworn to the mirror she would never do it again. The procedure left her feeling weak and ill, more and more. She'd get so sick she'd take to her bed for days, drawing the curtains and blocking out all sound. Even a thimble falling sounded like an earthquake. Opening her eyes made her feel like she was staring into the sun. Every bone in her body seemed to scream out in pain if she moved even slightly, and her head throbbed with a bone-crushing migraine like she'd never experienced before. It took days before she could sit up again, or even eat the smallest piece of bread.

But when her body returned to full strength, she could feel the difference coursing through her veins. The mirror was right: she was more powerful, smarter, and prettier than ever before.

Her handmaidens would marvel when she emerged from her quarters with skin so dewy she looked half her age. "A restful night's sleep does wonders for you, Lady Ingrid."

Ingrid would say nothing and keep walking, but she loved hearing their whispers.

"She looks younger than even the queen!" she once heard one say. "How is that possible?"

"Witchcraft!" someone else inevitably suggested.

Let them talk. They were just jealous. How could they not be? She looked better than she had in years. The calluses from her years of labor in the fields and the magic shop were gone. Her skin was now milky white and glowing instead of weathered. Her hair looked like spun silk. And the strength she felt—not just physically, but mentally—was the best high she'd ever had. Maybe the mirror was right: the nightmarish process was worth it.

At least that's what she told herself as she started the whole process all over again. She hadn't planned to give more of herself to the mirror so soon, but Katherine had become insufferable. All her free time now was spent with Snow White. The child didn't need the care she had as a baby anymore, and yet Katherine still preferred her company to her sister's.

"Come with us," Katherine always said when Ingrid would complain they never spent time together anymore. "Play with your niece." But Ingrid didn't have time to play. She wanted to make real changes to the kingdom and the infrastructure therein. She wanted Georg to be more commanding and stop letting other kingdoms walk all over them. But Katherine had different interests—she was a queen of the people, spending her time listening to their concerns and making sure farming conditions throughout the countryside were ideal. Being raised by the farmer had made her primarily concerned with the kingdom's agricultural trade rather than the things that mattered to Ingrid, like mining. There was so much more money to be made if Katherine opened more tunnels, leading to more diamond trading. But no. Katherine deferred to Georg when it came to the diamonds. And he, too, worried more about mining conditions than mining rewards. He was an inefficient ruler.

If Katherine couldn't see reason when it came to the mines, then Ingrid would find another way to get Georg's ear.

Everything comes at a price. More lifeblood is needed. Stop playing nice, the mirror told her.

So here she was again.

Ingrid had learned if she said incantations to herself while the lifeblood ceremony took place, it seemed to go quicker. That was how she missed hearing the doors to her chambers open, and Katherine calling her name. It wasn't until her closet doors swung open, letting in the bright light of day, that Ingrid realized she had company.

"Ingrid?" Katherine looked like a scared child. Her shoulders were drawn inward and her perfect mouth hung awkwardly in surprise. "Wh—what are you doing?" Her voice suddenly had a stutter.

Katherine looked from Ingrid to the mirror, noticing the pulsing light zipping from the glass through Ingrid's body like a lightning bolt. Horrified, Katherine started to run away.

"Wait!" Ingrid called.

We must resume, the mirror told her. *Let her go. Leaving now will mean your doom.*

"Wait!" Ingrid yelled louder, feeling like a prisoner in her own body. She could hear Katherine wailing in the other room. Any second now the guards would burst in and everyone would see her secret. They couldn't know about the mirror or its powers. Someone would certainly try to steal it from her if they knew what it was capable of.

Should she stay and complete the process or go to her sister? She had never heard Katherine this upset. She felt like she was being torn in two.

Ingrid, hear what I say. Take heed. Stay stay stay stay . . .

But she couldn't listen. She had to go to Katherine. She pulled her hand away from the mirror and the light burned out. In her weakened state, she couldn't get to the other room quickly, but when she did, she found Katherine hunched over, sobbing like she hadn't done since they were children. "Katherine—" she started to say.

Katherine whirled around, her face scrunched up with rage. "You're a witch!"

Ingrid stumbled backward, unsteady on her feet. "No." Her voice was barely more than a whisper. *Sleep.* All she wanted was sleep.

"Yes, you are!" Katherine was inconsolable. "Georg warned me. He said he'd heard rumors about what you did in your chambers, but I didn't believe him. I said you'd left that world behind when you moved into the castle and became my lady-in-waiting. I said you'd never practice dark magic, not with your niece sleeping under the same roof!"

"It's not dark magic," Ingrid said, but her voice wasn't as forceful as it normally would be. She sounded weak and she hated it. "It's something I dabble in during my own personal time, of which I have too much. You never need me for important matters."

"Liar!" Katherine lashed out, tears streaming down her face. Ingrid had never heard her this angry before. "You don't dabble. It's your craft. I'd heard you were performing rituals, doing dark deeds, practicing mind control, but I didn't want to believe it to be true."

Ingrid rolled her eyes. "Mind control? Please."

"Georg was right." Katherine started backing away. "Your heart is infected with black magic. What you were doing in there with that mirror—those incantations, the cold, strange lightning and black fog . . . it was unnatural. It felt evil."

"You're exaggerating," Ingrid told her. "What I do in my time is my business. It's never affected you! You have the perfect life, the perfect family. What right do you have to tell me what I can and can't do?"

"Your choices could affect Snow! I don't want her around that mirror," Katherine said. "It has to go! It's darkening your heart!"

"That mirror is mine!" Ingrid lashed out, her mouth tasting like blood. She had bitten down on her tongue. Tiny blood droplets dripped down her chin. Katherine moved farther away. "You can't touch it and it's certainly not yours to take away!" Her voice felt stronger now, like venom. Her master had tried to take the mirror from her, too, and look where that had gotten him. He was now in the ground. "You've taken everything from me. You shouldn't be the only one allowed to have love."

"Love?" Katherine questioned. "Ingrid, it's a *mirror*. It can't love you."

Ingrid's chest rose and fell quickly. She didn't have to explain herself. "You don't rule me!"

Katherine squared her shoulders, her face hardening. "Actually, I do. I am your queen, and if I say that mirror goes, it goes. Or you do."

"You're threatening to throw me out?" Ingrid said incredulously. How dare her sister behave like this! Ingrid had raised her. She had cared for her like a mother would. She had given everything to her sister and gotten nothing in return. Katherine loved her new family more than she had ever loved Ingrid. That would never change. And now, she finally had a deep, meaningful connection—for the mirror needed her in a way Katherine never did—and her sister wanted to take that away?

Katherine hesitated before speaking. "It's for your own good." She held on to the door. "I have to tell Georg about this. I'm sorry." She shut the door firmly behind her, and Ingrid collapsed to the floor in a heap.

This is what thou failed to see. It could have been avoided. I warned of what came to be.

Ingrid closed her eyes, feeling the pain seep into the backs of her eyes and the migraine begin. Even with only half the ritual performed, she still felt weak. She couldn't even answer.

You know what you could lose. Time marches on. Whose future will you choose?

Whose future? Ingrid thought, afraid to admit the truth out loud.

A single tear fell down her cheek as she thought about what the mirror was suggesting. In order for the mirror to survive, Katherine had to die. Ingrid had fought this for so long, but in the end, the mirror had been right. What had Katherine given her? A lowly title? She'd fought the mirror's prophecy for so long, but she couldn't anymore. If Katherine was going to threaten to expose her and the mirror, then something had to be done. It was always she who would rise to the occasion. She had gotten them out of their father's cottage. She had found them shelter with the farmer and brought them to the kingdom. She had raised

Katherine, and now Katherine was taking the one thing that mattered to Ingrid. Katherine had everything, while Ingrid had fought for every moment in her meager life. Why was it that Katherine was still living the life Ingrid was meant to live?

Choose you. Delay it no longer. If you want to be queen, you know what you must do.

"Yes," Ingrid whispered, a plan already forming in the back of her mind. Katherine needed to go, and she knew exactly how she would make sure that happened. Maybe the plan had been there all along, because the minute she accepted her sister's fate, the pain seemed to subside and the ingredients needed to take care of things sprang quickly to her mind. Where Ingrid had at first felt guilt and sadness, now she only felt anger. Katherine would finally get what she deserved.

There could only be one queen in this castle, and her sister wasn't the one meant to wear a crown.

Ingrid smiled wickedly. Long would she reign.

Snow

Snow froze. "You found my father?"

"Yes." Henri looked at her unwaveringly.

It felt like the ground was quicksand and she was going to be swallowed whole. Lately she had grown certain her aunt had killed her father. It had seemed more and more unlikely that he could be out there somewhere. "*My* father? Are you sure?"

Henri nodded. "I am certain. He told me about your mother and you, and the aviary your mother commissioned, and all the birds. He told me about the wishing well and the gardens." His blue eyes lit up with excitement. "He knew the castle grounds and the kingdom's terrain like the back of his hand. I truly believe it's him!" The dwarfs gathered round him to listen. "King Georg is alive and he misses you terribly."

At the words "King Georg," all seven dwarfs began to talk at once.

"He's alive?"

"We should have known he wouldn't leave us!"

"Where is he? Is he coming home?"

But Snow couldn't be so exuberant. She felt too conflicted. "If he misses me, then why did he leave me with the Evil Queen?" The dwarfs grew quiet. "Why did he abandon his kingdom? How could he do that to his people?" Her voice was shaking.

Henri took her hand and pulled her in close. They were practically standing nose to nose. She inhaled sharply. "He didn't *willingly* leave you or his people. You must understand: he was given no other choice."

"What *happened*?" Snow asked.

Henri cast his eyes downward, which was a relief because his gaze was almost too much for her to bear. "I shouldn't have blurted this news out like that. There's much I have to tell you, but not here." He looked around the ominous woods with a sharp focus he hadn't had when they'd found him.

"We can't go anywhere till we find the howling tree," Sneezy said, interrupting, and Snow and Henri broke apart.

"The howling tree?" Henri repeated uncertainly.

"The men heard rumors about a tree in these woods with a sap that can be used to make an elixir that allows a person to shape-shift," Snow explained. "Finding it might be the key to us getting to the Evil Queen without her knowing. It could be our chance at fighting her."

Henri's eyes widened. "You're going to fight the queen?"

"With our help," Doc declared, and they all nodded. "Which is why we need to find that tree."

"Do you mean this tree?" Henri asked. He led them a few feet away to a tree that truly looked like it had a face. Up close, Snow realized the ragged eyes and howling mouth were nothing more than hollowed-out parts of a tree with mangled branches that looked like claws.

She closed her eyes for a moment and pictured herself running past the tree, thinking it was actually coming for her. "Yes, this is the tree I saw."

Happy and Doc began to examine it, knocking on the tree stump and using their lanterns to peer into the hollowed parts. Grumpy used a carving knife to try to open up the bark and see what was behind it.

"This tree is dead," Grumpy declared. "There's no sap in this thing."

Snow's heart sank.

"Are you sure this is it?" Sleepy asked.

"I'm sure," Snow said sadly. She'd been so certain they had a lead. "I guess the rumor was just a rumor. The queen doesn't get her dark magic from this place."

There was a low grumble from somewhere deep among the trees. Henri grabbed Snow's arm. "We should leave."

"Yes. Why don't you join us back at the cottage?" Snow suggested as Grumpy sighed. "We have much to discuss and you must be tired from your journey. Where did you find my father?"

"At the border of my kingdom," Henri said, and the hair on the back of Snow's neck stood up. "A day's travel away."

"But that's not far!" she said. Had her father been this close the whole time? Why hadn't he tried to come back for her?

Henri seemed to sense her struggle. He grabbed her hand again. His fingers were callused but warm, and she felt her body relax slightly. There was so much she didn't know about the boy who stood in front of her. "I promise it will all begin to make sense once I tell you what he told me."

The two of them stared at one another. The dwarfs watched them silently, listening to the sound of a crow in the distance. "All right," Snow said finally.

"Are we going to get out of these woods and have dinner, or what?" Grumpy said, interrupting again.

Snow exhaled. "Yes. Of course. Let's go home," she

said, realizing that's what the dwarfs' cottage had become to her in a way the castle never could.

The journey out of the woods could not end quickly enough. By the time they reached the dwarfs' cottage, the sun was already beginning to dip. While Henri washed up, Snow and the men headed into the kitchen to prepare the roast for supper. Soon a fire was going, and the dwarfs performed their duties with Henri watching in wonder at how comfortable they all were together. Finally, he rose, grabbed a knife, and began chopping onions at her side. His hair was damp and pushed back off his forehead. He had changed into a beige linen shirt that was only laced halfway, revealing his chest and making her blush. Neither of them said anything for a while. Snow cut the carrots and peeled them, while Henri minced the parsley and cut the parsnips. Together they prepared the roast till all there was left to do was wait for it to cook.

Snow settled into a chair, a cup of tea in her hand, anxious to hear Henri's story. Although she had never expected to see him again, he was here, having come looking for her. If he had gone the long way to the castle, what would have happened to him? Would the Evil Queen have put him to death? Henri's finding her in the woods felt a little bit like fate, if she had believed in such things. Was it her fate to lose both her mother and her father and be raised by an aunt with no ability to love? She didn't know, but her heart told her Henri was someone she could trust. She wondered if he felt the connection like she did.

"Please, Henri, tell me how you came to find my father," she said, and all eyes turned to him.

"And you better be telling us the truth," Grumpy added.

"No lying to the princess!" Doc agreed, and the other men nodded as they sat on chairs, the couch, or the floor, ready to listen.

Henri took a deep breath and looked from Snow to the others. "I have no reason to lie. I wasn't looking for Snow's father. I knew nothing about King Georg being missing."

"Not missing," Sneezy corrected. "He abandoned his kingdom and daughter!"

Henri nodded, casting his blue eyes downward. "Right. After I saw Snow in the aviary, I tried to meet with Queen Ingrid, but she wouldn't hear of it without an appointment, and an appointment with the queen is hard to come by. I was told I'd have to wait months to have an audience, and even then, it couldn't be guaranteed. I decided to head home, feeling as if I'd failed my people." He looked at Snow. "I was so distressed. I didn't know what I'd tell them. Maybe that's why I pushed through my journey so quickly, traveling day and night to get home, not caring what the weather was. And it was treacherous. It rained for days and I was soaked to the bone. It was no wonder I took ill." He smiled grimly. "So ill I took a spill into a lake and nearly drowned."

Snow leaned forward. "What happened?"

"It was raining so hard I didn't see the cliff. My horse did, stopping short and throwing me off," Henri explained. "He ran away, which was a good thing, because that's how Georg found me. He spotted my horse and the baggage it was carrying, and knew there had to be a rider nearby. He went searching for me."

"Mighty brave of him," Sneezy blurted out, eyeing Snow. She didn't say anything.

"Yes," Henri agreed. "The current was fierce and I was fighting to get back to shore with my last breath. I was so tired I grabbed on to a tree limb that had fallen into the water. I was ready to give up when Georg arrived and pulled me to safety."

"Probably caught a good cold or even pneumonia in those waters," Doc hypothesized. "The weather has been pretty bad in much of our kingdom of late, too."

"Yes. I wish I had known this before I set out." Henri's face was grave. "Georg says I spiked a fever and slept fitfully for days. If he hadn't taken me into his home and nursed me back to health, I wouldn't have made it. I'm sure of that."

They were all quiet. Hearing Henri's story reminded Snow of a moment she'd had with her father as a small child.

A bird had fallen in the aviary and hurt its wing, and she'd tearfully rushed into one of his sessions with the royal court. He had stopped everything to listen to her story. Then he'd helped her make a nest in the aviary for the bird to see if it would get well again. One morning, when they went to check on the bird, it was gone. "We did all we could for him, till he could make it on his own," her father had said. Was that what her father had done for her as well? Had he thought she was strong enough to make it on her own?

"I'd been prepared to leave him right away, but I still wasn't myself and the weather was still bad, so Georg invited me to stay," Henri explained. "It was only when I was well enough that we got to talking. That's when I told him about my trip to your kingdom. As soon as I mentioned it, I could see the change in him. He seemed distressed, almost outraged, like a man consumed, and he began pacing the floor. When I asked what was the matter, he wouldn't say. Instead, he asked me to tell him more about my visit there. I told him of the queen's refusal to see me, and"—he hesitated, his cheeks coloring slightly—"about the beautiful maiden I met in the castle gardens."

"You did?" she asked, unsure why she was so taken with the fact that he'd mentioned her.

"Yes." Henri smiled shyly.

"Oh, brother," she heard Grumpy mumble.

"After I spoke of you, he started asking me all these

questions about the princess and her relationship with the queen. I said I didn't know anything about that, so he asked if the princess seemed happy."

"What did you say?" Snow asked.

Henri hesitated. "I said you were lovely, but you seemed sad."

"That is not untrue." She had been disheartened at the castle. But then again, she had also chosen to make the best of her life and not let the sadness consume her. She'd tried to find happiness in even the most ordinary ways—shining a castle suit of arms that a visitor might pass, or feeding the birds in the aviary. "But I tried to be happy as well."

"He would be pleased to hear you say that," Henri said with a smile. "When I didn't have more to tell him, he excused himself and went to bed. I was confused as to why he had this reaction when it came to you, so I tried to bring it up again, but his answer was always the same. 'Knowing the truth about my life will only put you in harm's way.' It had been so long since he'd talked about his kingdom, he started to think he'd dreamed his previous life." Henri paused. The fire licking the pot in the kitchen made a small popping sound in the quiet cottage. "Snow, your father never wanted to leave you or his people. He left because Queen Ingrid banished him."

"What?" Snow stood up.

"Yes," Henri said with conviction. "She tricked him

into leaving the castle one day. He said he doesn't remember leaving or why he agreed to go. In truth, he says he doesn't remember what possessed him to marry her in the first place."

"Dark magic." Snow was only just starting to understand her aunt's powers. She closed her eyes, feeling relieved. She had never been able to understand why her father would have married that woman.

"All he knows is that when he tried to return to you, he couldn't," Henri continued. "Any time he tried to reenter the kingdom, some strange force would prevent him from walking on your soil. He tried everything to get around it, going to every possible part of the border to get through, and the same thing would happen—a jolt of electricity so strong it would practically stop his heart."

"Black, black, black—*achoo!* Magic!" Sneezy repeated, and the others nodded in agreement.

"He's never stopped trying to get back here for you," Henri added. "He hated knowing you were growing up in that castle with a woman so wicked. He begged for mercy, hoping Queen Ingrid would hear him. He prayed she would take pity and give him you in exchange for his throne, but if she has heard his cries, she has done nothing. After years of trying, he gave up, thinking he was doomed to live in his own prison for the rest of his days."

Some of the men were crying. They all held their caps in their hands.

"I knew King Georg wouldn't abandon us," Bashful said with a sniffle.

Tears trickled down Snow's cheeks. So he truly hadn't left her. The Evil Queen had pulled the two of them apart, making each of them live their own personal kind of hell. All the while, Ingrid had lived in wealth and privilege upon her throne. If she could kill Snow's mother, was it so unbelievable to think she would banish her father? "I need to see him," Snow said. "If he can't come to me, I will go to him."

Henri smiled. "He was hoping you would say that. I will take you to him. I know the way."

"Then we will go," Snow said. "First thing in the morning."

Ingrid

At last, she had everything her heart desired.

As she stared down at the red heart on the carved wooden box in her hands, she couldn't help thinking the mirror had been right about everything. The heart inside the box beat no more, which meant not only was she queen, but there was nothing left to threaten her reign. *And* she was the fairest in the land. No one else could get in her way. *Finally.*

The mirror probably already knew what she had in her possession. She was so in tune with it that she could hear its thoughts without even being near it. And the mirror, in turn, knew what was going on in her head without her saying it out loud. Their two psyches, after all these years, were becoming one, just as the mirror had predicted all those years ago.

Just as her master had feared.

But there was nothing to fear from her mirror. It existed for her sake.

And so it no longer bothered her that she'd spent an agonizing week waiting to hear from the huntsman. Her practical side told her it would take him days to dispose of the girl's body. Besides, that absence gave her time to formulate her own plan about the princess's absence. She'd been smart to let that sentimental fool Mila get the princess ready for her day with the huntsman. It made her look like a caring aunt. When the pair didn't return at nightfall, she sent for Mila and asked her for word about the princess's day. She held her own, looking the picture of worry when Mila made it known the princess hadn't returned. She'd even pretended to send Brutus out to look for them. She asked the rest of the castle and her court to stay quiet about Snow's disappearance till they could figure out what had happened to the poor princess.

And now that Brutus had finally brought her the huntsman's gift, she was trying to decide what would be the best story to tell the people—that the girl was dead, or that she had abandoned her people like her father years ago?

"Is there anything else, my queen?" Brutus asked now.

"No," she said, trying to keep the excitement out of her voice. She gripped the box in her hands tightly. She couldn't wait to get back to the mirror and show it the fruit of their labor. "Keep the huntsman hidden till I decide what to do."

He bowed. "Yes, my queen."

Walking swiftly through the halls from the throne room to her chambers, she didn't look at any of the servants she passed. It wasn't like any of the fools would stop to speak to her anyway. They knew by now that when she approached, they should bow or curtsy and go back to their appointed chores. Closing the doors to her chambers behind her, she went straight to the hidden room and stepped onto the platform. She put the box down and raised her arms wide, calling to the mask in the mirror. The mirror began to smoke, thunder sounded throughout the chamber, and the mask appeared in the glass. Ingrid smiled wickedly.

"Magic Mirror on the wall, who *now* is the fairest one of all?"

She had done everything to hear the mirror tell her what she longed to hear once more. She couldn't stand it holding anyone's beauty above her own. She held her breath and listened closely.

The mask stared at her drolly. "Over the seven jeweled hills, behind the seven falls, in the cottage of the seven dwarfs dwells Snow White, fairest one of all."

Her eyes widened in anger. How dare the mirror play games with her! She tried to control her temper. She picked up the box and held it in front of the glass. "Snow White lies dead in the forest. The huntsman has brought me proof. Behold," she said, holding the box out with satisfaction, "her heart."

"Snow White still lives," the mirror told her. "The fairest in the land. It is the heart of a pig you hold in your hand."

Her hands trembled. It couldn't be. But then again, the mirror never lied. . . . "The heart of a pig! Then I've been tricked!"

Rushing out of her chambers, she headed back to her throne room, summoning the huntsman immediately. The queen handed him the box. "Show me her heart," she commanded.

The huntsman stood and shakily opened the latch on the box, showing her what was inside. The heart looked gray and lifeless. For a moment, she was almost happy . . . until she remembered the mirror's warning. Could this heart be that of a pig? There was only one way to find out.

Ingrid knocked the box out of his hands. "Liar! This is not her heart! It's a pig's!" She looked at Brutus. "Take him to the dungeon and leave him there to rot!" Brutus grabbed the huntsman roughly and began dragging him out of the room as Ingrid watched closely. Surely the man would protest his innocence.

"Long live the rightful heir!" the huntsman shouted at her. "Long live the future queen!"

Rightful heir? Future queen?

Ingrid began ripping at her hair, pulling out strands in anger and not even feeling the pain. *"No, no, NO!"* Ingrid let out a primal scream so raw she could feel the damage even though she could not see it.

For in her secret room, the magic mirror on her wall began cracking.

Snow

Snow and Henri journeyed to the border of the prince's kingdom alone.

At first, most of the dwarfs weren't thrilled with this development. They'd become a close-knit group in their time together, and argued that they had a lot of planning to do if they were going to take on the queen. But Snow agreed with Grumpy on this one—the men had diamond quotas to fill for the queen each day, and by keeping up their regular routine, they could speak with other miners frustrated by the tariffs. While Snow was gone, they could gather intel that would allow them to figure out which villages they should visit to gain allies in their fight. There was also the matter, as Grumpy pointed out, of making sure they continued to mine diamonds to squirrel away for a rainy day.

If things in this battle went south, they'd need something to barter with to get out of the kingdom. Snow didn't want to think about that option. She needed to succeed, not only for herself, but for all the people fighting with her. And now that included Henri.

"Are you sure you're not tired?" Snow looked down from the horse she was riding to Henri, who was leading the animal by the reins on foot. They had only one steed for this journey and Henri insisted the princess be the one to ride it. They'd been traveling for several hours and had barely spoken.

"I'm fine on foot," Henri insisted. There were quicker ways than the woods they were traveling through, but they were roads more traveled, and Snow could not risk being seen. "You need to rest up for your reunion."

"Why would a reunion be exhausting?" Snow wondered. Filled with anticipation, yes. Overwhelming, maybe. But exhausting?

Henri didn't reply. She had a feeling there was more to the story than he had revealed, but she didn't push. She wanted to hear it from her father, if it really was him. She prayed he would have some insight on the Evil Queen that she could use. In fact, she was counting on it. With their journey to find the elixir unfruitful, she was concerned they still had so little to go on.

"We've been traveling since early morning light," Snow reminded him. "You have to be growing weary by now."

He kept quiet. She wanted to learn more about this near-stranger who had dropped into her life. Snow imagined what her mother would have thought of Henri. This was what she did whenever she had something to work through: she envisioned the conversation they would have had about the things they'd never had the chance to talk about. She always pictured the two of them sitting in the aviary or on a garden bench, talking as if they had all the time in the world. Snow was grown in these visions, but her mother looked exactly as she had when she'd left this earth. They would talk till the sun was setting. She suspected her mother would like Henri. *A man who cares for the creatures of this earth has to be a kindred spirit,* Snow could imagine her saying. Henri helping her father would be something else she'd approve of. Snow snuck a glance in Henri's direction again. "Are you certain you're not tired?"

"Yes, I'm fine," Henri said again, and immediately started to cough.

He'd been coughing all morning, which led Snow to believe he was not 100 percent recovered from his recent illness. Had he pushed himself too far? "I will not take no for an answer. I think *you* are the one that needs rest," Snow said decisively. "There's room up here for two."

"It's not necessary," he said again, and coughed some more.

"It is to me," Snow insisted. "As the princess of this kingdom and the future queen, I command you to ride on this steed with me." He looked surprised at her tone, which she quickly softened. "It's fine, really. I don't mind."

Henri smiled. "Well, Princess, if I need to rest, then you need to eat. I know for a fact you've had nothing since we left. Doc insisted you have something in your belly when you see your father, and I'm a little nervous about not listening to orders from those men. They seem pretty fond of you."

"And I of them," Snow said with a smile. She could picture Grumpy giving Henri his long list of instructions for this trip. Her stomach growled at the thought of food. "Maybe we should stop for a spell."

Henri held out his hand to help her dismount. Their fingers stayed intertwined a moment longer than was strictly necessary.

Snow looked away. "I'll put down a blanket so we can sit properly." She laid it out and placed the satchel of food— fruit, breads, and cheese—from the dwarfs on it. They ate in silence for a bit, with Henri devouring his portion.

"I'm sorry I ate so quickly," he said as he finished his last piece of bread. "Before last night, I hadn't eaten since

I left your father, and before that I was still too ill to have much. Only broth."

"If you're still hungry, I have some apples for dessert." She held one out that was a mix of reds and greens with a hint of gold. "These are Red Fire apples."

Henri took a bite. "That's heaven. What did you call it? A Red Fire? I've never had anything like it."

"They're only grown in our kingdom. My mother was the one who created the hybrid," Snow said proudly.

She used to beg her parents to tell her the story of their courtship over and over. She could picture her mother laughing. *Snow, there must be something else you want to talk about!*

"It's what you get when you cross red apple seeds with some pears and green apple seeds," Snow told Henry now. "She came up with it at the apple orchard she helped tend when she was my age. My father loved them and had them planted all over the countryside." Snow picked up one and stared at it. "It was the Red Fire apple that endeared my mother to my father, actually. He adored her apples."

Henri smirked. "So it was love at first *bite*?"

She laughed. "I suppose so!"

Henri had some more. "I can see why. They're delicious, and I don't say that lightly. Apples are my favorite fruit."

"Mine too," Snow said, and they stared at one another for a beat. "I think I'll save some for our visit. I bet my father would love to have one after all this time."

"Then we'll share the rest of mine," said Henri, pulling a small jeweled pocketknife out of his belt. Carefully, he began to peel the apple in one long strand that didn't break. When he was done, he took the strand and wound it into a tight bud that looked like a rose. "For you, my lady."

"That's beautiful," said Snow, holding the apple peel in the palm of her hand. "Where did you learn to do that?"

"My older brother Kristopher taught me," Henri said, his smile fading. "He loved apples, too. This was his pocketknife." He held up the silver blade with the leather handle. His brother's initials were etched into the metal. "He died a few years ago during a battle and I was given his blade. He was my father's most trusted knight."

"I'm sorry for your loss," Snow said, immediately feeling a familiar pang. "Losing someone so soon . . ."

"Changes your life," Henri finished, and they looked at one another.

"Yes," Snow agreed. "I imagine my life has been different from the one my parents envisioned for me, but I've never lost hope, even when . . ." She faltered. She hadn't revealed the truth about her mother's death to anyone yet, not even the dwarfs. The kingdom remembered Queen

Katherine falling ill, and they had mourned her as such, but Snow knew her father deserved to know the truth. Maybe it would be easier if she shared it with Henri first. "I now know the Evil Queen—my aunt—had my mother killed."

"What?" Henri sat up straighter. "Do your people know? They couldn't possibly; how would they let her sit on the throne?"

"They don't know," Snow said. "No one does. The huntsman the queen sent to kill me told me the story. His father was the one tasked with killing my mother."

"But this huntsman didn't want to repeat his father's dark deeds?" Henri said, guessing correctly. "I'm so sorry, Snow. From what I've heard, your mother was beloved."

"She was, by everyone." Snow stared at the cloudy sky. "Everyone but her own sister. And for that dark deed, the Evil Queen will pay."

Henri looked at her curiously. "You seem different, somehow, from the girl I met in the gardens at the castle."

"I feel different," Snow said.

Henri shook his head. "I can't believe the queen tried to have you killed. I knew she was ruthless and difficult, but a murderer . . . You're not planning to face her alone, are you?"

"At the end, I believe it has to be her and me," Snow

said. "Maybe I can reason with her. Tell her I know the truth about my mother and get her to repent."

Henri appeared skeptical. "A woman that cold and calculating will never repent."

Snow looked at the apple peel flower again, seeing the beauty in something that would ordinarily be discarded. "I have to at least try."

"How will you stop her?" Henri asked.

"The men are trying to get new recruits to join our fight for the crown. But it is difficult. They can only do so in secret, and many are frightened of her and afraid to speak up. Hopefully we can convince them that there is power in numbers." She sighed. "As you can see, the battle plans are still hazy."

A raven landed on a tree branch nearby and cawed, startling them both. Henri frowned. "We shouldn't stay here too long."

There wasn't a single bird she disliked, but the repeated sightings of the raven were making her wonder. Was it indeed the queen? If so, what dangers did she have in store for them? Snow packed up quickly while Henri fed the horse the rest of his apple and some water. When she was done, he was holding the reins to again walk beside her.

"This time we both ride," Snow insisted, feeling bold, even though the thought made her slightly nervous. He started to protest, and she held up her finger to silence him.

Henri bowed. "Yes, Your Highness." She smiled as he continued. "I like your initiative. You're much like my brother Lorenz, who will take the throne from my father someday. I'm sixth in line to the throne, so I've never bothered to wonder what being a ruler would be like."

Being a ruler . . . She'd been so focused on overthrowing the Evil Queen and now finding her father that she hadn't stopped to consider what would happen after. The throne belonged to her father if he wanted it, and she would step up to the task of helping her kingdom, righting the wrongs that had been committed for too long. But she couldn't help thinking about what it would mean if it was her turn to wear the crown. . . . What type of ruler would she be? What new ideas would she bring to the table? It was startling and yet somewhat exhilarating to imagine all she'd be able to do for her people, to think of the change she would have the power to enact. She could bring the kingdom back to the way it had been when her parents had ruled . . . could maybe even make it better.

Henri held the reins tightly and the horse stopped, allowing him to climb up behind Snow. "But I'm sure someday you'll be a great ruler," he said, as though hearing her thoughts. He held out the reins to her and began to climb up, and in doing so, he had to put his arms beside her.

"Sorry," he said, his arm grazing hers.

"It's fine," Snow insisted, but she'd never been this close

to a young man before, and certainly never to one nearly this handsome. The guards in the castle, even the young ones, had permanent scowls on their faces, but Henri—whether he was worried, sick, or just being a gentleman—seemed to always be smiling.

They traveled in silence again for a while before Snow started to hum a familiar tune to pass the time. Henri joined in, and the two of them sang a song that made even the birds in the forest land on branches to listen.

As the sky started to dim, they approached the lake that divided Snow's kingdom from Henri's. On the outer bank of the lake, Snow could see a small cottage with smoke rising from the chimney. As they made their way around the lake, Snow noticed the abode wasn't much to look at—the cottage looked like it had been constructed quickly—and the shutters were drawn tight, as if there were a storm coming. But as the horse approached, the door to the cottage flew open. An older man shuffled out with a walking stick.

Snow gasped.

Thoughts and memories whirled around her mind. Could *this* be her father? His hair was white and much longer, but she noticed the familiar black mole on his left cheek. She held on to the horse's mane tightly, afraid she might fall off at the sight of him. She desperately wanted to get closer.

"Henrich?" Seeing the horse, the man held on to the doorframe with one hand and his stick with the other. He narrowed his eyes. "Is that you?"

"Yes, sir, I've found her!" Henri stopped the horse and jumped off, then offered Snow his hand to help her down.

She stood in Henri's shadow as he shook hands with a man whose voice she didn't recognize—it was hollow and tinged with age. If it truly was her father, he didn't sound the same, but then again, could she really remember his voice after having not heard it in over ten years?

"Let me look at my daughter," the man said, and Henri stepped aside.

Snow and Georg stood face to face. Neither of them made a move; instead they studied each other's features, as if looking in a mirror.

Snow stared at the man, with his white beard and cropped white hair. There was no crown on his head. No scepter in his hand or fine satin clothes on his body. He wore simple boots and a peasant's clothes, and his hands were dirty and free of the rings she remembered him wearing all those years ago. But when she looked into the man's weathered face she felt a sudden jolt. While the blue color might have faded from his eyes with age, there was no denying their familiarity. "Father?" she croaked.

He immediately started to cry, fat tears falling down his

cheeks. "Snow, my Snow. It's really you!" He grabbed her face in his two callused hands.

She immediately did the same, touching his face, his beard. "It's you! You're alive! You're really here." It was almost too much to take in.

"Yes, I'm here, my snowflower. I'm here!" he said.

They collapsed into one another's arms, alternately crying and laughing as they clung to each other like two marooned fishermen who had been lost at sea and found. Snow wasn't sure how long they stayed like that before Henri convinced them to go inside. She knew she should be worried the queen was watching, but it was hard to imagine danger when her father was by her side again. Inside the small cottage, with the fire going and her father's sparse wood furniture—all of which he proudly claimed he'd made himself—Snow felt like she could stay within those four walls forever, talking to the father she had been sure she'd lost.

"I'm so sorry, snowflower, I'm so sorry," he said over and over between offers of bread and wine and a place to rest her head. But Snow was too wound up to sleep. While Henri tended to the horse, Snow sat down with her father to ask him all the things she could think of and more. But he was one step ahead of her.

"I didn't leave you," he said, the minute she faced him. "I need you to know that. I would never abandon my daughter! If anything, I've spent a decade trying to get back to you, knowing you were with that woman." His face scrunched up with anger. "I was a fool to think she could ever be a surrogate mother to you, to be like my Katherine, but now, after all this time, I know I was no fool at all." His grip on her loosened and his face became resigned again. He looked broken. "I was under her spell, just like the spell that has kept me prisoner for a decade."

"What kind of spell?" Hearing her father confirm this was a relief. She'd never understood, however young she might have been, how her father could have loved someone like the Evil Queen. She was as different from her mother as another human being could be.

"A love spell." Her father looked embarrassed at this. "It would have been the only way she could have tricked me into marriage. Ingrid and I never saw eye to eye. It was your mother's love of her that kept her inside the castle walls. But the more I got to know Ingrid, the more I saw her for what she really was. Power hungry, and jealous. Consumed with her need to be in control of everyone around her, including your mother. I talked to your mother about it, but she insisted that her sister just had a strong personality and took some warming up. It was important to her that Ingrid live at the castle and be her lady-in-waiting. But when your mother finally saw through Ingrid's act, it was too late." His eyes cast downward. "She became ill so soon afterward."

Snow met eyes with Henri, who had just walked in, but the two said nothing. She had to know the whole story before she broke her father even more. "If she had you under a love spell, how did you wind up here?"

He let go of her hands and motioned to the room they sat in. "I've had a lot of time to think about this," he said. "The details are foggy, of course, but spell or no spell, I think there was always a part of me that resisted her, and maybe she realized that and finally decided to cut me loose. Why she didn't just have me killed, I don't know. All I remember is being sent on a diplomatic trip and winding up here. Once I arrived, I couldn't remember what I was sent to do, and the men who had brought me here disappeared." His weathered face was grim. "I felt almost a sudden surge of memories—marrying Ingrid, leaving you—and wondered what I had done. I immediately got a horse and prepared to return, but every time I try, an electric bolt sends me back to this very cottage!" Georg said, growing frustrated. "Henri tried to smuggle me through to the kingdom, too, but it's impossible. Even years later!" He swiped a cup off his table, smashing it to the floor. "I was desperate to get back to you." He glanced at the rafters and sighed. "To survive, I had to make my peace with the fact that I might not. I've become friendly with the nearby villagers after all this time. I make furniture like this table here to have enough to buy food and things." He pointed to the simple wood table in front of them. "It's a simple but honest life. I've bartered with an enchantress from time to time for spells to keep Ingrid from seeing me."

"An enchantress?" Snow asked.

"Yes," her father said. "She has traveled through these parts, which is how I met her. I'm not sure where she resides . . . or even if her spells are working, so I always take precautions when I can. I sometimes fear the queen is still watching me. I wanted Henrich to bring you through the forest so you wouldn't be seen on the roads. I know I am putting you in danger by bringing you here, but when Henrich described the castle, and meeting a fair maiden, I knew it had to be you. I couldn't help but beg him to help me see you and warn you about Ingrid. How did you get away from her?"

Snow grabbed her father's hands. "Father, she tried to have me killed. She sent me out with her huntsman, but he couldn't go through with it, not after . . ." She paused, her voice choked with emotion. "Father, Mother was not ill. Ingrid had her killed, too, the same way she tried to kill me."

"No." Her father's eyes filled with tears. "Your mother was sick. I saw her in bed . . . didn't I?"

Snow understood this fog. She'd felt it herself. Memories

filled her brain that weren't really her own. They felt almost tucked in there by someone else. "No. She wasn't. Not really. I fear Mother was poisoned. Aunt Ingrid tricked us."

Her father openly wept for some time before he spoke. Snow stroked his hand, unable to speak herself. "My darling Katherine," he finally whispered. "My love! I'm so sorry I failed you." Then his eyes sharpened and anger returned to his voice. "That woman is pure evil! After all her sister did for her. I told your mother she couldn't be trusted! The night before your mother died she came to me, worried about Ingrid's enchanted mirror. I knew we should have banished her right then! But she wouldn't let me. Her empathy for her sister was her downfall."

"Mirror?" Snow's ears perked up. "Why was she worried about a mirror?"

Georg looked confused again. "There was something about it . . . Katherine said Ingrid spoke to it. Like it was a person. She spoke of how evil it seemed, and how Ingrid seemed so attached. . . . Katherine and I had had many discussions over the years about whether or not Ingrid was using dark magic. But Katherine had always seen the best in her until that night. Ingrid was never openly warm to you, I'm afraid to say."

"Nothing's changed there," Snow said with a sigh.

Her father nodded sadly. "Ingrid seemed jealous of you

from the start. She never wanted to hold you or play with you like your mother or the handmaidens did. More and more Ingrid spent her days tucked away in her chambers doing lord knows what. When Katherine came to me that day after visiting her sister, she was extremely distraught. She wanted the mirror gone. Kept saying Ingrid and the mirror had become one and the same. I didn't understand what she meant. She told me to order it removed immediately, but then . . ." He turned away, holding his face in his hands. "I should have done it the moment Katherine asked. Why didn't I listen?"

"You didn't know what she was capable of," Henri said gently. "Who would think someone would kill their own sister?"

"An enchanted mirror," Snow repeated. Something about this was familiar. She just couldn't remember why. "I've never heard the servants talk about such an item."

"They probably wouldn't know about it," her father said. "Ingrid has always been very possessive and quite suspicious of others. Your mother said she kept it to herself."

They talked long into the night, Snow's father wanting to know what she did with her time in the castle. It angered him to hear she'd had to teach herself and spend her days cleaning. But he smiled wistfully when she mentioned she'd preserved the aviary. "Your mother would have loved that," he said, getting teary again. When she produced the Red Fire apple from her pocket, she thought he might cry a river of tears.

"I think we should turn in," Henri suggested as Snow consoled Georg. "It's been a long day, and we have a long journey back tomorrow."

"Yes," Snow said, but she was also disappointed. Her time with her father had been too short, and she still didn't know if they had anything useful for the fight with the queen. If no one knew about this mirror, how could it help them?

But those thoughts quickly faded as she fell into a deep sleep.

Ingrid

Ten years earlier

Even though she was on the other side of the castle, she could feel the mirror awakening. The simple gesture of the mirror coming alive had become as common as feeling the blood flow through her veins.

But the mirror never awoke unless she was near it—no one else alive knew of its existence, so it only called to her. That day, however, she could feel it speaking to another.

That person would regret it.

"Your Majesty?" her private advisor said, pulling her from her thoughts. He consulted the scroll in his hand again. "You were saying that it's time for the kingdom's flag to return to full height?"

"What?" Ingrid snapped, her fingers gripping the edges

of her throne so tight that her nails made indents in the gold-leafed wood.

She needed to get out of this room immediately and to her private chambers to see what was going on. But she noticed her court's reaction to her tone. They couldn't understand why a queen who wasn't of royal blood was allowed to rule. But those fears had been quietly dismissed when it was announced Georg had "abandoned" his people. She had argued that Snow was too young to rule, which was true. And since Georg's siblings had died of the plague years prior, there was no other heir. It was Ingrid or no one till Snow was of age, and many agreed. Those were the ones still standing before her. For now, if Ingrid was going to make changes, she needed allies, and she had to court sympathy for losing both her sister and her new husband in such quick succession.

"I'm sorry for my outburst," Ingrid said, holding her head. "I seem to have developed a terrible headache."

"Oh, Your Majesty!" Mila, her new lady-in-waiting, was at her side immediately. "We should get you to your chambers to lie down. We can't have you falling ill."

This insipid handmaiden had been like a hawk, following her around the castle, asking if she could be of assistance. Ingrid just wanted to be left alone! But then again, someone had to take care of her requests. So she had let this woman, who seemed so devoted to her, stay. Still, she had to learn boundaries, as they all did. She'd already dismissed half the staff. She didn't need so many people lurking around, knowing her business. What if one of them found the mirror? No, it was better to shrink the number of people who worked in the castle and continue shrinking it if need be.

"No, as I've said before, if I need something, I will tell you," she insisted. "I'm quite self-sufficient." Mila's smile faded and she retreated back into her corner of the room. "We were right in the middle of a session, so I will complete what we need to do, then attend to my headache."

"It can wait, my queen," said a member of the court. "Your health comes first. The kingdom needs you. You're all we have."

"Until young Snow is of age," another courtier piped up.

She glared at the man. Replaced by a clueless child someday? She thought not. But she had time to worry about that little problem. She softened her expression. "I will go, but first, please tell me what it is you were just saying about the flag."

Every nerve in her body was coming alive. She needed to get back to her quarters to see what was happening with the mirror. But she must be patient, too. She couldn't risk upsetting the court and losing the power she'd finally just attained.

"Yes, my queen," he replied, scratching his head, his white wig shifting slightly. She liked all of her court dressed the same, down to the white wigs. It was much more civilized, and besides, she hated being bothered trying to figure out who was who. This way they were just another number. "I was saying the flag has been flying at half-staff since Queen Katherine's death six months ago."

Queen Katherine's death. The words still felt like a knife to the heart. She glanced quickly at the dark recesses of the room. She kept seeing flickers of her sister, looking as young and as vibrant as she had right before she died. This figment of her imagination, which was what it must be—there were no such things as ghosts—sometimes comforted her, and other times made her feel sick. No one could trace the poison she'd had her faithful huntsman slip into Katherine's food. No one could have known *that* was what had caused her to fall ill.

Now she saw Katherine everywhere she went, just like she saw her master's image whenever things with the mirror were not going according to her liking. It was as if both of them served as an irritating reminder of what she had given up to gain her power. What choice did she have? She couldn't let her master keep the mirror, and she refused to allow Katherine to destroy it. And yet, there was still the unease she felt when she saw young Snow in tears, or refusing to eat her supper. Snow's mother's blood was on Ingrid's hands, and always would be, no matter how much she tried to convince herself otherwise.

"I suppose it's time we end our mourning, knowing that our former queen will always be in our hearts," Ingrid told the man.

She heard the mirror talking again. *But to whom?!*

He glanced anxiously at the other court members. "Shouldn't we keep our flag at half-staff a while longer, in King Georg's absence? What if he returns?"

Ingrid leaned forward, outraged. "The king is a traitor! He abandoned his throne, his people, and his daughter, not to mention his new wife. He does not deserve our sympathy. He will not be back, I assure you!"

The courtier looked down. "Yes, Your Majesty."

She looked around. Her harsh tone had shocked the others, but too bad. She had to be firm where Georg was concerned. "I'm sorry." She held her head. "This has all been so stressful for all of us, but especially young Snow." Ingrid rose and the others bowed their heads. "The flag flies fully again. Send a decree throughout the land that the mourning period is through. Any searches for King Georg should be abandoned, or there will be consequences. The man is mad and is not fit to lead us anymore. Remind the people what he has done and in what condition he has left his kingdom."

"Yes, Your Majesty," the members of the court repeated.

She flew out of the throne room and rushed through the castle, refusing to make eye contact with anyone. She didn't bother with small talk anyway. She could feel the mirror's movements and the hair on the back of her neck was standing on end. Who dared enter her chambers and speak to her mirror? Hadn't she said her rooms were off-limits? She didn't want food sent to her room; it was to be left outside it. She didn't want her chambers cleaned, either. No one could find the mirror. It belonged to her and her alone.

Whoever had engaged with it would pay dearly.

Locking the door to her chambers tight behind her, she made her way around her room, looking for the culprit who had dared invade her private space. Aside from a few pillows out of place at her window seat, the room was empty. She went to her closet, prepared to press the lever that revealed the dungeon-like room where she and the mirror convened—but she found it open.

Bursting into the dark room, she readied herself to sentence the intruder to death, but the words on her lips failed her when she realized what was happening. Through the green, smoky haze of the mirror's glow, she saw the outline of someone, their hand outstretched to meet the mirror's smooth glass. But the silhouette confused her, for it was so small, and appeared to be standing on its toes to reach the mirror. Then she realized . . .

"Snow!" she cried, rushing toward the girl and pulling her away from the mirror before the tips of her fingers could connect with its surface. "How did you get in here?" she shouted, shaking the girl by the shoulders so hard she wasn't sure who was more jittery—the child or herself.

Her niece burst into tears, which rolled down her round porcelain cheeks. The ivory gown she had on was covered with dirt from the chamber she had crawled through to get to Ingrid's private quarters. There were hidden passageways everywhere in this castle. Passageways that would need to be closed up immediately. Snow's bow, sitting atop her crown of black hair, was crooked. Ingrid distractedly wondered who had tied it in her hair that morning. It used to be Katherine; it had never been Ingrid. She wondered if it had been a few days or a week since she'd seen the child. Truthfully, she'd been trying to avoid her. After months of trying to bond with the girl at Georg's behest, she'd given up. Every time she saw Snow, the child was crying—first for her mother and now for her father. The tears that day came hard and fast, and the sob that escaped her throat was so raw that Ingrid let her guard down slightly. "Oh, child . . ." she started to say.

"It said I could see Mother!" Snow looked at Ingrid with big brown eyes that were the spitting image of Katherine's. "It said all I had to do was touch it."

"What?" Ingrid wasn't sure where to unleash her anger first—at the mirror that had betrayed her or the foolish child who had almost destroyed everything she had been working toward. "Snow, let's get you out of this room."

"No!" The tears were replaced by a flash of anger. The little girl began to pound on Ingrid's chest. "I want to see Mother! It promised! All I had to do was touch it!"

As long as she is allowed to live, your power will wane. She is the true heir in this game.

"Liar! You were trying to use her to help yourself!" Ingrid shouted at the mirror, and Snow stopped pounding and looked at her aunt in surprise. Then she tore out of the chamber.

Ingrid caught her before she could get to the bedroom door, but it wasn't hard. Little Snow crumpled like a paper fan the minute Ingrid touched her, and for a moment, she dissolved into tears again, burying her head in her aunt's chest. Ingrid was, again, caught off guard. Snow had never hugged her before. Not after Katherine's death, not after the rushed nuptials between her and Georg, which the young girl, only seven years old, could not understand.

She, too, had grown tired of this new role. Originally, the idea of marrying Georg had been a necessity—in order to have power, she needed the crown. But quickly she realized it wasn't enough to rule at a man's side. She wanted to rule on her own and not play second fiddle to his needs or affections. She had hoped adoration from the man would please her, but instead, she felt repulsion that the fool couldn't see through her spell.

She faithfully mixed the potion into his drink before bed each night, until one evening, she decided she'd had enough. His love wasn't real and neither was hers. It was a relief to have a guard take Georg away after she cursed him to a remote existence from which he could never return. She had the guard killed, of course, but let Georg live—not out of pity, but of necessity. As the mirror reminded her, she might need his royal blood someday—it was a powerful ingredient in many spells, which unfortunately would not recognize her blood as such, no matter how long she wore the crown. Better to leave him out there waiting.

But what did that mean for Snow? The mirror suggested she kill the girl, but every time she even thought about it, she saw Katherine's ghost. She argued that it was better to let the little thing grow till she could see for herself how twisted the world was. Maybe then Snow would realize the kingdom was better off in Ingrid's hands and stand by her side.

Don't be a fool. Carry on with the plan. The girl stands in the way of your rule.

Ingrid blocked the mirror's voice from her mind once

more. She wasn't a fool. She just wasn't ready to murder a little girl, no matter how much she hated the thought of mothering one. She'd done that with Katherine, and look how that had turned out.

But now, this child, whom she had all but dismissed, was in her arms, begging to be soothed, and she felt her hand cradle Snow's head. She started to stroke her hair and shush her. "Your mother is gone. No mirror can bring her back. And your father betrayed us. He wasn't right in his mind after your mother died. Now he's left you and me alone to fend for ourselves. Your father and my father did the same thing. Katherine and I lost our mother at a young age. Did she ever tell you that?" Snow shook her head. "Our father didn't raise us as he should, so we left." The story still stung, all these years later. "We relied on each other to make our way in this kingdom, and we did that together for a long time until . . ." *Another man came between us,* she wanted to say. "The point is, we don't need someone to lead us. We can lead ourselves. Your father underestimating us was a grave mistake."

Snow's crying subsided. Maybe this was their chance to find common ground.

"But no one will underestimate us in the future," Ingrid continued. "We are rulers, and strong ones at that. The fool who threatens us"—and this part was as much for the mirror as for her niece—"will suffer a fate worse than death."

Snow pulled away, crawling backward on her hands and feet like a spider. The look on her face was pure terror. What had just spooked her? The word *death*? Silly girl, so easily frightened.

"Snow, come back here," Ingrid said, growing irritated. "I wasn't finished talking to you." She patted her knee, where Snow had just been comfortably curled up.

"No!" Snow started to cry again as she backed to the door and unlocked it. "You're not my mother and you never will be!" She slipped out, slamming the door so hard that a vase fell off a table and shattered.

Ingrid felt anger course through her body. She closed her eyes tight, noticing a real headache coming on, and when she opened them, they were both there: Katherine. Her master. Staring at her blankly, before moving through the room and to the door through which Snow had just retreated. Then they both disappeared through it.

Rags cannot hide her gentle grace. Alas, she is more fair than thee, the mirror repeated, almost as if to mock her. *Lips as red as the rose, hair as black as ebony, skin as white as snow. Snow White.*

Snow

Snow's dreams that night at her father's cottage were restless.

She usually welcomed sleep. Not only was it a respite from her dull daily existence, but it allowed her a chance to visit with her mother. True, dreams couldn't replace actual time spent with her mother, but her dreams were so vivid sometimes that they felt like real visits. Tonight, though, her dreams were more like nightmares.

She was with her mother, but this time their time together did not feel jovial. It felt urgent and cold, like time was running out but Snow couldn't figure out why. In her dreams, the castle usually looked like it did in Snow's memories of her childhood—vibrant and blossoming with flowers and merriment. But this scene was different. Her mother was walking ahead of her in the darkened castle and smoke was filling the hallway.

"Follow me," her mother kept saying, leading the way by candlelight.

Snow didn't want to follow. The path her mother was leading her on was unfamiliar. She wasn't sure she'd ever been in this part of the castle before. It felt evil. Snow's legs became rooted to the spot and vines instantly wound around them. She struggled to move.

"Follow me," her mother urged again, ignoring the vines. "Quickly! It's important."

The vines disappeared and Snow had no choice but to listen to her mother. She started walking again and suddenly realized she was in Aunt Ingrid's wing.

"We shouldn't be here," Snow told her mother. "She could catch us."

Her mother turned and smiled sadly. "She already has. Come and see. It's important."

She led Snow through her aunt's bedchambers to a closet wall. As Katherine pressed her hand on a wooden heart carved into the doorframe, the wall clicked, revealing a secret passageway. Snow's mother motioned for her to follow. Snow did as she was told, finding herself in a darkened room with dungeon-like walls.

"Look," her mother said, and pointed into the darkness.

Snow didn't want to look, but her mother kept calling her name till she opened her eyes.

There, on a platform, was a large mirror.

It had a ghastly masklike face that appeared almost human and yet not. Thunder seemed to rumble from inside the chamber, where smoke thickened.

Snow stared at the mirror in wonder and felt the urge to touch it. It looked so familiar. Had she been in this room before? Why did the mirror seem to call to her?

"She knows you live. This much is true. She's coming for everyone you love. She will try to hurt you," the mask in the mirror said.

Snow woke up, gasping for air.

"Snow!" Henri jumped up from the floor near the fireplace and shook her from her stupor. Her father was right behind him. "Are you all right?"

She looked at Henri. "I saw it! The queen's mirror! The one my mother was talking about!"

Her father and Henri looked at her worriedly.

"It came to me in a dream," Snow explained. "Well, Mother led me there." She looked at her father pleadingly. "I know where it is hidden. It's in the queen's chambers." She lowered her eyes. "I think it knows me. I remember seeing it before."

"What?" Her father's voice sharpened. "She's taken you to see this dark magic?"

"No, I went there on my own," Snow said, pulling the distant memory into focus. "It called to me once, much like my dream. I was a child. I think it was after Mother died. It led me straight toward it like it wanted me there, but Aunt Ingrid came in at the last moment and took me away. She was furious." Snow looked at Henri and tried not to sound alarmed. "This dream, though, was different. The queen knows I'm alive. The mirror told me. She's coming for me."

Henri exhaled slowly.

"Then you will stay here," her father insisted. "I will defend you."

Snow touched his arm. "No, Father. You know that won't work. If she knows I'm alive, she will find me. She may even come here first."

"Let her come!" her father thundered. "I am ready to face her."

Henri and Snow both looked at him, and she knew they were thinking the same thing. Her father had aged, and the queen had magic on her side. Besides, if there was one good thing her aunt had taught her, it was that she didn't need a man at her side to fight. She had lived in Ingrid's shadows long enough. It was *her* turn to do the protecting. She'd just found her father again. She didn't want to lose another parent to the queen. This battle had to be hers.

"We need to get to that mirror," Snow said decisively.

"Yes, before she finds either of you," Henri added.

Her father started to protest, but Snow cut in. "It is our best chance at stopping her. If I were to get ahold of that mirror and hold it hostage in exchange for her undoing her spell on you, she might agree to leave the kingdom and never return. . . ."

"No," her father said flatly. "She cannot be allowed to just leave! She's too dangerous. Too reckless! She's done too much harm and destroyed our kingdom's resources." His voice weakened. "It has to be an eye for an eye. We must avenge your mother, and to do so, the queen must be killed."

"Two wrongs do not make a right," Snow said. "Didn't you and Mother teach me that?"

Georg looked furious. "She killed your mother! She tried to kill you! The Evil Queen must die."

Die? Snow wasn't sure she could kill someone in cold blood, but she wasn't going to argue with her father at the moment. Time was running out. "First, I must get to the mirror. Threaten to destroy it. Break it. Do whatever it takes to be rid of it."

"If she's that attached to it, she won't allow you to harm it," Henri said. "Maybe she will go quietly if you let her keep it."

"She will never go quietly," her father said sadly. "This I know." He looked at Snow. "If you won't stay here, I can't even help you fight her, my snowflower. Not while I'm prisoner."

Snow grabbed his hands again. "You won't be a prisoner for much longer. I will break this spell. I will rid the kingdom of the Evil Queen and save our people. I will not let her continue to hurt the ones I love. I promise you that."

He held her face in his hands and she saw his eyes well with tears. "Be careful what you promise, my Snow White. Be careful."

Ingrid

Snow White was alive.

The mirror was cracking.

In a fit of rage, Ingrid flew out of her quarters and descended the castle steps to the first floor unseen. It wasn't that hard to do. She had recently dismissed several more servants after they were found in her private wing. She trusted no one. Now the mirror had failed her, too. How had Snow White survived? The huntsman was the son of the man who had helped poison Snow's mother years ago. How had Snow convinced him to let her go?

Furious, she went straight to her lair deep in the castle dungeons. In fact, there were two dungeons in the castle basement—the one where the guards put enemies of the kingdom and left them to rot, and the one she'd had walled off with her own private staircase. It led to a few cells for her own personal use, as well as her potion room. Since no one knew it was there, it wasn't often cleaned. Cobwebs decorated the walls, and rats scurried along the floor, but even they could be of use if the potion called for it. The important thing was that no one knew this place existed but her.

Ingrid threw the box with the heart in the corner in disgust. "The heart of a pig!" she yelled to the only one who could see her: a raven. Whether it was the same one that had been appearing at her window each day for the last week, she was not sure, but the bird comforted her somewhat. It seemed to share her darkness and lend its ear to her struggles in a way the mirror no longer could.

She looked around the lab, where several potions she had been brewing were bubbling in various flasks and bottles. None of them would work on the girl. There were memory loss spells, meant for those who needed tricking. And then there were the tonics meant to keep Ingrid youthful. Things she and the mirror had worked on together. Nothing she had on hand seemed like it would work with the girl. In fact, she couldn't rely on the mirror or a huntsman or anyone else to do this deed for her. If she wanted Snow White truly gone, she had to do away with the girl herself.

But how?

Looking around the lair for inspiration, her eyes landed on the dusty bookshelf in the corner of the room. A spine with simply the word *Concealments* caught her eye. *Yes!* She knew where the girl was. All she needed to do was go to the dwarfs' cottage in disguise and take care of Snow White once and for all. But it needed to be a good disguise that could mask the beauty she had worked so hard for. Of course, it would be temporary. But it also needed to be believable.

Pulling the book off the shelf, Ingrid flipped through it till she found just the right potion. *Yes.* This was the one. An old hag. Those little men had probably warned the girl not to open the door for strangers. But if Snow was anything like her mother, she'd take pity on an old woman who happened on her doorstep. She quickly read the instructions. It was a high-level spell and required only the rarest of ingredients. She'd raided her master's shelves after his death and took whatever she thought she might need. But the things that were required for this particular potion were so rare that one use might be all she got out of each vial she had. Ingrid read over what was required for the reverse spell, and many of the ingredients were the same. Would she have enough? Where would she get more mummy's dust? Or black of night?

The raven cawed at the sound of thunder in the distance.

The lair had a small dungeon window, which showed a world of blackness outside. Rain was coming.

Snow White is the fairest one of all, she heard the mirror say.

She couldn't waste time worrying about where she'd get more ingredients to reverse the spell. She needed to use what she had before the girl appeared to claim her crown.

Ingrid gathered each vial on the list and went to her cauldron. One by one, she repeated the steps laid out for her in the spell and dripped the ingredients into the cauldron, making sure to announce her intentions out loud. Her master always said appealing to the darkness was what bonded a spell.

"Change my queenly clothing into a peddler's cloak." She dropped the powder into the bubbling cauldron that always sat full of oils, waiting for use. "Mummy dust to make me old. To shroud my clothes, the black of night. To age my voice, an old hag's cackle. To whiten my hair, a scream of fright!" The potion was thickening and bubbling. It was beginning to turn green, as the spell book said it would. For the final touch . . . "And a thunderbolt to mix it well!" The thunder boomed almost as if on cue.

Quickly, Ingrid scooped some of the liquid into a goblet and put the bubbling green concoction to her lips. She hesitated for half a second as she looked at the youthful hands she had spent so many years perfecting. In a moment, they would be veiny and decrepit. She wasn't sure she could stand it.

Snow White is the fairest one of all.

Bracing herself, Ingrid swallowed the contents of the glass. The potion tasted like bile. It was so wretched she choked it down, then immediately wished she hadn't. She became woozy and the room started to spin. The glass slipped from her hands and shattered on the floor as she began to choke. She couldn't breathe. Something was very wrong. As she slipped out of consciousness, she grabbed her throat and began to sink to the floor.

But then she felt a change stir inside her. Slowly, the hand around her throat began to wither. Her beautiful gown began to fade away, replaced with a wretched black dress like the one the farmer's wife had always worn. Her hair grew long and scraggly, turning white from the roots to the tips. Her nose seemed to lengthen and sprout warts. She was veiny all over, and it was glorious! She was not dying. The disguise had worked! She let out a laugh. It came out like a cackle.

"My voice! My voice!" she said, listening to the broken sound. Snow White would not suspect a thing.

But now, what to do to the girl once she was in front of her? Her actions needed to be quick and uncomplicated, as she was working alone. Concocting a poison tonic like she had used on the girl's mother would take days. She needed something fast. Something enticing the girl couldn't resist. It needed to be a special sort of death for a girl so fair.

She went to another spell book—her wrinkled, speckled hands looking like someone else's—and turned the pages. The "sleeping death" in the form of an apple. How poetic. Katherine's life had changed because of those Red Fire apples, and now, in turn, her daughter's life would end because of one. She read the steps in the spell book. "'One taste of the poisoned apple and the victim's eyes will close forever in the sleeping death.'" It was perfect.

She sighed, frustrated that her body moved slower because of her temporary new age. Youthful was the way to be. With all the speed she could muster, she gathered the ingredients into the cauldron and let it brew. Thankfully, she had fruit on hand. She grabbed a rotting Red Fire apple and dunked it in the cauldron.

"Dip the apple in the brew!" Ingrid proclaimed. "Let the sleeping death seep through!"

One minute later, she pulled the apple back out of the cauldron and looked to see if the spell had done its magic. As the green potion dripped off the apple, Ingrid imagined a poison symbol appearing on it.

"Look!" she said to the raven. "On the skin. The symbol

of what lies within. Now turn red to tempt Snow White, to make her hunger for a bite!" Slowly, the apple changed shades. Ingrid laughed to herself with delight and held the perfect apple out to the raven. "Have a bite!" The bird flew away and she cackled. "It's not for you! It's for Snow White. When she breaks the tender peel and tastes the apple in my hand, her breath will still, her blood congeal. Then I'll be fairest in the land!" How strange. She was suddenly talking in rhyme, just like the mirror always did. It was almost as if it were speaking through her now, though this time she was working alone. She held up her handiwork to admire it some more.

This was an apple Katherine would have proclaimed worthy of a king. Of a princess. It was ruby red with swirls of green and shaped as perfectly as a heart. She nestled it into a basket with more apples, placing it on top so that Snow would see it first. If she left now, through the trapdoor in her dungeon floor, under the cover of darkness, she'd be at the dwarfs' cabin near the woods by early light, just when the men left for work. Who needed the mirror to guide her? She could manage every step on her own! She was headed to the trapdoor when a sudden thought stopped her. She looked back at the raven, which had returned and was eye-ing her curiously.

"There may be an antidote." Ingrid headed back to the

dusty book and read the spell again. "Nothing must be over-looked." She found the footnote she was looking for: *The victim of the sleeping death can be revived only by Love's First Kiss.* Slamming the book closed, she cackled with delight as she picked up the basket of apples and opened the trapdoor. Well, there was no fear of that. The dwarfs would come back to think her dead. She'd be buried alive!

Satisfied, Ingrid disappeared through the trapdoor without a trace.

Snow

Leaving her father felt like losing a piece of her soul. After being separated for a decade, their one evening spent together felt far too short, and the future was still so uncertain. While her father didn't know if they'd see one another again, Snow vowed that they would.

"I'm coming back for you," she told him, hugging him goodbye.

Her father didn't argue as he had earlier. "Take care of each other," he said instead, looking at both of them.

"Yes, Your Majesty," Henri said, and Snow smiled. Even in exile, without a crown or people to call on in times of need, Henri honored him with his title. Snow had assumed he'd leave after fulfilling his promise to reunite her with her father, but Henri insisted on taking her back to the dwarfs. She didn't protest. She enjoyed his company, and she relished the chance to spend more time with him.

Her father placed something small in her hand and closed her fingers around it. "Take this with you," he whispered.

She opened her palm and looked down at a delicate blue jeweled necklace.

"It was your mother's," her father said. "It was the first gift I ever gave her . . . early in our courtship, as I recall. She wore it faithfully till our wedding." He smiled at the memory. "After she died . . ." The words caught in his throat, and Snow took his hand. "I started carrying it on me in my breast pocket. It may seem silly, but it felt like I was holding a piece of her near my heart. I had it on me when Ingrid banished me here. Somehow, she didn't know about it. It felt as if your mother had given me one last gift. I always hoped one day I'd be able to pass it on to you."

"It's beautiful." Snow's fingers traced the etches of the stones, which were cool to the touch.

"While I may not be able to journey with you, this necklace may still be of aid," her father explained. "Others will recognize it. The enchantress did when she came my way once." He smiled. "That necklace has kept me safe from harm this far and it will do the same for you."

She wanted to wear it, but it was too fine a piece of jewelry for the peasant she was disguised as. The jewels would stick out if they encountered others on their journey. Instead, she tucked it into her shirt pocket, like her father had done, holding her mother close to her heart. "Thank you." She hugged him again. "Someday soon, I will wear it. When the queen is gone, and you have safely returned, and I am. . . ."

I am what? Coronated? She paused. Would her father want the crown again when this was all over?

Her father smiled, clearly understanding her hesitation. "Yes, my snowflower. You will wear it when you are crowned queen. My time has passed. You are this kingdom's future. And if you rid the kingdom of the Evil Queen, as you plan to do, they will demand you become their new leader." He clasped her hand. "I can advise you in the beginning, of course, and be there at your side, but your time has come now."

Your time has come. Her father's words echoed in her ears, full of weight. Could she find the strength within herself to be a good leader? She thought about it for a moment, but she already knew the answer. Yes, she could. Her mind raced with the potential. She would return the kingdom to its time of prosperity, as it had been under her father and mother's reign. She would right the wrongs done to the miners. She would set up new infrastructure so the agriculture would thrive once more. She would open up trade agreements with other kingdoms, like Henri's. The possibilities were endless.

If she could get her aunt to renounce the throne.

The only thing that still troubled her was her father's declaration that the Evil Queen must die. No matter how angry they both were at what she had taken from them, Snow wasn't sure she could take a life. She suspected her mother would agree with her.

The journey back to the dwarfs' cottage felt much longer than the one to see her father. She was desperate to tell the men about the mirror and learn of their progress. Thankfully, she and Henri had both begun to open up more, and they talked the whole way back. She spoke about life with the dwarfs, while he regaled her with stories of Georg nursing him back to health. Apparently he'd stubbornly refused to let Henri die, waking him every hour to feed him water or broth, and talking his ear off about Snow's childhood to keep Henri awake.

"I think I know more about you at age seven than you do," Henri teased.

"Oh, do you now?" she asked, happy he couldn't see her blushing since she sat in front of him on their steed.

"Yes," he said confidently. "I know you always preferred

the colors blue and yellow to any other. You were excellent at hide-and-seek. You hated cold porridge, and my personal favorite—you named every horse in the royal stables *and* liked to put bows on them when allowed."

She colored some more and burst out laughing. This she did not remember! "I did not! Did I?"

Henri laughed, too. "Apparently you did, driving the royal seamstress crazy with your requests for ribbons and bows for the royal steeds."

"And what of you?" Snow demanded. "It's only fair you tell me what you were like as a child, since you know so much about me."

She could feel Henri's arms around her waist as they rode through the forest. "Fair enough. Let's see . . . I found a mouse in the castle once and tried to keep it as a pet. Kept feeding it. My mother almost passed out when she caught me giving him cheese, but I couldn't abandon Ol' Croxley."

"Croxley?" Snow found the idea quite sweet. She'd often begged to have a pet, but her mother said having an aviary full of birds was enough. "You named him Croxley?"

"Why not?" Henri sounded indignant. "It's not like I made him clothes and taught him how to sing. But I was always getting into mischief. One time Kristopher and I broke a castle window when we had a sword fight in the palace hall. The weapons were the guards', but they were eating their supper and didn't know we had gotten ahold of them. I'm not sure who got a louder talking to—us or them. Probably us, because of the window. My mother made him go easy on us *that* time."

"There were more times?" Snow asked incredulously.

"Well, when I was ten, I stole my father's crown and tried selling it to the highest bidder in the village square." Henri chuckled. "I told Father I got sick of him being so busy and wanted him to give up being king so we could play."

"*No!*" Snow roared with laughter. "You didn't."

"He was amused, and yet not," Henri said. "None of my brothers ever pulled a stunt like that one. My mother called me 'boisterous.' Says I still am a bit strong-willed."

"Nothing wrong with that," Snow noted. "I wish I had been more so the last few years."

Henri grew quiet. "You didn't know. You can't torture yourself, Snow."

"I know." Snow tried to sound positive. "The past is done. What I need to concentrate on now is how I will change the future."

"I have a feeling you're going to figure that out," Henri said.

He was right. She would. By the time they got back to the dwarfs' cottage, she was already forming a plan. Her reunion with the men was a festive one. They were elated to see the pair safe and to know that the king was well. And they'd had some success talking to a couple of other miners—their friends Kurt and Fritz—who'd suggested they all travel to their hamlet to discuss plans for overthrowing the queen with the other villagers. But Happy insisted they save the details for after dinner.

Everyone was in such a good mood that as soon as they finished eating, Bashful and Sleepy broke out their fiddles and started to play. Snow, who hadn't danced in years, jumped up and joined Dopey on the dance floor, spinning around the small room with abandon. When Dopey was tired, Henri stood and offered her his hand. Snow hesitated for the briefest of moments, hearing Grumpy sigh, before she accepted. Her heart beat rapidly with every turn, and she struggled to maintain eye contact with Henri, her face rising in color every time he looked at her. But soon she got lost in the moment, forgetting to be nervous and just letting go. As the men struck up a new tune, Grumpy interrupted the merriment.

"Enough celebrating! We haven't won yet!" he bellowed. "We still have a queen to stop!" He looked at Snow and Henri. "Tell us what you learned."

"And how King Georg is," Bashful added.

Snow smiled softly, her pale cheeks glowing in the

firelight. "He's in good health." The men appeared relieved. "Seeing him, it felt as if no time had passed, and yet, so much has. He's missed the kingdom terribly, but is cursed to remain outside our borders." She explained what her father had told her about the queen's cruel trickery and then told them about the magic mirror.

"Your mother showed you where it was in your dream?" Doc asked, rubbing his chin. "Interesting."

"How so?" asked Happy.

"It's as if she's trying to help Snow take back what's rightfully hers, even from the other side."

It was a nice idea, and Snow hoped it was true. She'd never felt closer to her mother than this past week. She'd have given anything to have her near. If this was her attempting to help, then she'd accept it gratefully. She looked at Henri. "It's best I tell them about my mother, too." He nodded sadly.

The men were heartbroken when they heard how the Evil Queen had poisoned Katherine. If anything, the news only made them want to thwart her even more.

"The mirror must be how she gets her dark magic," Grumpy said. "She seems obsessed with it. If she didn't want Snow near it, it must be quite powerful."

"Sounds dangerous," Bashful said.

"Sounds like she's possessed by it," added Doc.

Possessed. Obsessed. Jealous. Her aunt was all of those things, and the mirror seemed to bring out her worst qualities, as if . . . "Doc, do you think it's possible for a person to become one with an object?"

"How so?" Doc asked.

"The Evil Queen seems to have given herself over to the mirror completely," Snow said. "Perhaps she's even taking commands from it."

"Don't you let her off the hook," Grumpy warned. "She did this all herself!"

"True, but she's had help," Snow said. "Maybe the reason she's so attached to the mirror is because she cannot function without it. She gains her power from it and it gains power from her as well," she guessed. "If that's true, then one cannot survive without the other."

Did that mean if they destroyed the mirror they would kill the Evil Queen along with it? Snow still wrestled with the idea of rising to power because of her aunt's death. Wouldn't that be stooping to her level? There had to be another way.

"Snow may be right," Henri agreed. "I've heard the darkest wizards and witches put pieces of themselves in their most treasured objects."

"That's why we need to steal her mirror," Snow declared. "We'll hold it for ransom. She'll have no choice but to leave the castle and let my father come home in exchange."

"You can't leave that thing in this world!" Grumpy sounded like Snow's father. "It should be destroyed."

"But it could kill her!" said Happy.

"So?" Grumpy countered. "Think of all the people she's tried to kill. She tried to kill Snow!"

"But . . ." Happy tried again.

"For now, we focus on getting to that mirror," Snow said. "Stealing it may be the only way to convince the queen to release my father from his prison."

"What are you going to do?" Sleepy asked with a yawn. "March into the castle and just take it off a wall?"

"The mirror will know you're coming for it," Grumpy said.

"I sense it already knows I'm alive," Snow agreed. "Our time to act may be shorter than we think."

"Which is why we must hurry," Henri said.

Snow looked at him. *"We?"*

Henri smiled. "You don't think I'm leaving now, do you? My people need this queen gone as much as you do. It's the only way to bring our two kingdoms together again as allies. An evil like this must be stopped. Let me help you."

Snow couldn't help feeling a flush of excitement at the thought of him staying to assist her cause. "Thank you, Henri. We need all the help we can get." She looked at the others. "We must go to your friends at once and talk to everyone in their villages about joining our cause."

"We will leave at first light," Grumpy vowed. "There is no time to lose."

"Tomorrow morning," Snow agreed, "we begin to make our way to the castle."

Ingrid

Her overnight journey had been a fool's errand; the wretched girl was not at the cottage.

After leaving her dungeon, she took the hidden passageway out of the castle by boat, then went the rest of the way through the woods on foot. She wasn't alone. The raven from her dungeon followed her, leading the way at points. This shell of a body she was now taxed with made walking difficult, but she finally arrived after first light. And the cottage was empty.

She'd expected the men to be gone. (In truth, she was happy that they were already on their way to the mines. She appreciated the work ethic, especially when it benefited her.) But where was Snow? Why wasn't she there? Ingrid walked around the cottage, swatting squawking birds away as she tried to peer in the windows. For some reason, several deer had come to graze nearby, too. She shooed them away as well and rested her weary body, but when the girl didn't return after a long spell, she became agitated and forced her way inside.

The cottage was clean as a whistle: not a bowl out of place or a crumb on the long table with the little chairs. The sink was empty, the floors spotless, and the seven tiny beds made. She hobbled back downstairs, feeling her knees creak as she walked, and went to the fireplace. Embers still glowed softly, and a sinking feeling crept in as a thought dawned on her: what if the wretched little men somehow knew she was coming and had hidden Snow away?

Ingrid put her basket on the table and screamed angrily at the thought. Her voice sounded hoarse and weathered. If this was true, her elaborate hag spell had been for naught! The girl was still out there.

Her heart still beats, her skin is still fair. Without action, our future will tear.

The mirror? Her large eyes widened. The mirror had awakened? Immediately all anger she felt toward the object vanished. She needed to go to her companion and repair any fissures that had started after their last encounter. How could she have been so foolish as to leave it? She grabbed the basket and began the arduous walk back to the castle, cursing her old legs.

It took the entire day to get back to the dungeon, and by the end, she wasn't sure she could take another step. She couldn't wait to find a way to replenish the ingredients and reverse the blasted spell. She finally snuck through the castle to her quarters, knowing she couldn't chance being seen in her hideous disguise.

Striding to the mirror, she ran her hand along the crack in the glass. She grabbed the renewal tonic she kept for just this reason and dabbed it on the cool surface. It lessened the deepness of the fracture, but did not repair it completely. She'd have to go to her lair again to create a stronger batch. For now, it did its job, the mirror springing to life, the colors of the glass swirling black and green before it started to smoke and the masklike face came into view. If it noticed her new appearance, it said nothing.

"My queen."

"Mirror," she demanded. "Have you led me astray? You said Snow White should perish, and yet she lives and breathes! And now she is gone from the dwarfs' cottage!"

"My queen, you had the chance to change fate," the mirror replied. "But instead you let that babe grow. And now it may be too late."

"She was just a baby!" Ingrid said, feeling desperate.

"Now she is fully grown and ready to take her crown," the mirror told her. "If action had been taken, this future would not have been found."

"What do I do now?" Ingrid asked. Why did the mirror have to rub her failure in her face? "I have concocted the strongest of spells to throw her off my scent and created a poison apple that will finish her with one small bite! But if I can't find her to fix things, my work will have been wasted."

"Her death would be mourned, and the people would rally en masse. But to have a deeper impact, perhaps it is her love that should be dashed."

The girl had found love with that insipid boy? She should have dispatched him when she first spotted him. Ingrid let out a scream so primal she wasn't surprised to see the fracture in the glass begin to grow. She quickly stopped shouting, her heart racing, her hands suddenly feeling very weak. In her withered state, if she wasn't careful, she would fall over. She held the wall and peered into the darkest corner of the room.

Katherine and her master were watching her. Her master looked angry, but Katherine did not appear alarmed. In fact, she looked quite smug. What did Katherine know that she did not?

"Her hope grows like a weed," the mirror replied. "As does her resolve. Learning her father lives has given her new vigor to proceed."

Ingrid tried to steady herself at this unexpected information. *She found him? How?!*" Her eyes went to Katherine and her master, both watching her with interest. She quickly looked away again.

"The prince you dismiss showed her the way. Armed with this knowledge, a spark in her has been reignited. And a new path is being forged straightaway."

Forget about reversing her hag spell. If the girl was attempting to reach the mirror, that meant she was coming to the castle with that boy. She needed to buy herself some time. "Show me the girl," she told the mirror.

The mirror's smoky view cleared and there were Snow White and her handsome prince, leading the group of little men through the forest. They were nearing the mines. Ingrid smiled to herself. An idea was slowly forming. It was a complicated one, and in her condition, she didn't know how easy it would be to pull off. But it was of the utmost importance that she did. "Perhaps there is a way to bury the girl alive after all . . . along with her prince and the little men!"

Snow

She was on her way back to the castle, but this time she wasn't alone. For the first time in her life, she had friends by her side. Friends, and maybe someone who could be more . . . someday. But there were more pressing things to focus on now.

"What are you thinking about?" Henri asked as they rode side by side through the countryside.

Snow lowered her blue hood. "Too much," she admitted. "My mind is cluttered with thoughts."

The dwarfs had bartered an illegal diamond or two to gather enough horses to take them all to Kurt and Fritz's village, but they'd had to pick the animals up at a farm half a day away. The time spent had been worth it. They wound up making camp and speaking to the farmers—a man named Moritz, and his wife, Lina—about their quest. Lina actually cried in relief when Snow told her who she was. "We need you now more than ever, Your Highness," Lina told her, explaining how difficult it had been to make a profit in the fields when the queen demanded more and more of their supply. Within the hour, Moritz had returned with several workers in the area, and together, Snow, Henri, and the dwarfs told them what they were up against. The others had immediately agreed to gather supplies and wait for word to storm the castle. Snow was so grateful for their service she could have wept.

But the unexpected delay at the farm meant they were now a day behind. *The queen could be watching us,* Snow thought as she saw a raven fly overhead. Time was of the essence, and they needed to get to Kurt and Fritz's village to gather more reinforcements. The dwarfs had first suggested they take the more rural roads and passes to the hamlet, to avoid drawing attention to themselves. But since a party of nine was sure to draw attention anyway, Grumpy insisted they travel as close to the route they took each day to get to the mines as possible. "At least if we have to turn around, we know exactly where we're going," he'd told the others, and they'd agreed.

They'd been riding for hours now and were finally

nearing the mines. Snow should have been used to so much travel by now, but she found it tiresome. It didn't help that she was so on edge. She felt her breast pocket, where her mother's necklace was safely secured, and wondered why her mother had led her to the mirror in her dream. Did she want Snow to kill her sister? Or was she just helping her find a way to stop Aunt Ingrid? Without her mother there to confer with, there was so much she was unsure of. But what she remembered about her mother was that she was always concerned with doing what was good for *all* people. She would want Snow to find a way—as *peacefully* as possible— to take back what was theirs. Of that, Snow was sure. Of course, when it came to the Evil Queen, things never went as planned. . . .

Snow looked around the rolling countryside. Since they'd left Moritz and Lina's homestead, they hadn't seen a home or a person for miles. They had passed the men's mine entrance ages ago, but Doc explained there were several caves in which miners from different villages could enter. She'd had no idea there were so many mountains in this part of the kingdom. How could Aunt Ingrid have said the diamond mines were all dried up?

"Are you all right?" Henri asked.

"Yes, but there is so much to worry about," Snow said. "I feel responsible for all of you and my people. I don't want any harm to come to anyone."

JEN CALONITA

Henri smiled kindly. "It'll be all right. We know what we signed up for on this quest."

And what of the huntsman who had spared her life? Snow couldn't help thinking about him. Had he given his life to save hers? An eye for an eye, in a way, considering what his own father had done.

Snow shuddered, then took a deep breath. It was time to refocus. No good would come from all that worrying. "Okay, let's tackle one thing at a time—today, it's getting to the village. Tomorrow, it's gathering more fighters. Before the queen tries to stop us."

"I doubt she will leave her castle to search for you," Henri said. "Her castle is her fortress and where her mirror is. Hopefully we have nothing to fear till we reach the gates."

"I see smoke up ahead!" yelled Doc, pointing to the tree line in the distance. "Should we go another way?"

"No, stay the course," Grumpy told the others. "I'm sure it's just someone making camp. No one lives in these parts. We won't get to Kurt and Fritz's village for miles yet. We're only just reaching the entrance to the mines."

Henri and Snow looked at one another as if they were both thinking the same thing. There was something about the smoke that looked odd. It didn't billow up in a single line, or spiral like a twister. It seemed to be spreading wider and wider, becoming darker with each plume. Soon it spread clear across the tree line, till it filled the sky with darkness.

"I don't think that's smoke. . . . They seem to be dark clouds," said Happy. "I think a storm is coming."

Suddenly, the horses they were riding grew restless. Doc's stood on its back legs, almost tossing him off. The wind picked up, sending tree limbs flying with the sudden gust. Branches bent and twisted in their path, as if they were trying to scoop the riders up. One tree's limbs seemed to stretch out toward Snow as if it were trying to grab her. Snow had a flashback to her time in the Haunted Woods. Something was definitely wrong.

"We need to find shelter immediately!" she shouted over the wind.

But it was too late.

The clouds spun toward them like a venomous fog and soon overtook them, turning the sky pitch-black. The wind's howl made it almost impossible to hear what anyone was saying. A giant crack of thunder sounded as a lightning bolt struck the earth mere feet from Bashful's steed. The horses took off in various directions. Dopey's took off so fast he was almost thrown from the horse, but he clutched his stirrups.

"Hang on!" Henri yelled over the wind.

Snow looked desperately from Dopey to Henri and dismounted, knowing she could do more good on the ground. The rest of the men did the same, and they helped Dopey untangle from his steed. The horses disappeared into the darkness. The air was too full of debris to even see her hand in front of her face. Rain came down so fast and hard it felt like hail. They needed to get inside . . . but where?

"Into the mines!" Grumpy shouted over another clap of thunder. "This way!"

Snow followed the sound of his voice, struggling to move forward in the wind. She looked for Henri but couldn't see anyone, so she kept her eye on the rocky mountain in front of her, hoping she'd find the entrance to the cave.

A bolt of lightning hit a tree next to her, and the large limbs began to fall in her direction. Someone reached out and grabbed her, pulling her out of the line of fire before it was too late.

She looked up. "Henri!" she said, holding on to him for dear life.

"The entrance to the cave is that way," he shouted. "Don't let go of my hand!"

"Or you of mine!" Snow shouted back. It would take both of them to find their way in the darkness. She could hear shouting and her name being called in the darkness, but the wind was too strong for her to even turn her head and look around. The two of them held on to each other, making their way slowly toward the large shadow that loomed in front of them. Snow pulled her cloak over their heads, trying to keep the rain off their faces. It fell harder, hitting their backs and leaving welts. Lightning struck again and again, closer and closer as she and Henri pushed forward, hoping to find somewhere to escape the storm. Suddenly, she saw the entrance to the cave. Grumpy was already inside.

"This way!" she shouted, and they took step after painful step till they reached the entrance, collapsing against a cave wall in relief. She wiped her eyes and looked around. Doc, Happy, and Dopey were there, too. Two seconds later, Bashful, Sneezy, and Sleepy stumbled in.

"Thank the heavens, you're all safe," Snow said.

Another crack of thunder sent a tree limb falling toward the entrance of the cave. Everyone jumped back.

"Witchcraft!" Grumpy declared. "There's something strange about this storm."

"The queen! She's following us!" Bashful shouted.

Snow feared they were right. "Let's get away from the entrance. It isn't safe."

Grumpy grabbed a lantern in the cave entrance and lit it shakily. "Follow me below," he said, and the group made their way deeper into the caverns, each man grabbing a lantern to help them see. They could hear the storm howling outside. It felt like it would be upon them at any moment. "Quickly! Quickly!" Grumpy said, seemingly sensing the same thing.

Snow took a lantern, as did Henri, and they hurried

forward. The air was colder the lower they descended, and Snow felt her breath quicken in the darkness. Grumpy kept shouting out directions. There were so many passageways Snow feared they'd get lost.

"We will ride out her storm down here," Grumpy said as they reached a hollowed area where mine trains full of diamonds glistened in the darkness. Pickaxes and small crates that served as tables were scattered about the cave as if the men had left in a hurry the night before. An assembly line of tables was set up along one rocky wall to clean the diamonds before they were placed in the carts. The space was musty and dank. Condensation dripped down the rocks and stalactites hung like daggers. Snow might have found these things beautiful if she hadn't been so worried about the storm outside. Was this really her aunt's doing? She could still hear the howling wind whistling through the cavern as if it were following them down the shaft. Snow and Henri took a seat on the crates at the edge of a nearby tunnel and placed their lanterns on the ground for light.

Doc smiled at Snow reassuringly from across the room. "We will be safe down—"

That was the last thing Snow heard him say before the ground started to rumble and rocks fell from above. Snow and Henri moved into the tunnel to avoid getting hit by falling debris.

"Cave-in!" someone yelled.

"Get to the walls!" came Grumpy's muffled shouting.

Snow and Henri covered their heads and crouched against a wall, waiting for the avalanche of rocks to stop falling, but the debris kept coming, making it hard to breathe.

So this is where I die, Snow thought as the world around her turned to black. *The Evil Queen finally gets her wish.*

Ingrid

Ingrid stepped away from the mirror, the last of her strength leaving her body. She'd given more of her lifeblood to the mirror, and in her elderly state it felt more draining than it ever had before. The headache was instant and her aged hands were literally shaking, but it had been worth it. The mirror had given her the power she needed to conjure that storm. It was a storm like no other, designed to track the girl. And it had worked brilliantly.

The timing felt fated. When the storm struck, Snow, her hapless prince, and those little men had no choice but to take cover in the cave. That's when Ingrid sent repeated lightning strikes to the entrance, till it finally caved in. The girl had been buried alive after all.

She let out a cackle that petered out as the headache she felt began to strengthen. She sank to the floor, unable to even find the strength to make it to her chambers.

"Magic Mirror on the wall," she whispered. "Who is the fairest one of all?"

Katherine began to take shape in the corner of the room, but this time she did not appear droll.

Let her spirit come, Ingrid thought as her eyes fluttered and she forced them to stay open. She was so tired. *I have won.*

The mirror spoke. "Lips red as the rose, hair black as ebony, skin white as snow. Snow White still lives, and soon all will know."

"No!" Ingrid choked out, but her voice didn't seem to work. Neither did her limbs.

As Katherine stood watch, Ingrid succumbed to the pain and fell into a deep sleep on the cold floor.

Snow

When the debris finally stopped falling, the only thing Snow heard was deathly silence.

"Henri?" Snow called out frantically, coughing hard as the dust settled around her. Her right shoulder was throbbing, but she was in one piece.

"Snow?" Henri was coughing hard, too. He stumbled toward her and she noticed the gash on his forehead. He fell into her arms and the two held each other.

We're alive! Thank you, Mother! Snow thought before she saw the wall of rock in front of her.

Henri began trying to pull the rocks down, but most of them were small and he barely made a dent. He tried a different tactic, pulling hard and grunting against the weight of a larger boulder, before finally collapsing against the wall.

They were trapped.

"Grumpy?" Snow frantically searched in the darkness, tripping over the rocks that lay at her feet. "Doc? Sleepy? Sneezy? Bashful?" Her voice grew more and more urgent.

A light suddenly illuminated the wall ahead, and Snow realized Henri still blessedly had his lantern. It lit up the small area of the cave they stood in. Otherwise, they were surrounded by darkness.

"Where are they?" Snow was beginning to feel as if the walls were closing in. "Dopey? Dopey, where are you?" But Dopey, of course, wouldn't speak. He couldn't, as far as she knew.

The men were missing. She and Henri were trapped in a darkened tunnel. The entrance to the cave was on the other side of that rocky wall. Her father had no clue where she was and would never know why she didn't return. She took a shaky breath, trying not to let an overwhelming feeling of failure consume her.

Henri took her in his arms again. "Snow, it's okay."

She gripped his shoulder. "We don't know these tunnels. We have to find a way to get back to them."

The two of them started to feel around the collapsed tunnel entrance for anything that might indicate loose stone or rubble that could be cleared for a path.

Henri suddenly had another coughing fit.

"Henri, please," Snow said, reaching toward him. "Sit. I will continue looking. But you must rest."

"If we cannot get out . . . then at least my life was not lived in vain," he said softly.

She looked up at him in the low lantern light. "What do you mean?"

"When Kristopher died, I felt a certain burden to take his place in the family, and yet, no matter what I did, I couldn't step out of his shadow." He smiled sadly. "Going on this journey with you, and helping you try to change your kingdom, has given me purpose. If this is where I die, I want you to know that."

"Henri," she said, feeling overcome. Suddenly, she became aware of her arms wrapped around Henri's neck and his arms around her waist. She was close enough to see the soot and the dirt in his hair and the smudge on his left cheek, and yet he'd never looked more beautiful.

Henri brushed away the tears trickling down her cheeks and leaned in closer. His lips were inches from hers. She closed her eyes and waited for their lips to touch. Instead, she heard a clinking sound. They both jumped back in surprise.

The clinking became louder and louder until a boulder in the wall began to wobble and a hole appeared, letting in light from the other side. Half of a face came into view.

"Dopey!" Snow cried, reaching her fingers through the small hole to touch him.

Suddenly, he disappeared from view and Grumpy's familiar scowl appeared. "Are you all right? Is Henrich?" he shouted.

"We're fine!" Snow cried with relief. "Is everyone all right on your end?"

"Everyone is banged up but fine," Grumpy said. "We're lucky Dopey grabbed his pickax when the sky started falling. His is the only ax we can find. The entrance to the cave is closed in. It's going to take a while to dig ourselves out. But I think you and Henrich can get to the back entrance."

"The back entrance?" Henri came in closer to hear what Grumpy was saying. "This tunnel has a way out?"

"Yes!" Grumpy said. "You don't think us miners come down here without having a backup plan, do you? Just follow the path down till you hit the lake. You'll see the tunnel of light that leads you back out the other side of the mountain."

"But what about all of you?" Snow asked.

"This tunnel is closed up tight," Grumpy said. "It would take us longer to dig a way to you than to dig a way out the way we came in. You get out of here and we will meet up with you again. Get to Fritz and Kurt's village. It won't be far from that side of the mountain."

Snow reached her fingers as far as she could to touch

Grumpy's hand. She hated the idea of leaving them. "Are you certain?"

"Yes, I'm sure!" Grumpy said, sounding annoyed. "Now go! Before the Evil Queen makes another tunnel cave in. And make sure that prince of yours takes good care of you."

"I will," Henri said. "I promise. Till we meet again, friends."

"Till we meet again," Snow and Grumpy repeated, and then they let go of each other's fingers.

Henri held up his lantern and offered Snow his free hand. She took it, and together, they once again made their way out of the darkness.

Ingrid

When she finally awoke on the floor, she let out a scream so loud she thought she'd wake the castle.

Too bad. Let them wake during the dark of night. She was awake. She would not sleep, would not rest, would not stop till the girl was dead.

She pushed herself up on her veiny arms and slowly rose to full height. Katherine was still there, watching. Always watching. As was the mirror. It came to light, showing her an image of the girl walking with the prince by lantern through the darkness.

"While you slumbered, the fairest and her prince found a way out. Gather your strength, or your future will remain in doubt."

The mirror's words only made Ingrid want to scream louder. This time it came out as a deep, throaty cough.

She couldn't believe this. She'd given the last of her lifeblood to the mirror and the girl was still coming for her? How had that monstrous storm or a cave-in not been enough to stop her? But there was the girl in the mirror, walking through a tunnel into the light and heading off with the prince on foot. Where were the little men? Had they perished? She didn't see them. Well, good. At least her storm had done one thing right. Snow and the prince seemed worried.

"Tell me what they're saying!" Ingrid croaked at the mirror. But by now, she already knew its response.

"My queen, that I cannot do," the mirror replied. "But her purpose is clear as the face on the glass. She will not rest till she comes for you."

"You keep saying that, but never how I can stop her!" Ingrid knocked several potions off the nearest table in disgust. Katherine moved in front of her, and her master appeared then, too. Both of them watched her pace. Ingrid looked seemingly through Katherine back to the mirror. She needed to control her anger and think.

The mirror continued to smoke. Its masklike face was solemn. "Thy heart and head have resisted my aid. My powers only reach so far, and only ever when you bade."

"Enough!" Ingrid shouted. The girl could not have her crown. She wound up her arm, prepared to destroy more of her things. Then she stopped. "Rain and wind may not deter the princess, but I know something else that might." She smiled wickedly, thinking about the little she knew of Snow's pitiful everyday life. What she did know, though, might be enough. She rushed out of the cavernous room and through her bedchambers. She opened her door a crack and yelled to the guard outside her door, hiding her face behind her hood.

"Guard! I have a royal decree that must be issued at once."

"Yes, my queen," the guard said, appearing bewildered. Her voice sounded different, but he wouldn't dare question it.

"Summon the royal court and have them issue this news at once," she said. "The princess is not missing. She is on the run. She is a coward, like her father was before her."

The guard's eyes widened.

"Tell them to issue a decree that the traitorous princess, and anyone who pledges their allegiance to her, shall pay with their lives." She smiled. "And offer a reward to anyone who brings her—and her companions—to me."

Snow

When Snow and Henrich emerged from the cave, the storm had ended and the air smelled like pine. Their horses—if they had stayed, which she doubted—were on the other side of the mountain. They'd have to make their way to Fritz and Kurt's village on foot. Without food rations, the journey felt particularly long. Finally, as the sun was beginning to dip below the mountains, they saw smoke. This time, however, it wasn't apocalyptic. It was billowing out of an actual chimney.

"We made it," said Henri, his voice relieved as he pointed out the row of cottages just over the next hill. "Let's hope these friends of the men are hospitable. We need water."

"I'm sure they will be," said Snow, bending down to gather a bunch of wildflowers.

"What are you doing?" Henri asked, amused.

"Bringing them a gift," Snow said. "One should never show up somewhere without an offering of some kind. Unfortunately, the cured meats we packed are lost, but flowers are always nice." She bunched the purple flowers together and held them up for Henri to sniff.

He took a whiff and looked at her in surprise. "They're lovely."

They stared at one another awkwardly and Snow could feel that familiar rush of color come to her cheeks. Her heart seemed to beat harder the closer she stood to him.

"You there!" a man called. They looked over and saw he was leading a donkey loaded with supplies over the hill. "Are you looking for someone?"

"Yes," Snow said, rushing forward. "We're here to see Fritz and Kurt. They should be expecting us."

"I'm Kurt," the man said. He was not as short in stature as the dwarfs, but he was diminutive. He also had a splatter of freckles across his nose, and bright red hair. "Where's Grumpy, Doc, and the others?"

"I'm Snow," she said, rushing forward and presenting him with the blooms. "And unfortunately, it's just us."

"You're the princess?" Kurt raised one eyebrow, and she nodded.

She could only imagine how the two of them looked—Henri with the cut on his forehead, and both of them covered in dirt. Neither looked much like royalty.

"Why aren't the men with you?" Kurt asked. "They said you were traveling together."

Snow frowned. How could she explain this without scaring him off? "They couldn't make it, but we have their blessing to come on our own to speak with you."

Kurt seemed to consider this. "Where're your horses?"

Henri and Snow glanced at one another. Neither wanted to say exactly what they'd just been through.

"They ran off," Henri explained. A rumble of thunder in the distance jolted them, and Henri and Snow exchanged looks again. Was another storm coming? "Unfortunately, our time is limited. Is it possible for us to speak?"

Kurt looked at them for a moment, then nodded. "Follow me."

He wasn't the most talkative man, so Snow didn't prod. Instead, they followed him the rest of the way into the village. It was quite small, with only one farm in the distance and a cluster of cottages that had seen better days. As they walked, Snow could see people peering out their windows or in doorways. She wasn't sure what to do, so she just smiled. When she did, people seemed to drift back into the shadows, which she supposed she could understand. It was a technique she had used herself, especially when she was uncomfortable. But now things were different. She had to be the leader her people needed her to be. And she was *this* village's potential leader. At least, she could be, if they let her.

Kurt turned to them. "I will gather the others and we will meet you in that barn over there." He pointed to the farm in the distance and his expression hardened. "It's the only place large enough for us to gather unseen. The Evil Queen's guards burned down the two other farms in the area when we failed to produce enough crops to sell for her."

"I'm sorry to hear that," Snow said.

Kurt looked away. "We do our best to avoid her now." He pointed again, and there was another rumble of thunder. "You should get going before you're seen. She has eyes everywhere, and the weather today has been unusual, to say the least."

"Oh, yes, we know," Snow said without thinking, and Kurt waited for her to say more. She didn't.

"Thank you for your hospitality. We will wait for you there." Henri pulled up his hood. Snow did the same.

The weather held off till they were inside the barn. In a corner, a few cows munched quietly, seeming less concerned with another storm than the people were. Several horses pawed at the ground nervously in stalls filled with hay. There was also a coop where chickens clucked quietly, and next to it, a water jug. She and Henri went to it, grabbing two tin mugs from a nearby shelf and drinking thirstily before collapsing on some bales of hay. Thunder rumbled in the distance, and after a while they heard the sound of light rain hitting the roof. Time passed slowly, and Snow's eyelids felt heavy. She willed herself to stay alert, but the exhaustion of the day seemed to have caught up with her. When she awoke a short time later, she realized her head was on Henri's shoulder. He opened his eyes when she sat up.

"Hello." He smiled.

"Hello," Snow replied. "We fell asleep."

"We did." Henri looked around. Rain was still falling and the barn was dark. Evening had come. "And we're still alone."

Snow frowned. "Where could they be?"

"I don't know." Henri stood to go to the barn doors.

As he did, a group of people with lanterns entered with Kurt. There had to be a dozen or so men and women, as well as children, who hid in the folds of their mothers' skirts. All eyes were on Snow and Henri.

She rose to greet them. "Hello! Thank you so much for coming."

Kurt held out his arm. "This is the princess and . . . ?"

"Henrich," Henri told them. "I'm the princess's traveling companion."

"We thought Grumpy and his men were the princess's traveling companions," another man said. He was small in stature as well, and had jet-black hair and a long beard. Snow suspected this must be Fritz. The glow of the lanterns in the darkened barn illuminated his face. He looked angry.

Snow took a step forward. "Yes, that's true. Unfortunately, we were separated during the storm and they asked us to go on without them. We will meet up with them again near the castle." Fritz didn't reply.

Just then, a woman holding a small baby rushed forward. She held out a few blankets. "Here, Your Highness. These are for you. You must be tired from your journey."

"Thank you for your kindness," Snow said to her and the others. "We are so grateful for this barn and to all of you for agreeing to meet with us. I know Grumpy and the others aren't with us tonight, but it is important that I speak with you about the queen." The room was silent, so she decided to go on. "I know times have been difficult. I'd had no idea how much so till I left the castle. But now that I've learned so much about the queen's behavior, I know I must take back the kingdom." Still there was no response. "But to do so, I will need help."

"Help?" Fritz questioned.

"Yes," Snow said, and Henri squeezed her hand encouragingly. "I am prepared to lead my people. The queen was only supposed to reign till I was of age anyway.

I don't believe she will go quietly, so we feel there would be strength in numbers. We are hoping to force her out and take over the castle."

Fritz stepped forward. "You expect us to lay down our lives to save yours?"

"No, that's not what I want to happen—" Snow started to say.

"We should trust in your leadership when you've never led?" Kurt asked. "What if you're just like your father?"

"I pray I am," Snow said fiercely. "He was an excellent leader." They started to laugh, preventing her from explaining her father's situation.

The crowd of men moved in closer, and Snow realized she and Henri were actually surrounded. A baby began to cry, her wail barely audible over the thunder.

"Good people," Henri interrupted. "This is the princess. Please show some respect."

"Respect?" a man asked. "Like she had for us? She has abandoned her kingdom. She doesn't want to help us!"

"I do!" Snow protested.

The man raised his knife. "Liar!" Snow flinched as Henri pulled her closer. "You show up here without the dwarfs, on foot, and in the middle of another storm— perhaps it is *you* who curses us! Where are the other men? What have you done with them?"

"They are safe," Henri said. "We assure you."

"Then why aren't they here to vouch for you?" Fritz questioned.

Kurt pulled out a scroll from behind his back. He let it unravel, and Snow gasped in surprise. There was a painting of her on it. Above her head it said WANTED. "There is a bounty for your capture, Princess. You have abandoned your people, hurt our friends, and refused your crown. You're coming with me to the queen before she blows down this whole kingdom trying to find you! These storms are no coincidence. They're happening because you are here in our village!"

"Let me explain," Snow said as they moved in closer. There was nowhere for her to go. "It is the queen who deceives you."

"The queen is the one in charge in this kingdom!" Fritz thundered. "Your father allowed that to happen, and now we are under her rule. Don't you know she has dark magic? We cannot spare you and hope to live. Grab them!"

"Please! Wait!" Snow cried as the closest villagers grabbed each of her arms.

Henri tried to kick out from his hold. "Let go of the princess!" His treasured pocketknife fell from its holder and landed in the hay, where Fritz picked it up and held it out.

"I'm so sorry," cried the woman who'd handed Snow the blankets earlier, her eyes glistening. "We have no choice. The queen shows no mercy. We must take you in."

"And we will be paid well for our find," Kurt added.

Snow sensed this would not end well. As lightning lit up the cracks in the barn and thunder roared, she looked around for an escape. Some of the men were shouting at one another, while others, along with several women, were trying to make them see reason, but none would. Snow's head was swirling. *Mother, help me,* she prayed as the baby in the woman's arms cried harder.

And then Snow had a moment of clarity, amid all the shouting and words of hate: *These people are scared. They don't want to hurt me. They feel they have no choice.* These folks weren't evil. They were her people. Snow thought back to the beggar woman she'd met with her mother so many years before. *Always remember your past, Snow, and let it help you make decisions on how to rule your future,* her mother had said.

"Please!" Snow tried again. "Let Henrich go and I will let you take me to the queen. I don't want anyone getting hurt."

"Snow, no," Henri started to say, but she shushed him and spoke only to Kurt, whose pale face lit up in the glow of the lightning striking outside.

"All I ask is that you listen to me for a moment more," she begged.

"No! You will just spin more lies!" Kurt declared.

"Let her speak!" someone thundered, and everyone turned around.

A person stepped forward then and removed a heavy hood to reveal a tan face, long curly brown hair, and big brown eyes.

Snow gasped in surprise. "Anne?"

The girl smiled. "You know my name?"

"Of course I do," Snow said. "You're the royal tailor's daughter."

"Don't listen to her lies, Anne," Fritz started to say, but Anne cut him off.

"I have seen the princess from afar my whole life," she told the others, "and I can assure you, she is not evil. She is very much alone. The queen has allowed her no one. She has been abandoned, much like the rest of us have." Anne turned to look at her. "If she says she wants to help her kingdom, then I, for one, believe her."

Snow's eyes welled with tears. For so long she'd observed this girl, and it turned out Anne had been doing the same thing. "Thank you," she whispered.

Anne nodded. "Surely, men, you can give your kingdom's princess a moment of your time before returning her to the queen for a bounty?"

These words shamed Kurt, Fritz, and the others, and they hung their heads. The women looked displeased with them, she could tell. Buoyed by Anne's faith, she felt a renewed vigor to explain herself.

"It is true I am on the run, but not because I've abandoned you," Snow told them. "The queen tried to have me killed, as I am a threat to her crown." The room was quiet except for the sound of the rain falling outside their doors. "I escaped and have been planning my return to the castle with the help of Grumpy and his men, and Henri here." She smiled at him. "Instead of running, I am choosing to fight for your freedom and my own. For too long we've been under the strangling rule of Queen Ingrid, who cares only for herself and nothing for her people."

"That's true," she heard one of the men mutter.

"She doesn't care that you work yourselves to the bone through weather such as this to bring in crops," Snow continued. "She taxes you excessively and gives you little reward. My parents taught me the castle was meant to be shared with those who needed shelter. If you had an issue with your land, they wanted to hear it. If you needed a bit of joy, there was always a party to celebrate our kingdom's good fortune."

"I remember," said the woman with the baby, jostling the child and trying to calm her. It was still thundering and her voice was soft, so Snow listened hard. "Queen Katherine always greeted her subjects. She had a kind word for everyone. I remember her giving me a flower once as a child. She was very kind."

"Yes, she was." Snow's face softened. "But our new queen is not. She has taken our kingdom's wealth and squandered it while destroying our relationships with our neighboring kingdoms. For our kingdom to survive, her reign must end."

"And how are you going to do that?" Kurt asked, looking unconvinced of her sincerity. "You are just one girl."

"I may be one girl, but I have friends now, and that makes all the difference. Grumpy and the others are on their way to the castle as we speak," Snow said. "We plan on overwhelming the guards so that I can get into the castle and make my way to the queen. Our numbers may be small, but our hearts and our word are true. We will do whatever it takes to put this kingdom back in capable hands." Fritz looked thoughtful, then glanced at the others.

"It is still no matter," Kurt said. "She has a price on your head now. You won't get far."

Snow's heart sank. She couldn't deny that with the queen's decree, their job was going to be even tougher than they'd anticipated. Everyone would be looking for her now. How was she going to get into the village undetected?

"No one can get into the castle," said another. "No one."

"You forget, that castle was my home . . . once," Snow said. "I know its secrets. I can get back in there unde-tected . . . if you give me the chance. If you fight at my side, I won't forget it. I promise if you do, I won't let you down."

Kurt glanced at his wife. "Let her try, Kurt," the woman said. "She's our future."

Our future. Snow smiled. Her mother would have liked this woman's spirit. "Help us take back what's ours. Who's with us?" At first, everyone was quiet.

"I am," Anne said, and she smiled.

Snow beamed. "Even one more is a help. Thank you."

"We cannot let this queen continue to ruin our lives," Anne told the others.

"Your mother would not want you to risk it, Anne," said one man.

"This is for our livelihood," Anne told him. "It's worth any risk. I know my mother would agree."

Fritz stepped forward with Henri's knife, using it to cut his binds. Then Henri quickly freed Snow.

"I will help you," Fritz said, lowering himself to one knee.

"So will I," agreed Kurt, and he, too, bowed down before her. Several of the other men did the same.

Snow laughed through tears. "Please rise! We have much work to do! I cannot thank you all enough for your faith in me." The people in the barn let out a cheer, which buoyed Snow's rising spirit.

"We will fight with you, Princess," said Kurt. "Don't let us down."

"I won't," Snow declared.

Ingrid

She watched the mirror obsessively for the next several hours for word of the girl's capture, but there was none.

"Show me the girl again!" she would shout at the mirror in her leathery new voice, which she was beginning to despise. But she would do nothing to change it till she had the girl. She would not get distracted.

"In the village she slumbers, my queen, but she's ready to rise. Her goal guides her like a beacon—to take you and the castle by surprise." The mirror showed her an image of Snow and the prince sleeping on a bed of hay like animals. How had no one captured her yet?

"She won't get far," Ingrid said yet again. "Her people will hand me her head on a platter!"

"The princess is loved by all that she meets," the mirror said. "To best her you will have to find a new method of defeat." The mirror's smoky haze lifted and an image of the dwarfs appeared.

Ingrid gasped. "They're alive!" The little men were marching in a line over a hilltop. They looked dirty and tired, but they were all there . . . and it seemed there were several more men with them, carrying pickaxes and other weapons. Not a large number, but a growing one to be sure. "Their group is no threat to me," Ingrid declared, but inwardly, she worried.

"We both know that not to be true," the mirror replied. "Do not attempt to wear a mask. Your fears betray you."

Ingrid didn't reply. She was lost in her thoughts. How had the men survived her storm and lived to tell the tale? How were the others not intrigued by her reward? Money and power usually changed everything.

"Love is the key to her undoing," the mirror advised now. "Harm her dear ones. That is the plan worth brewing."

The smoke cleared and showed Snow again. The little men might have no longer been at her side, but the prince still was. His presence was beginning to become a nuisance. The mirror was right.

Something would have to be done about that boy, indeed.

Snow

Their new friends did not have horses to spare, but they did have fruit, bread, and water, and they packed some up for Snow and Henri's journey. Kurt and Fritz vowed they'd gather more men to meet the dwarfs at the castle, with plans among both groups to stop at other like-minded villages along the way. Snow was grateful for their change of heart and hopeful that their growing ranks would make a difference. They were small in number compared to the queen's army, which there was still the matter of getting past once the fighting began.

Anne approached as Snow and Henri were getting ready to leave.

"I'm coming with you," she told Snow.

Snow blinked in surprise. "What about your mother and your work in the castle? Won't the queen be angry if you don't arrive as scheduled?"

"I have told Mother I am ill and cannot join her," Anne said. "She will cover for me, Your Highness."

Snow blushed at the term. "Please call me Snow."

"Snow," Anne repeated shyly. "We have to ensure you get to the castle in one piece, with that price on your head. It will be difficult for you to move about the kingdom unnoticed."

"If your village has already seen that 'wanted' scroll, then I suspect there must be dozens more just like it around the kingdom," Snow mused. "I won't be able to go anywhere."

Henri bit his lip as he stared at the cloudless sky. "And the queen was already tracking our every move. A new storm could appear at any moment. How will we get by her?"

"I think I have an idea," Anne said. "To allow you to continue to spread your message, and get you the rest of the way to the castle unseen. And your prince, too."

Snow blushed. He wasn't exactly *her* prince, was he? "How?"

Anne's brown eyes looked playful. "We have to make the two of you become invisible . . . and I know just the person who can make that happen: Sorceress Leonetta. She's an enchantress people in the village sometimes go to."

"An enchantress," Snow said in surprise. "My father mentioned one, as well." Snow quickly explained the truth about him.

"This explains so much," Anne said. "And if this enchantress is one and the same, then she will want to help you as she has him. She's a bit out of the way of the castle, but I believe it will be worth the trip."

"Let's go see this Sorceress Leonetta, then," Snow agreed.

Anne held out a sack. "I've brought you both some new clothes. One of the men lent some things for Henri, and Snow, I made yours," Anne told them. "Things the queen discarded. Mother usually makes me leave the clothes she doesn't want behind, but I don't like to see my creations go to waste." Anne's eyes twinkled.

Snow pulled out a lovely blue dress with a gold sash. There was even a tan traveling cloak to go with it. "Anne, you're very talented. But I knew that when I saw that green velvet gown you made, with the red cape."

Anne's eyes widened. "How did you see that? The queen hated it!"

Snow smiled. "I heard you talking to your mother the day the queen told you to do away with it. It was too lovely to go to waste. I took the extra fabric to make into curtains."

"I *thought* I saw those in passing! But you always close your door so quickly."

Snow blushed. "My aunt would grow angry when I

conversed with others, so I shut myself away. But you were someone I always suspected I would enjoy speaking with."

"I always thought the same thing about you," Anne said, and they both smiled.

Once dressed, Snow, Anne, and Henri headed off. Snow learned a lot about Anne in a short amount of time. Her father had passed away when she was a baby, and she was close to her mother. Anne wasn't as familiar with bird-calls as Snow or Henri, but Snow taught her a few. Before they knew it, Anne said they were nearing their destination.

"I'd heard rumors about the enchantress for years, but had never been brave enough to go see her myself," Anne explained. "When you showed up, I asked someone in the village who had been here before to tell me the way. I think this is the spot."

They came to a halt at a small cottage that was built into the side of a small hill. Covered in green moss, with a roof that looked like it grew grass, it seemed to blend into the mountain and fade away from existence. Anne pulled a small scroll out of her pocket and consulted it.

"Redwood trees in a circular pattern," she said. "A weeping willow orchard on top of the hill . . . yes, this is the place. Come on!"

Anne approached the door and knocked three times in quick succession.

It opened seconds later. The small woman had long

white hair and skin so wrinkled it appeared fake. Her grayish-blue eyes were so cloudy Snow thought she might be blind.

"What do you want, Princess?" she asked, revealing a mouth of yellowed, rotting teeth.

Snow's eyes widened. Anne got down on bended knee and beckoned the others to do the same. "Sorceress Leonetta, the princess, her prince, and I seek your wisdom."

"Humph," Leonetta grunted, and she tried to shut the door again. "You won't make it to the castle like this, that's for sure."

"Wait!" Anne cried. "We know that. That's why they need your aid."

"I don't get involved in the politics of this world," Leonetta said, eyeing Snow with interest. "And this one right here should already be dead like her mother."

Snow shuddered. "I almost was, but I got away. Please help us find a way to continue unseen. We are told you can make such things happen."

"I can, but it will be difficult," the woman said. "There is a mark on your heads. Both of them," she said, gesturing toward Snow and Henri. "And one may not fare as well as the other in the end."

"Please," Snow tried again, and she pulled the blue necklace out of her breast pocket. "I believe you may have once helped my father—King Georg."

The woman raised one black eyebrow in surprise. "It is the necklace he kept close to his heart! If the king has given it up, then you truly must need my help. That necklace has protected him for years. Come in." She looked at the sky again. "Before she sees. Quickly!"

She ushered them inside her cramped abode. It was a single room. Herbs and roots, either by design or nature, hung from the ceiling, and a cauldron bubbled in the center of the room. There was a large table with pots and containers holding worms and various creatures, alive and dead.

"I met the king when I journeyed through the kingdom he was banished to," Leonetta said, walking toward the table and examining a jarful of worms. "His life of late had been filled with such sorrow, and yet he never lost faith." She looked at Snow. "He knew you'd make an excellent ruler if given the chance, and begged me to watch over and protect you from afar. I have tried my best, but the queen makes it difficult. Her dark magic is very powerful and you have been locked away for so long. Is he right to put his faith in you?"

"Yes," Snow promised. "I will not let my kingdom down."

Leonetta studied her for a moment. "I believe you." She began pouring things into a pot. The liquid turned blue as she added water. "Just as I believed him. Why do you think I used magic in that necklace to cloak his movements from her? I sent the spell that would keep him from being seen inside his abode. The king deserves some privacy until he is finally free." She pointed to Snow. "You are the one who can do that."

"I know. I won't fail." Snow paused. "I will take her dark magic and use it to force her off the throne and return my father home."

Leonetta scratched a wart on her chin. "And if you succeed, and wear the crown, will you help me if I call? As I am willing to help you?"

Snow wasn't sure what to make of this request. What would Leonetta ask of her? It was a difficult decision, but her instincts told her she could trust this woman. "I will."

Leonetta flashed a yellowed grin. "I know you will, my future queen. Let's get you and the prince to the castle unseen." She chopped several herbs and threw them in the pot. It made a small explosion, but she seemed unconcerned.

"Sorceress Leonetta, how long will this spell take?" Anne asked. "We haven't much time, and I suspect a spell like this will be complicated."

"It is!" Leonetta agreed. "That's why I don't need any interruptions." She wagged a finger at Anne. "There may come a day when you also need me, but it's not today. You wait outside. I need to concentrate."

Anne looked at Snow, and she nodded. Then Anne went to the door.

"I must warn you, you will only remain unseen until you set foot on the castle grounds. Once inside, you are on your own." Leonetta spoke again once the door closed, her face grim. "The queen controls the magic within those walls. I suggest you trust no one but each other, and even then, don't be fooled by appearances."

Snow wasn't sure what she meant by that, but she nodded all the same. "How do you plan on making us invisible?" This seemed the most impossible idea in the world.

Leonetta smiled as she dropped four mealworms into the pot. Henri began to gag. "Not literally invisible, my dear princess. Instead, I will cloak you from her. She will not be able to find you, for you will look completely different than you do to me or anyone else you encounter." She ladled the bubbling concoction into two mugs and handed them to Henri and Snow. "Drink up!"

Henri looked into his cup of broth and dead mealworms and started to gag again. "I'll go first."

"No, I will," Snow said. He was doing this for her, so she should be the one who took the risk. *One step at a time.* With that thought running through her mind, Snow drank the concoction. It was tangy and tasted like ginger, but it wasn't as bitter as she'd imagined.

She looked at Henri. He took a deep breath and chugged. They looked at one another. Neither's appearance had changed.

"It didn't work," said Snow.

Leonetta tsked. "Ye of little faith! Look at yourselves through this!" She went digging in a box on the floor and came up with a small dirty mirror. She wiped the glass on her apron and handed it to Snow. Henri walked up behind her and the two stared at their reflections. Or at what *should* have been their reflections. Snow's eyes were now green instead of amber. Her hair was now a wispy mop of long blond locks in two braids piled on top of her head. Her body looked thicker than her own and shorter, while Henri seemed to have sprouted two inches and had her jet-black hair instead of his normal brown. His eyes were a deep chestnut, and he had long lashes that blinked anxiously at he stared at the man in the mirror.

"This is . . . hard to get used to," he said, touching the hair on his head.

"Enjoy it!" Leonetta said. "Tomorrow you face the consequences that come with challenging the queen. You will need all your wits and your strength about you, so today you should continue to let your relationship blossom. You will need to draw on its power."

Snow didn't understand what Leonetta meant by that. It felt like something was about to go wrong, and if that was the case . . . "If you can see what comes next, wouldn't it help us to know?"

Leonetta busied herself cleaning up the cauldron. "Why, I can't predict the future! Futures change depending on who tries to change them." She pointed to both of them. "Remember your feelings for each other." Snow and Henri looked at one another and then away. Snow's face felt very warm. "Your hearts are stronger than you realize," Leonetta said.

And with that, the enchantress unceremoniously pushed them out the door. Within seconds, vines grew over the entrance, obstructing it from view.

Anne blinked at them in wonder. "Snow? Henrich? Is that really you?"

Snow took Anne's hand so she wasn't frightened. "Yes! It truly is!" They all started to laugh. It was almost too impossible to believe.

"You are truly disguised!" Anne said. "There's a small hamlet right outside the castle village where we can celebrate. Hopefully the others will begin to arrive in the area tomorrow and we can discuss how we will descend on the castle."

The warmth of the sun felt good on Snow's skin after so much rain.

"Come on, you two," Anne said, beckoning them to follow her down the path that would lead them to their destination. A blue jay flew over their heads and began to lead the way. Snow and Henri filled Anne in on the rest of their visit with the enchantress, including the fact that the spell would not hold once they reached the castle—though they both carefully avoided the woman's advice about their growing feelings.

It was just growing dark as they made their way to an inn, where a sign offering a reward for Snow's capture had been torn in half on the door. Snow wondered if this meant the people inside were friends, not foes. Either way, she would not give herself away. Anne decided it was safer if she was the one who made conversation with people at the tavern to see if they could add to their ranks, while Henri paid for two rooms for the night, giving one to Snow and Anne and taking the other for himself. It would feel strange being so close to the castle and placing her head on a pillow that was not her own. The tavern sounded boisterous.

"I've met two men already who are here to help aid the princess," Anne said with a pointed look when she returned to Snow. "They said there are growing numbers of folks arriving and camping out in the woods. A group of little men are said to be leading the charge, but are waiting on word from the princess to storm the castle." She raised her right eyebrow.

The dwarfs were safe. Thank the heavens. "We should send word that the princess is safe and ready to take back the castle with them at noon," Snow said. Midday was usually when most guards took their main meal, if they had one to eat. Perhaps it would give her friends an advantage.

"I can tell the others to be ready then, but there is still the problem of getting you in the castle unseen," Anne said.

"Maybe you could take us separately. I could sneak in first so that I'm there to provide a distraction if needed once Snow gets inside," Henri suggested.

"It's too dangerous," Snow protested. "You've done so much already."

He took her hand. "And I would gladly do more. I believe in you. Please believe in me and let me do this." He looked her straight in the eye.

"I believe in you, too," she said softly. Snow didn't want to let go of Henri's hand. "But you must be careful. Find safe haven until it is absolutely necessary to intervene."

"I'll be safe," he said.

"The kitchen," she said quickly, thinking of Mrs. Kindred. "Say you are her new baker. The queen fired the old one. You'll be all right there."

"Okay. Tonight, I'll go find the others and tell them our plan," Anne said. "I'll come back and take Henri at first light so we can enter unseen. Then I can slip back out and come for you."

"All right," Snow agreed. There was a lot placed on Anne, but Snow had faith she could do it.

Anne placed her hood over her head. "I'll meet you in our room later, after I go see the men. Try to keep your mind at ease while I'm gone."

Snow hugged her. "Be safe, my new friend."

Henri led Snow to a table, and food was set down before they knew it, as were their drinks. The tavern grew louder as people kept drifting in—travelers, locals, even beggars. Some were turned away and others were not. Henri raised his glass.

"To storming the castle, tomorrow," he said.

She held up her glass and clinked it with his. "To tomorrow and all the days that will come after."

Ingrid

Who was this boy? A prince from a neighboring kingdom. That much she knew, but how she regretted declining his request for a meeting at the castle when he'd come. She'd worried he'd want to ask for Snow's hand, so she'd sent him away, never knowing he'd find her again. How was it even possible?

Like so much that she had anticipated, she had been wrong.

The huntsman had failed her.

Snow had found safe haven.

Now the princess was returning to the castle for her crown.

What did the boy get out of her escorting her like this?

She'd been watching them since they'd emerged from

the cave unscathed and made their way to a nearby village. She had been certain someone there who had seen her generous reward proclamations for the princess's capture would turn her in, but no.

Instead, Snow had embarked on the road again, nearing the castle with each step. And this time, she didn't just have the boy with her. She had a girl, too. It was hard to tell who she was with the hood raised above her head, but Ingrid would find out. She couldn't sleep, couldn't eat, couldn't breathe till she figured out what to do with Snow and her prince.

"Show me Snow White," she requested for what was surely the tenth time that day.

The mirror began to smoke and she watched the glass begin to swirl, turning violet then pale green. Then the masklike face appeared.

"Alas, something is not right. The fairest and her beau are mist on a bright summer's day. They have vanished in plain sight."

"You can't find them?" Her whole body tensed. "How is that possible?" Ingrid began to pace back and forth in front of the mirror, feeling like a large cat about to pounce. Suddenly, Katherine appeared and began to walk in her footsteps. Ingrid flicked her cape out, making the image of Katherine disappear. Momentarily.

"As though under the snow for which she's named, their footprints are gone. And magic is to blame," the mirror replied.

"No!" Ingrid swept her arm across a table, knocking over several seeping vials. They crashed to the floor and shattered. "How do I break the spell?"

"They must pass the castle gate. Only then will their true selves emerge. It appears you must wait."

"Someone must be hiding them! Who?" she snapped. "There is a price on the princess's head. The whole kingdom knows that! Who dares disobey that? When will I see them?"

"The magic has been planted like a powerful seed," the mirror replied, and Ingrid let out a low growl that turned into a cough in her old hag voice. The mirror continued, "From an enchantress. One who helped the king in his time of need."

Ingrid had a sudden urge to throw things against the wall. Instead, she steadied her breath. "Georg?!" Instantly, Katherine appeared by her side again. She was the thorn that would not go away. "But how? He can't be inside our borders! He's bound by magic. Show him to me."

A blurry image appeared in the mirror, and for the first time in the last few days, Ingrid breathed a sigh of relief. Yes, there he was, pacing in his dank cottage, looking very much worse for wear. She realized it had been many years since she had last seen him. But he was still where she'd left him. And yet, he'd found a way to help Snow. . . .

"How did this happen? What do I need to do?"

"Choose," the mirror said simply.

"Choose?" Ingrid repeated, confused.

"The crown or your mirror, which will you choose?" the mirror replied. "If you try to keep both, you will surely lose."

"I am not choosing!" Ingrid thundered. "I earned this crown! I have given everything I have to you as well! I am not being banished or made to choose by a young girl who doesn't know what it takes to rule!"

"Life is not fair, this you know," the mirror replied. "Try to keep all you have obtained and you will lose everything—including me—to Snow."

"But how?" Ingrid cried. "She's only been in your presence once, and she was just a small child. No one even knows you're here. How could she possibly imagine what you're capable of?" Ingrid stopped pacing and clutched the mirror's gilded frame for strength. "Unless . . ." The image suddenly came to her so strongly she could see it in her mind's eye. "Of course. Georg told her."

"The ties that bind are strong," the mirror said. "The

fairest in the land has consulted her father; she has the people on her side. She can do no wrong."

"Stop calling her that!" Ingrid screamed, and she felt the crack before she heard it. She looked up to see the fracture in the mirror growing. She felt a sudden sharp pain in her right arm and she clutched it, gasping in horror as a blue-gray vein trailed from her fingers up her arm to her elbow, growing and spreading like a weed. "What is happening?"

"We have become one," the mirror replied. "My fate is yours. And yours is almost undone."

More damage to the mirror would cause her death? Was that what the mirror meant?

She didn't want to know for sure, but she suspected as much. Were they *too* close now? In the recesses of her mind she'd allowed herself to wonder, but never fully, as the mirror could hear every thought. It knew her every action, and she had given it that privilege. Now her body was paying for it. "What do we need to do?" Ingrid whispered, holding her arm, which was burning.

"Choose."

"No." Ingrid was firm. "I won't. I need both." She tapped her chin, which had a single hair sticking out of it. "There has to be another way." She glanced at the smoking mirror and had an idea.

Smoke the girl out.

Yes.

The girl was already coming. There was no stopping that. So then let Snow come. She would be ready for her.

Ingrid glanced at the poison apple that remained unused, lying on top of a basket of fruit. Its potency was still strong.

Snow knew what Ingrid most wanted: the mirror and the crown. What did her niece most want? Not the crown. No, the girl never seemed to ache for power the way she had. The girl had lost her mother and her father. She'd raised herself. What she most wanted was . . .

"Love," the mirror replied.

Love. Such a foolish thing, to love another. It made a person weak.

Which was what she was counting on.

So she couldn't get to Snow via the dwarfs or the prince. No matter, there was another loved one she could use to her advantage. It was time King Georg returned to his castle . . . or more precisely, became comfortable in the dungeons, where Snow would never find him.

She picked up the poison apple and looked it over. The girl would come for her father. And the poison would still work if she could get the apple to her.

Ingrid smiled. She had a plan, and she was prepared to follow it through to the end.

"Magic Mirror? Keep an eye out for the princess," Ingrid said. "For the first time in a long while, I'm looking forward to having visitors."

Snow

Just before dawn, while the rest of the inn and the kingdom slept, Snow, Henri, and Anne made their way to the edge of the forest, where their forces were waiting in the dewy early morning light. There was a light fog, making it hard for Snow to see, but she kept moving forward. She was desperate to see the dwarfs again and whatever villagers they had gathered. Perhaps they would have as many as twenty. But when she reached the hilltop, she gasped in surprise.

There weren't twenty villagers waiting for her.

There were hundreds—women and men, old and young.

Seeing Snow, they raised their weapons.

"Who are you?" Grumpy thundered.

And that's when Snow remembered—she didn't look like herself.

Henri put his hand on his sheath, his pocketknife within reach. Snow reached out and touched his hand. "It will be all right."

"I bring the one you seek," Anne announced, leading the way. "You may not be able to see her clearly with your own two eyes, but I know for certain that the one you are looking for is here in front of you. All you need to do is listen to the sound of her voice."

"What is this hogwash?" Grumpy blustered. "I don't know those two! Who are you? And what are you doing here?"

"Where's the princess?" someone in the crowd shouted.

Snow feared their voices would soon give their gathering away. She stepped forward before things could get out of hand. "She's right here," she said, and the men looked at her. "The same one who cooked and cleaned by your side in the cottage stands before you. But thanks to a bit of magic, I look nothing like myself, which is how I'm able to walk through our kingdom unseen." As though further proof was needed, a cardinal landed on Snow's shoulder and tweeted happily.

"Snow?" Grumpy repeated.

"Yes," Snow said with a pleasant laugh, clearly her own. "It is me! I'm so glad to see you all. I was so worried after the cave-in. Where is Dopey? Is he all right?"

Dopey jumped from the crowd and hugged Snow's waist fiercely.

"Dopey! I'm so glad you're all right," she cried.

"It *is* you!" Happy cried, rushing toward her and giving her a quick a hug.

"You look better with brown hair," Grumpy said to Henri before shaking his hand. "Thanks for getting her here in one piece."

Henri eyed Snow. "I assure you, she's more than capable of doing that on her own."

Grumpy turned to Snow. "It's good to see you . . . well, sort of see you."

"The magic only lasts until I reach the castle gates," Snow explained. "We were helped by an enchantress. It was Anne's idea."

"Who's Anne?" Doc asked.

Snow turned to the girl, who remained hidden under her hood to avoid being seen. "My friend." Both girls smiled. "She has agreed to take Henri to the castle now so that he will be inside waiting for me, should I need backup getting to the queen's chambers. I will slip in once the fighting starts. The diversion will give me a chance to get in unseen and make my way to the queen."

Grumpy sighed. "Are you sure you don't want us coming with you?"

Snow clasped his hand. "I need you at the castle, leading the rest of the men. It's because of you and the others that a group of this size has gathered here to help us. You must be a strong speaker."

Grumpy blushed. "I just told them the truth. We need the Evil Queen gone."

"Maybe *you'd* like to say a few words?" Doc suggested.

Snow looked around at the group of people, with their varying sizes and strengths. Some had nothing more than a slingshot, but they were all there, ready to fight for her. She felt overcome with emotion as she stepped forward. "My faithful subjects, I know it doesn't look like it, but I am the lost princess. I say lost, because that is how I've felt the last few years living under the Evil Queen's rule. I accepted my fate, thinking there was nothing to do to change it, but I realize I was wrong. As the daughter of King Georg and Queen Katherine, I am this kingdom's rightful heir, and it is my job to fight for my people. I want all of us to live as happily and harmoniously as we can, and we cannot do that under the current regime. I will do all I can to change that." She looked around at their solemn faces. "Your presence here means more than I could ever convey. We have something the Evil Queen will never have—friendships, families, allies. In short, each other."

There could be no clapping—not if they didn't want to be heard—but one after another, men moved forward to shake the hand of their princess. By the time Snow made her way back to Henri and Anne, they had both been moved to tears, and Grumpy was dabbing at his eyes with a handkerchief.

"That was beautiful, Snow," Anne whispered.

"Spoken like a true leader," Henri agreed.

Grumpy grunted. "Let's stop sitting around and help her become one. When do we move out?"

"He's right," Anne said. "It's time I take Henri to the castle."

Snow nodded. "Grumpy, will you gather the rest and hide near the castle? When the clock strikes at noon, it will be time for you all to burst from the shadows and invade the castle. Meanwhile, I'll travel with Anne and slip inside once the invasion starts."

Grumpy nodded.

Snow looked at the prince. "Henri . . . that means you'll be alone in there for hours."

"I know," Henri said. "But I had an idea. Anne? Do you think we could get ahold of a guard's uniform? Then I'll be cloaked even once I'm inside the castle walls."

"That could work against the guards, but the mirror could know you're there," Snow argued. "You still must stay hidden."

"I will," said Henri. "I will find somewhere safe. But the uniform will help."

"The kitchen," Snow reminded him. "Look for Mrs. Kindred. She is a kind soul. And no one comes to the kitchen."

"Then the kitchen is where I will be," Henri promised. His eyes never left her face.

The sky was already a bright pink and the fog had begun to lift. Clouds were parting and the dark blue of night was giving way to morning. Anne tightened her hood.

"We should hurry. Everyone will be up soon." She hugged Snow tight. "Be safe. I'll be back as soon as I can."

"You too, friend," Snow said, and then turned to Henri.

She wasn't sure what to do. Hug him? Shake his hand? No. What could she say to the boy who had protected her and slowly become her most trusted confidant? Seeing him prepare to leave left an ache in her heart she'd never felt before. "Be careful," she said.

"You too," he said with a soft smile. "I want you to have this." Henri placed something cold in her palm. She opened her hand. It was his pocketknife. Her fingers brushed against the engraving of Henri's brother's initials. "To keep you safe while I'm gone."

"No." Snow tried to hand it back to him. "I couldn't. You'd have no weapon!"

Henri shook his head. "I don't need one. I know you're coming, and you'll look out for me." He touched her hair and she felt her cheeks warm. "You're kind and clever, Snow. One of the best I've ever known. I feel safe in your care."

Snow placed the knife in a pocket in her skirt. "And I yours. Will you hold on to this for me, then?" She pulled her mother's necklace out of her pocket and put it in his hand. "We will exchange them later."

He placed the necklace in his leather vest pocket. "I will guard it with my life. Till I see you again." He reached out and kissed her hand.

She blushed. "Till I see you again."

She watched Anne and Henri disappear into the tree line, knowing she'd count the minutes till that moment.

Ingrid

Finally, the tide was turning in her favor.

King Georg was locked in the dungeons next to a skeleton that had fared far worse than he. She couldn't even remember who the poor soul was, but she knew Georg the moment she saw him. Even after all these years, his blue eyes were still brazen.

"Who are you?" he asked.

Ingrid cackled, her voice sounding so unlike her own. "Who do you think, darling Georg? It is I, your wife."

"My wife died at your queen's hands when Snow was merely a girl!" Georg thundered.

Ingrid rattled the bars. "And your new wife stands right here in front of you, masked in the ultimate disguise."

"Dark magic!" He pointed a wobbly finger in her direction. "You're a witch!"

"Yes, you should know that by now," Ingrid said with another laugh. "Have you missed me?"

"You will not win this fight, Ingrid," Georg said. "She will kill you."

"I'd like to see her try." Then Ingrid turned on her heel and left him there to rot.

By the time she reached her chambers, the mirror was alive with news.

"She is still in shadows, but the boy has stepped into the light," the mirror revealed. "He is here in your castle, in plain sight." The mirror showed the prince sneaking in through a door with the help of the same girl who had been with Snow the day before. Ingrid watched as the girl lowered her hood. She recognized her immediately. It was the tailor's daughter. She and her mother would pay for this disloyalty. Later.

So the cowardly girl had sent the boy in first. She looked at the apple still in her possession. Maybe she didn't need to use it on the girl, after all. The boy wouldn't even see it coming. She could finally get to him, picking off Snow's allies one by one. This would only motivate the girl to get to the castle quicker. Her end would then be imminent.

Poison the boy instead, the voice in her head said. Or

maybe it was the mirror. She could never be sure anymore.

Katherine's smoky image appeared again. It stared at Ingrid somberly, making her feel uneasy. There wasn't a moment of the day that she didn't see her dead sister now. She was going mad, wasn't she? Snow had done this to her.

Ingrid watched the boy descend the steps to the kitchen. The tailor's daughter slipped back up the stairs again and out of view. Perhaps she was going back for Snow—which meant the boy was alone. The situation couldn't be more perfect.

"The end is near, the sun is high," the mirror said. "If you don't choose, we shall surely die."

Never.

She had a better plan. She laced her fingers together and smiled wickedly. "I think it's time I met Snow White's prince."

Snow

Something was wrong.

The sun was now high in the sky and Anne still had not returned. The others were growing anxious and so was Snow.

Had Anne been caught sneaking Henri inside the castle? Was she in danger? Was Henri? Snow couldn't bear the thought of either of them in the queen's clutches.

"I think we should begin to make our way to the castle," Grumpy said.

"But Anne has not returned," Snow reminded him. The woods were so quiet she could hear passersby talking as they approached. Every time she heard a voice, she thought it was Anne.

She had a sudden urge to rush to the castle to see for herself, but that was foolish. She'd give herself away the minute she stepped onto the grounds. She needed to wait here and trust that Anne would come back for her.

"It is getting too busy in these parts to stay here," Grumpy told her. "We must start to disband and make our way into the village without rousing suspicion."

That made sense. But where was Anne? She heard rustling in the bushes, and she and Grumpy turned around. Several men moved in closer with their weapons. Anne burst through the trees, sounding breathless.

"Anne!" Snow ran to her. The two quickly embraced. "I'm so glad you are safe."

"Yes," Anne assured her, holding her close. "And so is Henri. He's in the kitchen."

Snow exhaled slowly. "Good."

Anne pulled away. "I tried to get back sooner, but there was a commotion in the castle. Guards were moving quickly and gathering weapons. For a moment, I thought they knew you were coming." Grumpy and Snow looked at one another. "But then I saw them bring a man in to the dungeons." Anne licked her lips nervously. "Snow, I think it was King Georg!"

Snow steadied herself. She should have known the queen wouldn't go without a fight. She'd tried to have her killed, sent weather to destroy her, and put a price on her head. Now she had reclaimed Snow's father. It worried her to know he was in the queen's possession, and yet there was a part of her that was a little pleased by this development. If the king had returned to the kingdom, then his curse had been lifted.

Yes, he was in the dungeon, but she was certain Aunt Ingrid wouldn't kill him. She knew Snow was coming, and her father would be used as bait.

"He will be all right," Snow assured her. "We all will be once this is over." Anne looked confused. "Let's just get to the castle."

Ingrid

The ragged cloak she had on would not do, but that was an easy fix. Moving to the pile of discarded clothing she had from the tailor, she pieced together something more peasantlike. She pulled her dry white hair back under a handkerchief and hoped the brown sack of a dress she had on looked more kitchen appropriate. The thing itched like crazy. How did people wear such things? She had long forgotten.

Slipping through her corridor, she found a guard and spoke to him in the shadows, making like one of those incessant maids who used to always be hovering about till she'd had most of them dismissed. "You! The queen wants you to fetch Mrs. Kindred at once and send her to the market for fresh herbs. Her Majesty would like roast duck for dinner and she won't like it if I tell her no for an answer."

"Yes, miss." The guard hurried off.

If the woman did come back with a roast duck for dinner, it would be a feast worth savoring. By evening, Ingrid would have triumphed, and the mirror would know she had been right to fight for all the things she had worked for.

Ingrid clutched her basket of apples as she rushed through the shadows. She went down the stairs, feeling the air grow cooler as she reached the basement. She smelled a stew bubbling on the hearth when she entered the room. Mrs. Kindred was gone and the room was empty. Or so it seemed. Quietly, she walked around, looking for places large enough for a prince to hide.

Her eyes landed on the large cupboard. They'd had one just like it in her home with Katherine as a child. It was always almost empty, never holding the things she needed to make meals. But this cupboard should be full of flour and sugar and other necessities. Ingrid glanced at the table. All those items were on top of it instead of locked up tight.

She walked to the cabinet and opened the door. There was the prince, crouched down inside, looking sweaty and worried. Perfect. "What do we have here?"

The prince jumped out, wearing a guard's uniform. Where had he procured that?

"Please don't say anything," the prince said. "I'm not here to steal anything. Mrs. Kindred said I could stay here for a spell."

That woman would be dismissed immediately.

Well, after the roast duck was served.

"Of course!" Ingrid croaked. "But it's much more comfortable out here than in a cabinet. Come!"

The boy hesitated. "I'm not sure I should be seen."

"Nonsense!" Ingrid said. "I'm Mrs. Kindred's assistant and I'm the only one who will be down here while she's gone. Come. Sit. Eat something! You look dreadful."

The boy laughed good-naturedly. "It was hot in there. Thank you, kind woman."

"You're welcome," she said, and made herself look busy around the kitchen, moving spoons and bowls and not doing much else. Her eyes never left the basket of apples on the table. "So, are you hungry?"

"A little," he admitted. "But, please, don't go to any trouble. Just giving me somewhere to stay right now is all I need."

Ingrid waved her arm in the air. It burned as she made the motion; she was still in pain. "I insist." Moving to the basket of apples, Ingrid eyed the poison one on top of the pile.

Choose, the mirror called to her.

She ignored it, her hands shaking as she reached for the basket. She held out the poisoned one in her wrinkled hands. "Here. A lovely apple. Do you like apples?"

The prince smiled as he stared at her outstretched hand. He was a handsome boy. Such a pity the princess had dragged him into this mess. "Yes, I do. They look delicious."

"Wait till you taste one, dearie." Her voice dropped to a whisper. Her heart started to thump and she felt every nerve in her body tingling. "Go on, take it."

The prince took the apple from her hands. "Thank you for your kindness."

"Of course! Fairest apples in the land!" *They're to die for.*

She held her breath as he brought the apple to his lips. She watched anxiously as he bit down and took his first—and last—bite. The change in his face was instant.

"I think there is something wrong with this," he said.

He stumbled backward, falling into a pile of pots and sending lids clattering to the floor. He reached for something in his pocket, but pulled out nothing. If it was supposed to be a weapon, he had lost it. She stood there, lacing her fingers with pleasure, and watched him collapse on the floor.

"I feel so strange." He looked at her. "Help me."

She watched as the apple fell from his hand and rolled across the floor. It landed with the bite mark visible. It was already beginning to brown.

Ingrid let out a cackle so loud she thought it might wake the dead.

Snow

Snow followed Anne through the forest, her mind on her father and Henri and the castle looming in the distance.

They had planned for everything one could plan for, and the rest would be up to fate.

Stay with me, Mother, she thought, watching a flock of birds fly overhead, making their way to the castle and possibly the aviary. *Help me save our kingdom.*

Her mother didn't reply, of course. Snow hadn't seen her in her dreams since the night she'd dreamed of the mirror. Her father was now imprisoned and Henri was hiding somewhere in the castle, his life in danger. All of their lives were. The men had set out in different directions to slip into the village unnoticed and were ready to fight for her.

Everyone had put themselves in the line of fire for her. She refused to do anything but succeed.

But what would a successful outcome truly be? She felt Henri's knife in her skirt pocket and patted it as if to remind herself it was there. Her father wanted the Evil Queen dead. Would it come to that? She couldn't even imagine holding the knife in her hand, let alone trying to harm someone with it. She wasn't her aunt. She didn't kill in cold blood. She hoped for the thousandth time that taking the mirror would be enough to make her aunt leave and never look back. If not, she'd have to reassess.

They made their way down the rural path, through the brambles, for what felt like an eternity, the castle looming above them.

"This way." Anne beckoned, leading Snow through an entrance to the village that was unusually quiet. The streets that she'd thought would be bustling were empty. She noticed a proclamation nailed to a wrought iron post. There was to be a celebration at noon and all villagers were expected to attend. The timing of this unexpected occasion filled her heart with dread. Did this have to do with her father?

Before she could even really begin to wonder what it was about, they heard shouting, and the sound of someone running. Had Grumpy started the invasion too soon?

A man rushed past them with a wild look in his eyes.

"The queen is a witch!" he shouted, getting in Snow's face. "Steer clear of the town square—run! Hide! Or Queen Ingrid will curse you, too."

Curse?

Snow took off running, ignoring the cries of Anne and the wailing in the streets. She pushed her way to the front of the crowd and saw him lying there.

It wasn't her father. It was Henri.

Her Henri. Lying in a glass coffin.

"No!" she cried, pushing her way inside the gates and up to the platform, where he lay as pale as death. His body was on display in its glass tomb. She choked down a sob as she reached him, knowing full well her magic had dissolved the minute she'd entered the castle gates.

"It's the princess!" someone cried.

"Snow! Wait!" she heard Anne shout.

But she couldn't. She had to reach Henri. She opened the glass coffin lid and lay her head on his chest, listening for the most important sound in the world: his beating heart.

She didn't hear it. Instead, she felt herself being ripped off the platform and dragged toward the castle by a guard, who was laughing in her face. "Welcome home, Snow White."

Ingrid

From her window, she could see the pandemonium, and she drank it in like the most wondrous elixir. The boy's body was on display for the entire village to see, and the fear on their faces was palpable. She watched as Snow White was dragged away from the boy's glass coffin. The princess would be delivered to her chambers at any moment. Snow White's "army," if one could even call it that, had been scared away.

Ingrid turned away from the window with a feeling of smug satisfaction. The mirror had been wrong. She *could* have it all.

Choose, the mirror surprisingly implored her again. Ingrid looked toward the mirror's room and saw Katherine and her master watching sadly. She ignored them and went straight to her door, where she heard a sudden commotion.

Seconds later, a guard opened the door, tossed Snow White inside, and quickly shut the door behind him, as instructed.

Ingrid watched as Snow fell to the floor, a look of horror written on her face. Her plan had worked. Snow White was broken. Now it was time to finish her off.

"Get up!" Ingrid croaked, and Snow lifted her head in surprise.

"Who are you?" Snow whispered, staring at Ingrid.

Ingrid rolled her eyes. Sometimes she forgot she hadn't had time to reverse the hag spell yet, despite her wrinkled hands. "I'm the one who cursed your prince," she cackled, and Snow's face paled. Ingrid's voice deepened. "Yes. It is me. I am your queen, child! You're not the only one who knows how to cloak your appearance with magic. Now rise and show some respect." Snow White stood. "Come with me!" Ingrid beckoned. Katherine and her master walked silently alongside her, but Ingrid wasn't worried. *The mirror needs to see how this all ends,* she thought. *Then it will never question me again.*

The chamber was dark except for the mirror, which was smoking and glowed green and yellow.

Snow stared at it in horror. "So it's true. This is the source of your power. A magic mirror."

"*I* am the source of my power," Ingrid declared. "I have spent decades working for this crown! Do you think I'd really be so foolish as to let a child take it all away?"

"Is Henri dead?" Snow whispered. She held her breath as she waited for the answer.

Ingrid pressed her lips together. "He's as good as dead. He had no right to enter this castle and aid you in taking away my throne." Her eyes blazed. "How dare you challenge me?"

"That throne belongs to my family," Snow said shakily, but she stood straighter. Katherine moved to stand right beside her. "I know what you did to my father. I know, now, that he didn't abandon me."

"That fool was in no position to run a kingdom! He was weak!" She hobbled closer, the whites of her eyes blazing.

Snow inhaled sharply. "If you harm him . . . if you hurt him like you did my mother . . ."

Ingrid laughed the threat away. "I don't need to harm him. He will harm himself, without anyone to live for! He couldn't survive without your mother!"

"Who you had killed!" Snow cried.

Ingrid felt a sharp pain in her right side and grew silent. She looked from Snow to Katherine, who stood so close she could've touched the girl if such a thing were possible. If it had been possible for Ingrid to regret one thing, it would've been her sister's death. But Katherine, like her daughter, hadn't been able to leave well enough alone. "It's not as simple as you make it out to be," Ingrid said quietly.

"She was your sister," Snow argued. "She'd brought you to the castle to have a good life, and you betrayed her. You left me motherless as a small child. You broke my father's heart, then put a love spell on him and banished him!"

Ingrid refused to look at Snow or Katherine when she spoke. "You were a child and couldn't understand the ways of the world. Your mother threatened my future and gave me no choice."

There was a pounding at the door and both Snow and Ingrid jumped. No one had ever dared enter her chambers before, let alone make their way to her secret room and try to enter.

"My queen!" Ingrid heard a muffled voice shout. "They've broken through the castle gates! We can't hold them off; there's too many of them! We must get you out of here."

Ingrid looked at Snow, who suddenly looked wiser than her years.

"We all have choices," Snow said, her voice stronger. "You chose to put Queen Katherine in the ground to protect your precious mirror."

Ingrid flew at Snow. "Do not say my sister's name to me!"

"My queen! You must hurry!" the voice said again.

"Choose," the mirror uttered for all to hear.

"The mirror can speak?" Snow said, mesmerized by the masklike face that began to appear in the glass.

"Soon it will be too late. Act now. Remedy your mistake!" the mirror told Ingrid.

Ingrid covered her ears, unable to think clearly in the commotion. Snow moved in on her.

"I know the truth now, and the rest of our people soon will, too," Snow declared. "About all of us—King Georg, Queen Katherine—"

Ingrid ripped at her coarse white hair, her face scrunched up with anger. "I said, do not mention my sister's name to me!"

"My queen! You must hurry!" the guard outside the door said again.

"Katherine!" Snow said again, her voice louder and clearer than it had been moments before. "Katherine! Katherine! Katherine!"

Ingrid couldn't take it anymore. She began to scream, the sound so loud it vibrated off the walls. The cracks in the mirror began to grow.

Snow

Her aunt's scream was so shrill it forced Snow to cover her ears. Her aunt was doing the same thing, the sound of her own voice seemingly tearing her frail body apart.

The once mighty Evil Queen had transformed into a hag, and Snow could not fathom why she had not turned back. The spell, Snow realized now, must be draining her.

Now, Snow. Now! a voice inside her commanded. Now *what?* she wanted to ask. The voice felt like her mother's. Perhaps it was her own. For some reason, in this cold dark room where so much evil reigned, she could feel her mother's presence guiding her. And she could also feel a strong, building self-assurance that she had never experienced before. Despite the danger. Despite the loss, she did not feel afraid.

The guard had said her army was invading the castle. Someone would find her father in the dungeons and set him free. Aunt Ingrid would be stripped of her crown. But what of the mirror? From the moment Snow had entered the chamber, she could feel it pulling at her, beckoning her to come closer. This mirror with the masklike face had darkened her aunt's soul. It had convinced her to kill her sister, trick Snow's father, and sentence Snow to death. Yes, those were Aunt Ingrid's actions, but the mirror obviously had an influence over her. Something so heinous should not be allowed to exist. *Now, Snow! Now!* she heard the voice in her head say again.

When she looked up, she could see the mirror's glass cracking. The fissure was spreading in various directions, like a spider's web. As it cracked, Ingrid's wails grew louder. It was almost as if the mirror was tearing her apart, and despite all that had happened, Snow felt pity for the woman before her.

If she destroyed the mirror before it destroyed Aunt Ingrid, would that be enough?

Snow's heart began to pound in her chest. She reached for Henri's knife to see if it was still in her pocket. The cold steel was there. Her fingers grasped the handle.

Now, Snow! Now!

She might not have been able to strike a knife through her aunt's heart, but she had no qualms about breaking a mirror. Snow stepped forward, the knife raised above her head.

Her aunt slowly turned around. "What are you doing?" she cried.

"Snow White, the fairest in the land," the mirror spoke, and Snow faltered. "You could be so much more if you put your fate in my hands."

For a moment, Snow hesitated.

"Don't talk to her!" Aunt Ingrid screamed, but her legs seemed to fail her. She fell to the ground on her hands and knees.

"Touch the glass and let me show you the way," the mirror said. "You are stronger than your queen. With my help you could rule this day."

"NO!" Aunt Ingrid cried, and she lunged forward on her knees. "Don't touch it!"

Snow did not need her aunt's guidance. She would not be fooled by the mirror's lies.

Snow plunged the knife deep into the fractured glass, cracking the mirror's surface even further. The glow from the mirror began to brighten and the green soon turned to red as Snow struck the mirror again and again. Her aunt screamed, but Snow kept striking until the mirror finally shattered into a million pieces. The glass exploded, a strong wind and a sound like a roar accompanying it. It blew the

Evil Queen backward and sent Snow to the ground. She covered her face as fiery red glass flew through the room, shattering the windows and plunging the entire castle into darkness.

Ingrid

When she opened her eyes, all she felt was sharp pain. She held up her hands and saw blood trickling down her scaly arms. She wasn't sure where she was.

Ingrid looked up, startled to see the woman standing over her.

"Katherine?" she croaked, not recognizing her own voice.

"It's Snow White," the woman replied. "You will be tried for your crimes. Guards, take her away."

"What?" she cried as two men raised her to standing and pulled on her arms. The guards were not in uniform. In fact, they looked like peasants! She tried to pull her arms away, but they held firm. It hurt to be touched.

The windows in the chamber were blown out, letting in the light of day. Her eyes adjusted and she noticed the glass littering the floor. She looked at her precious mirror's frame. It was empty. The glass had been completely destroyed.

After all the sacrifices she had made to get here—leaving her master and watching him die, having Katherine poisoned, banishing Georg, ordering the huntsman to kill Snow White, poisoning the prince—she was left with nothing. Her mirror, her most trusted companion and faithful servant, was gone and her life was in ruins. She stared down at her old hands, which were shaking. She couldn't stay a hag a moment longer. Her eyes darted to her potion table, where several bottles were overturned and the liquid was dripping onto the floor. "Just give me a moment." She needed to reverse this spell. The men wouldn't let go of her arms. "I'm the queen! I deserve respect."

The men scoffed. "Doesn't look like the queen to me. Have you seen her, Princess?"

"No, I have not." Snow stared at her. "This woman did away with the queen. Please take her to the dungeons, where she will think about her crimes in solitary confinement."

She wasn't being sentenced to death?

Solitary confinement didn't scare her. She'd spent her entire life on her own.

But then the mirror had always been by her side.

Snow was watching silently. Outside Ingrid's chambers, some of her faithful guards were being taken away and the halls were filled with villagers, congratulating one another and cheering. She wanted to shout that they didn't belong in her castle, but she knew no one would listen. No one even bothered to look at the old hag that passed by them on the way to the dungeons. The men said nothing to her as she was placed in the darkened cell she'd had Georg sent to only hours before. She was alone.

For a moment, at least.

As Ingrid's eyes adjusted to the light, she saw her master and Katherine appear beside her. Their ghosts—or the figments of her imagination, or her deranged mind, or whatever they truly were—were there to keep her company. Her master's ghost quickly disappeared, but Katherine's remained.

How poetic that, in the end, Katherine was there for her. Her heart gave a sudden lurch as she realized all that could not be undone. And yet, it was Katherine who was at her side now. Ingrid reached out her hand to touch her sister's specter. She watched her image slowly give a sad smile, then disappear like smoke, never to be seen again.

Snow

Snow emerged from her aunt's dim chambers shaky but alive, and found everyone celebrating in the darkened halls. Someone was reigniting the torches and lanterns in the hallway, flooding them with light, but Snow didn't want to stay. She couldn't wait to get as far away from her aunt's quarters as she could. She suddenly felt so tired.

"Snow! Snow!" Anne came rushing toward her and Snow collapsed into her arms, the two girls in tears. "You're all right. When we saw the windows shatter, we feared the worst."

"I'm all right," Snow assured her, and pulled back to look at her friend. "But Henri . . ."

Anne clasped her shoulders. "I know." Snow's eyes welled with tears.

"You're hurt," Anne said, lifting Snow's arms, which were nicked and dripping with blood from the broken glass. "I'll clean you up. Stay right here."

"No," Snow said. "My wounds can wait. I want to see him."

"Your father?" Anne asked. "He's already here."

Snow had meant Henri, but then she caught sight of him—her father, back at the castle. He rushed toward her with Grumpy and Doc and the other little men. Anne let go, and Snow raced toward him, falling into his arms.

"You're safe!" her father said, stroking her hair like he had when she was a little girl. "I have been so worried."

"As I have been about you," Snow said, choking back tears. "When I heard she had you, I wasn't sure what to think."

"I'm fine, but Snow . . ." Her father's eyes searched hers hesitantly. "Henrich is . . ."

Dead. "I know." She couldn't bear to say the word.

"Is that the former king?" she heard someone say, and they both turned around.

"King Georg? Have you come back for us?" another shouted as a crowd gathered around them.

"Yes! The Evil Queen banished me long ago, and I am finally free of her curse, thanks to my daughter," her father told the people assembled.

"Get the king fresh clothes," someone shouted, and they pulled him away.

People all around started to cry, hugging one another and cheering, and Snow, for all her happiness for them, felt numb.

"Snow?"

Snow turned around and saw Happy, Sleepy, and Sneezy standing with Dopey. They removed their caps.

"When we heard what happened to Henrich, we couldn't believe it," Sleepy said. "Had to see it for our own eyes."

"A glass coffin." Sneezy shook his head. "Snow, we are so sorry for your loss. The guards told us they brought him up from the kitchen. It must have happened down there. Dopey found this, and he wanted you to see it."

Dopey stepped forward, holding up a bright red apple with a single bite taken out of it. The bite mark had turned black as coal, as if touched by magic. Snow knew then that Ingrid must have tricked him into eating a poison apple, and sent him to his death.

"We are so sorry for your loss, Snow." Happy shed a tear. Snow felt a lump begin to form in her throat.

"Someone should alert his kingdom so they can come take his body," Doc said.

"Henrich deserves a hero's burial," Grumpy said in

agreement. "He was a good man." He, Doc, and Bashful removed their caps. Sneezy blew his nose into a tissue and cried. Dopey, however, kept pointing to the apple. Snow couldn't understand what he meant to show her. It was poisoned—that much she could guess. The queen had done it. What more was there to know?

He's as good as dead, she remembered the old hag saying, and something about the words struck her as odd. *As good as dead.*

"As good as dead" didn't mean he was actually dead, did it? Dopey smiled at her as the realization crossed her face.

Snow rushed out of the hallway past the others.

"Snow! Where are you going?" Anne cried.

The little men called to her, but she kept running.

She needed to know for sure. She pushed her way out of the castle doors and ran to the podium, where Henri's still body lay in the glass coffin. A crowd remained gathered outside the gates, watching.

"It's Snow White!" several voices cheered. "It's the princess! She's saved us!"

Snow wanted to go to her people and assure them the Evil Queen was gone and wouldn't return. But at the moment, all she could think about was Henri. As she neared his coffin, she slowed her walk. The sight of him lying there filled her with so much dread and grief, but she also felt a glimmer of hope. If there was any chance he could be alive, she had to know.

She opened the glass lid and pressed her ear to his chest one more time. Then she held her breath and waited for a sign. Something, anything that would tell her "as good as dead" wasn't *actually* dead. If she had a sign, she'd go to the enchantress. She'd tried to find a cure for this magic. But she heard nothing. Tears began to fall down Snow's cheeks.

"Henri, I'm so sorry," she said, and she slipped his knife back in his pocket. She reached inside his jacket and felt her mother's necklace. Pulling it out, she held it in her hands. His knife had helped her, but her mother's necklace hadn't protected him.

Her mother had loved her father so much she would have done anything for him and Snow. True love was like that. Was that what she had been starting to have with Henri before he was ripped away from her? He looked so handsome and peaceful lying there, like he was only sleeping. She felt an urge so strong come over her that she couldn't stop herself.

"Till we meet again, Henri," she whispered in his ear, and then she leaned over and kissed him softly on the lips. When their lips parted, she prepared to close the lid for the last time.

She heard a gasp, like a fish trying to find water.

Henri's eyes fluttered open and found hers.

"Snow?" he croaked.

"Henri!" Snow cried, the tears flowing harder. She pulled him to a sitting positon and heard the commotion start up around her. The dwarfs came running, as did her father and Anne. As news spread of the prince awakening, a cry of joy rang out inside the castle gates, and soon outside them as well.

Henri looked around in wonder as Snow helped him out of the glass casket.

"She saved him!" Happy cried, with tears of joy.

Henri looked at Snow, who was still crying herself. "You saved me," he repeated.

"True love saved you," Doc told him as Georg looked on with tears in his eyes.

Snow and Henri looked at one another and smiled.

Perhaps it had.

Snow

A few months later . . .

"Presenting Her Majesty, Queen Snow White!"

The throne room erupted in thunderous applause.

Her father stood in the finest of velvet robes, his crown perched atop his head where it had always belonged, but today he took it off and placed it on Snow's own. He held her hand as she rose and stood at the edge of the throne room podium, looking out on hundreds of people. Anne was there with her mother, both of whom were now officially the royal tailors. Mrs. Kindred stood with her family, who had joined her in the kitchen. Grumpy, Sleepy, Sneezy, Dopey, Bashful, Happy, and Doc were front and center, applauding in their new uniforms. They had been made official envoys of the queen, and it was their job to journey to villages throughout the kingdom to talk to the people and learn of their needs and problems. Snow knew they'd be grand at it (even if they would have to rein in Grumpy's attitude from time to time). After years of spending their days in the darkest mines, they deserved to live in the light.

As she stood in front of her people and basked in all of their newfound happiness, it seemed like she'd lived this before. She could see herself standing beside her parents in this very spot as a child, and the feeling was very much the same: she felt loved.

After months of transition, she was on her own.

Snow was ready. Her father had prepared her for this.

With the Evil Queen vanquished, the kingdom welcomed change. Snow and her father had spent the last few months working together to right the wrongs done to the kingdom during Ingrid's reign, and Snow's ideas for improving the kingdom were put into practice. Borders were reopened and trade was welcomed, with people coming from far and wide to express their hopes for a fruitful exchange. Taxes were made more manageable, and farmers and miners enjoyed the opportunity to profit off what they'd sowed and found in the ground. Safety measures were put in place in order to make the mines less hazardous for the workers. Official forums were established so communication between the various hamlets and villages would be more open and free, and so folks could benefit from being part of larger communities.

But perhaps most important, the biggest change they made was opening the castle up to their people again. Those seeking employment there were welcomed with open arms, and Snow smiled at seeing the many new faces in the halls. Her mother's garden parties had been reinstated, with children happily running around the gardens and marveling at the birds Katherine and Snow had always loved so much. They no longer resided in an aviary—Snow felt it was time for all who lived in cages to be free, and the birds were no exception. And yet it surprised her how many birds still graced their garden walls and visited the castle windows. With their freedom, they had found a home, just as she had.

Today would be yet another party, this one for her.

After years of being the forgotten princess, she was now the queen.

"Are you ready to meet your people, Your Highness?"

Snow looked down at the handsome young man on the step below her. He was dressed in a royal blue jacket with a red cape and looked as beautiful as the day she had first nervously watched him from her castle window, listening to him call to her. His arm was outstretched to take hers, and this time she didn't hesitate.

"Yes, I truly am," Snow said, and she smiled up at him as they walked out of the throne room to loud applause.

Henri gave her a proud look. "I can tell."

Snow couldn't help laughing. He made her infinitely happy, and she was so thrilled he'd agreed to stay in her kingdom. His official duty was acting as a trade liaison between neighboring kingdoms, including his own, but unofficially he was her heart and soul, and she wouldn't be surprised if a day came in the not-so-distant future when they announced their intentions for marriage.

But for now, she had important work to do.

As they reached the entrance to the gardens, where more subjects were waiting, a cardinal flew down and landed on the stone steps that she had cleaned so many times in her life. It tweeted a song of happiness, and Snow could only imagine it saying one thing: *I love you.* For her mother would always be with her.

"I feel as if I've been waiting for this moment forever," Snow confessed to Henri.

But now there would be no more waiting.

Snow White's moment had arrived.

And if it wasn't quite "happily ever after," it was pretty close.